PALESTINE + 100

Deep Vellum Publishing
3000 Commerce St., Dallas, Texas 75226
deepvellum.org · @deepvellum

Deep Vellum is a 501c3 nonprofit literary arts organization
founded in 2013 with the mission to bring
the world into conversation through literature.

In memory of Tom Hurndall
1981–2004

LIBRARY OF CONGRESS CONTROL NUMBER: 2021950252

Support for this publication has been provided in part by
Amazon Literary Partnership.

Cover design by David Eckersall

PRINTED IN THE UNITED STATES OF AMERICA

PALESTINE
+ 100

EDITED BY BASMA GHALAYINI

DEEP VELLUM PUBLISHING
DALLAS, TEXAS

Contents

CONTENTS

Introduction

WHEN I WAS A CHILD, my grandfather would tell us about his shop in Yaffa, a business he owned with his brother until 1948 before being expelled to Egypt. He told us that, on their departure, they only packed a few days' worth of clothes for him, his wife and children, having been told they would be able to come back as soon as it was safe. They left their sheets on the clothes lines, chickpeas soaking in water, and toys in the yard. He locked the door, put his key in his pocket, and headed to safety as instructed. They never returned, and his key stayed in his pocket until he died in Cairo sixty years later.

On the fifteenth of May 1948, Israel declared itself a new-born state on the rubble of Palestinian lives. In the months before and after this date, Palestinians were forced from their homes across the country; those who weren't driven out fled in fear of execution, having heard of the horrors which took place during massacres carried out by the *Haganah* (Israeli militia) in villages nearby.[1] This event would later, and begrudgingly, be known as the Nakba (or 'catastrophe'), as Palestinians slowly came to terms with the fact that this was not a temporary displacement and that no one was going home any time soon. Eighty percent of Palestinians (over 700,000 people in total) were expelled, and their land taken over and occupied in what can only be described as an act of ethnic cleansing by the Zionist movement. They were all placed in refugee camps in Gaza and the West Bank, or in neighbouring Arab countries (Jordan, Syria and Lebanon), or displaced within the occupied lands of Palestine itself, now known as 'Israel'.

Four generations on, any Palestinian child can tell you all about their great-grandfather's back garden in Haifa, Yaffa or Majdal. They can tell you about their great-grandmother's kitchen, the patterns on her plates, and the colours of the embroidery on her pillows. They can tell you about their great-grandparents' neighbours, the musky smell of the local shop and all the handmade goods it sold. This child has never been to any of those places, of course, but so long as they keep the memory of them alive, then, should they ever get to go back, it would be as if they had never left; they could pick up exactly where their great-grandparents left off. Indeed, wherever Palestinian refugees are in the world, one thing unites them: their undoubted belief in their right to return.

Palestinian refugees are, in this sense, like nomads travelling across a landscape of memory. They carry their village in their hearts, like an internal compass where 'north' is always Palestine. They pass this compass down to their children, who sketch in the details on an ever-fading map – the hills and trees and *wadis* – from their own imagination. Every day spent away from Palestine, in the life of a Palestinian refugee, is one that they believe brings them a day closer to their return.

The Nakba didn't end in 1948. It continued. With every brick built in this newly declared country; with every wall, watch-tower, gun-turret, or segregated road in the occupied West Bank; with every confiscation of land or demolition of Palestinian property (my own grandmother's 800-year-old farmhouse in Khan Younis was bulldozed as part of a 'security' operation on 26 November, 2000); with every restriction on Palestinians' ability to travel, and with every new attack on Gaza (what the Israeli Defence Force calls 'mowing the lawn'); with each of these acts, the Nakba has continued. Israel's seventy-year programme of systemic ethnic cleansing is one long, ongoing extension of the event that took place in 1948, the origin of which lay in the liberties that Israel took that year when Zionist militias, supported by the British, took more than 78 percent of the Palestinians' land. Since then, countless Israeli government policies have furthered this gradual ethnic cleansing, building on the more comprehensive land-grab accomplished in 1948, and again in 1967. The ideology that continues to underpin the legalised destruction of houses in Jerusalem and settlement areas in the West Bank, and the slow strangulation of Gazans (through the now twelve-year-old blockade) is the same ideology that first destroyed 531 villages and eleven cities in 1948, an ideology that transforms each Palestinian into a potential target, myself and my two-year-old daughter included.

This 'ongoing Nakba' is also continually evolving. We are forever entering new stages of it, whether it's the isolation of Negev Bedouins into smaller and smaller ghettos, the further separation of the Gaza and West Bank governments, the use of explosive bullets in the 'shoot to cripple' response to last year's March of Return, or the subjection of Palestinians in Jerusalem to increasingly restrictive, discriminatory policies.[2] These systematic aggressions towards the Palestinian people continue on a daily basis in countless small, localised cases, making it difficult, or simply too unspectacular, to report on. Yet they are all part of a process that began in 1948.

You can see the repercussions of the Nakba throughout the diaspora in the neighbouring Arab countries, where refugees first fled, and beyond (as of 2003, there were 9.6 million descendants of Palestinians living outside Palestine). Its influence is not just geopolitical, but also profoundly cultural. When Palestinians write, they write about their past through their present, knowingly or unknowingly. Their writing is, in part, a search for their lost inheritance, as well as an attempt to keep the memory of that loss from fading. In this sense, the past is *everything* to a Palestinian writer; it is the only thing that makes their current existence and their identity meaningful. And the Nakba, of course, sits at the heart of this. Whether it is Jabra Ibrahim Jabra's novels, *A Cry in a Long Night* or *In Search of Walid Masoud*, or Ghassan Kanafani's *Men in the Sun* or *Returning to Haifa*, Palestinian authors have all felt obligated to, as well as inspired by, the Nakba. They have a cultural duty to remember it.

It is perhaps for this reason that the genre of science fiction has never been particularly popular among Palestinian authors; it is a luxury, to which Palestinians haven't felt they can afford to escape. The cruel present (and the traumatic past) have too firm a grip on Palestinian writers' imaginations for fanciful ventures into possible futures.

Another reason why science fiction might not have been popular among Palestinian writers is it doesn't offer an obvious fit to the Palestinian situation. In classic SF, the battle lines are drawn quickly and simply: the moral opposition between a typical SF protagonist and the dystopia or enemy he finds himself confronting is a diametric one. But in Palestinian fiction, the idea of an 'enemy' is largely absent. Israelis hardly ever feature, as individuals, and when they do, they are rarely portrayed as out-and-out villains. In Ghassan Kanafani's *Returning to Haifa*, for example, we follow the unlikely visit by two Palestinians, Said and Safeyya, to the city they fled twenty years earlier, where they get to know the Israeli woman, Miriam, now occupying the house that was stolen from them. Instead of portraying her as a zealot, a woman self-convinced of her people's holy right to the land, Kanafani presents us with a sensitive, compassionate individual, someone who, when confronted by it, is ashamed of what her people did to the Palestinians.

The absence of an 'enemy' isn't the only absence in Palestinian fiction. You might even say absence *generally* is one of the defining features of Palestinian fiction – which is where science fiction might be able to contribute. Absence, and the feelings of isolation and detachment that come with it, are easy to magnify in a context of galloping future technology. In the twelve stories specially commissioned for this project, absence is everywhere. In Saleem Haddad's 'Song of the Birds' and Rawan Yaghi's 'Commonplace', young protagonists are haunted by the voices of their dead siblings. In Anwar Hamed's 'The Key', Israelis are plagued by nightmares about Palestinian ghosts. In Abdalmuti Maqboul's 'Personal Hero', the absence of a grandfather in her mother's life inspires a scientist to make a game-changing invention. In all cases, the future's technology, though designed to ease conflict or ameliorate trauma, manages only to exacerbate it.

Perhaps another defining feature of Palestinian fiction is the cultural disconnect felt between different sets of refugees and, within those, different generations of refugees. Once more, science fiction – in this case its love of alternate realities – offers surprising opportunities for exploring this. In Saleem Haddad's story, the existential boundary between Aya's world and Ziad's provides a metaphor for the author's own dilemma as a Palestinian in exile: do you accept your condition and make a home for yourself where you are? Or do you return, fight, and give up all the comforts of your life abroad? In the story, 'N', by Majd Kayyal – a writer whose grandparents were displaced inside what became Israel but never left it – we are presented with a cosmological solution to the Arab-Israeli conflict: the creation of two parallel worlds – one for Palestinians, one for Israelis – both occupying the same geographic space. In this future, only Palestinians born after the establishment of the parallel worlds are allowed to travel between them; thus a deep cultural fissure opens up between the eponymous 'N' and his father when he leaves to study in the Israeli world. Once again, we see how even the most extraordinary future technology can do little more than mirror or reframe the current, real-world impasse.

But that's what science fiction does; it uses the future as a blank canvas on which to project concerns that occupy society *right now*. The real future – the *actual* future – is unknowable. But for SF writers, the mere idea of 'things to come' is licence to re-imagine, re-configure, and re-interrogate the present.

In the wider Arab context, this act of reframing the present may become increasingly important. In Egypt, for example, where under President Sisi writers are regularly jailed for what they have to say about the present, the option of recasting that present – reframing it through fantasy or science fiction – is becoming more and more popular, especially among women writers (Basma Abdel Aziz's *The Queue* uses SF; Eman Abdelrahim's 'Two Sisters' uses supernatural horror). Likewise, for a Palestinian living in the West, writing about the present (or rather, the present back home) risks exposing them to automatic accusations of antisemitism. In these contexts, the act of reframing the present in the form of allegories (and not just future-set ones) may become more of a necessity than a luxury. Indeed, if infringements on free speech get worse, this re-framing may even need to become a conscious act of disguising.

Not that the disguise of science fiction would be that drastic a costume change for Palestinian writers, especially those based in Palestine. Everyday life, for them, is a kind of a dystopia. A West Bank Palestinian need only record their journey to work, or talk back to an IDF soldier at a checkpoint, or forget to carry their ID card,[3] or simply look out their car window at the walls, weaponry and barbed wire plastering the landscape, to know what a modern, totalitarian occupation is – something people in the West can only begin to understand through the language of dystopia.

Hopefully, most readers in the West will never know what this kind of occupation feels like first-hand. But feel we must, *all* of us – even if that has to start with metaphors and allegories – if there is ever to be any hope of peace.

Basma Ghalayini, June 2019

Notes

1. Depending on the sources and the definition, between 10 and 70 massacres occurred during the 1948 War. These included the Deir Yassin massacre (9 April, around 112 killed), the Abu Shusha massacre (13-14 May, between 60 and 70 killed), the Lydda massacre (12 July, approximately 250 killed), the Al-Dawayima massacre (29 October, between 80 and 200 killed, leaving 455 people missing), and, between 30 October and 2 November, three massacres in the villages of Saliha (between 60 and 94 people killed, having taken refuge in a mosque), Safsaf (between 50 and 70 already-bound men killed, and four women publicly raped), and Jish (numbers unknown; a mass grave of two dozen bodies was reported to have been found by Archbishop Elias Chacour when he was 8 years old).

2. During 1967-2014, the Israeli occupation withdrew residence cards from more than 14,000 Palestinians living in Jerusalem. Research conducted by the Association for Civil Rights in Israel has revealed the number of Jerusalem Palestinians living in poverty had reached 79.5% in 2013. According to the same research, Palestinians are allowed to build on only 14% of East Jerusalem, equivalent to 7.8% of the total area of Jerusalem. Since 1967, one third of Palestinian land has been expropriated in East Jerusalem, onto which thousands of new apartments have been built for Jewish settlers.

3. All Palestinians are issued ID cards with unique numbers by the Israeli government that keeps track of their movements, marital status, mothers and father's names, religious practices, and number of children.

Song of the Birds

Saleem Haddad

In Memory of Mohanned Younis, 1994–2017[1]

THE UNRAVELLING BEGAN ON the beach. Since Ziad hanged himself the year before, Aya had felt haunted, saddled by the weight of things. The violence of his death only reinforced how unreal everything seemed, like she was trapped in someone else's memory. But as she stood on the shore under the late afternoon sun that day, the haunting had felt much closer, like it had suddenly crawled under her skin and decided to make a home for itself there.

Behind her on the sand, Aya's father was dozing under a giant yellow umbrella. Like all grown-ups, her father slept a lot, although no one slept as much as her mother, who was barely awake these days. Whenever life got a bit complicated, it seemed that all these grown-ups could do was just drop off to sleep.

Taking one final look back, she walked into the water, leaving behind all the business of the beach: the loud, cheesy music blasting from the drone speakers in the sky, the smell of shisha and grilled meat, the screaming children and half-naked bodies running up and down the sand. *Just another headache-inducing summer day in Gaza,* she thought to herself as the waves softly lapped at her shins.

She made her way deeper into the calm blue waters, her feet navigating the occasional piece of coral on the otherwise sandy seabed. The sea was so blue, the sky so clear. When the water reached her stomach, she turned around in slow circles, her fingers gently grazing the surface.

Time passed more slowly by the sea. She learned that in physics class: the hands of a clock placed at sea level run a fraction slower than those of a clock placed on a mountaintop. Sometimes, she thought that she should go up and live in the mountains. That way, she would stop being fourteen more quickly. Time would pass faster and she'd be a real grown-up, do all the things she wanted to do. By the sea, she felt herself a prisoner of both history and time.

But the good thing about time moving slower by the sea was that, if she stayed there, she would remain closer to the last time she saw Ziad. Maybe, if she descended deep enough into the water, she could find a way to grind time to a halt and then push it back, back to the period before he left. Maybe then she would find a way to stop her big brother from dying.

She lay back and closed her eyes, allowing her body to float in the water. She could hear the song of the birds in the sky, the slow, familiar chattering: *kereet-kereet . . . kereet*. She dipped her ears below the surface, listening to the rumble of the sea. The sea, warm and inviting, seemed playful that day, licking the sides of her face. But underneath this playfulness she felt something more sinister. She imagined the blue waters swallowing her, dragging her deeper, until her body hit the seabed to join the thousands of bodies that had drowned in these waters throughout history.

She wasn't sure if she fell asleep, but a sudden putrid smell overcame her. She sensed something cold and slimy wrap itself around her neck. She opened her eyes, took in a gasp of breath. The stench made its way down her throat, and her body shuddered in response. She reached for the thing around her neck and pulled it off: a soggy piece of yellowed toilet paper, disintegrating between her fingers.

She flung the paper behind her and stood up in the water. Her feet found the seabed, which now felt spongy and slick. The water around her was a brownish green sludge. Sewage and excrement bobbed on the surface. A rotting fish carcass floated by her right arm, casually bumping into an empty can of Pepsi. To her left, white foam gathered and bubbled on the surface of the water.

Her body contracted as a giant retch escaped her. A crackle of gunfire erupted on the horizon. She turned to the noise: four or five gunboats bobbed further out in the sea, as if warning her not to advance any further. She turned back to the beach. The beachfront was unrecognisable. The string of hotels and restaurants were replaced by decrepit buildings wedged alongside each other, aggressively jostling for space. Smoke blooms hung in place of the colourful beach umbrellas, the music and chatter drowned out by gunfire. Above her, the sky was a furious grey.

'Baba,' she shrieked, wading through the dirty water. She pushed aside bottles, soiled tissue paper, plastic bags and rotting animal carcasses. Her body jerked and convulsed continuously with what was something between a gag and a sob. A sharp stabbing pain tore through her body, like someone twisting a knife deep inside her stomach.

Stumbling onto the shore with seaweed in her hair, she looked like a deep-sea monster emerging from the depths of the waters. The sand was littered with plastic bottles, burning tyres and smouldering debris. The sunbathing bodies had disappeared. Above her jet planes roared, leaving in their wake trails of black smoke like gashes in the sky. A thundering explosion threw her to the ground. Her tongue tasted sand and blood.

'Baba . . .' she whimpered, barely hearing herself. The pain in her belly intensified. Up ahead, three people were lying on the sand. She crawled towards them. The bodies were small,

3

too small to be adults. As she got closer, she realised the bodies were of three children. They looked asleep but there were pools of blood, limbs contorted into impossible positions. A punctured football lay beside the lifeless bodies. There was a loud screaming in her ear, and she realised the screaming was coming from her.

She stood up, looked down at her feet. A trickle of blood ran down her left leg.

'It was likely the shock of the blood that caused her to faint,' the doctor said. Aya was vaguely aware the doctor was placing a bandage on her forehead. 'Sometimes, in young women, their first menstruation can be scary. Has her mother not prepared her for this?'

Aya's father hesitated. 'Her mother is . . . not well.'

The doctor did not press further. 'These bio-therapeutic bandages should heal the wound by tomorrow.'

'Habibti Aya,' her father said, stroking her hair. 'You're a woman now.'

'Do you remember what happened before you fainted?' the doctor asked.

'I was thinking of Ziad . . . I was in the water, thinking of Ziad . . .'

'Ziad is my son,' her father explained. 'Aya's brother . . . he . . . he passed away last year.'

'There were these three boys . . .' Aya said, suddenly, recalling the bodies on the beach. 'Little children . . . their bodies . . .'

'Habibti Aya,' her father interrupted.

The doctor looked at Aya. 'Three boys?'

Aya's head moved in a vague resemblance of a nod. 'There was dirty water . . . rubbish everywhere and burning tyres and . . . and the bodies of three boys . . . next to a football . . . their arms and legs were twisted and . . .'

'That's enough,' her father interrupted. He turned to the

doctor. 'It was a hot day yesterday . . . it must have been the heat . . .'

The doctor nodded. 'Trauma can lodge itself deep in the body, emerging when we least expect it . . .'

'I understand,' her father said. 'It's just . . . first her mother, then her brother . . .' His voice trailed off.

The doctor prescribed some pills, which he said would help her rest. That night Aya quickly fell into a deep and dreamless sleep. In the morning, she woke up with the feeling of having emerged from a dark cave of infinite blackness. The doctor was right: the bandage had disappeared overnight and the deep gash above her forehead had healed. She took a long, hot shower and tossed the remaining pills down the toilet.

She got dressed and put on the pad the doctor had given her. She recalled her father's words: *You're a woman now.* Something inside of her felt changed. It was an awakening of sorts. She felt it in her body as much as in her mind, a strange disquiet that had settled inside her, a tingling sensation.

Returning from school that afternoon, she found her father in the living room listening to the news. He seemed to be in a dream-like state, sitting down on a chair and staring out of the window, barely listening to the newscaster, who was reporting on the spike in teen suicides across Palestine.

'Baba?'

Her father jumped in his seat, his hand pushing over the glass of tea next to his chair. The glass crashed on the floor and shattered into pieces.

'Aya you scared me!' he said, irritated. The robo-cleaner – responding to the sound of the crash – emerged from the cupboard and began to clean up the glass on the floor.

'I'm sorry . . .'

He sighed and anxiously picked at the skin around his fingernails. 'I should probably take a small sleep.'

Aya nodded. Her father stood up and went to his bedroom.

He was always so absent-minded, as if he lived in another dimension and was just trying this world on for size. She didn't blame him. From that moment last year, when she saw Ziad hanging there, she had felt as if a hole in her chest had opened up, leaving all her insides to tumble out like a spool of thread. Since then, some days she felt okay, and would wonder whether the worst of the pain was over. Then, when she least expected it – when she'd be sitting in class or else walking along the corniche – that image of Ziad would flash before her eyes: his limp body swaying, his head leaning lifeless to one side.

Aya shook her head to erase the image from her mind. She walked to her mother's bedroom and opened the door. Her mother was asleep, as usual. The last time Aya had seen her awake was perhaps twelve days ago. She had emerged from the bedroom for a brief moment to grab a couple of figs. She ran into Aya in the hallway and they spoke for a few minutes. She asked Aya how school had been, and whether she was happy. Aya said she was, and her mother smiled.

'Good,' her mother said, giving Aya a kiss on the cheek. Then she returned to bed.

That night Aya dreamt she was walking through an enormous field of olive trees. The sky appeared much closer to the earth, the moon so large and bright the entire field twinkled like a sea of diamonds. Sounds had an intense clarity: she could hear the rustling of each olive branch in the wind, the crickets chirping at a deafening volume.

There was shuffling behind her. Turning around, she recognised the familiar figure – tall and lanky – and the unmistakable tangled mess of brown hair.

'Ziad?' The name caught in her throat.

'It's me,' he said, in that voice that was so deep for an eighteen-year-old.

He was wearing a black T-shirt and jeans. He looked tall

and strong, not like the last time she saw him. She ran up to him and threw herself against him, half-expecting him to disappear, and for her to simply fall through him and onto the ground. Instead her body crashed into his solid frame. His arms wrapped themselves around her and she sunk into his chest.

'Ziad, it's really you!' She looked up into his face. He smiled down at her, that familiar half-smile, the bottom two front teeth slightly crooked.

She hesitated. 'But you died?'

He shrugged. 'In your world, death isn't really dying. In a way, I guess it's more like waking up.'

'But I saw you! If you didn't die, then where have you been?'

'I've . . .' He paused, considering his words carefully. He had always taken his time to find the most precise way to describe his thoughts and feelings. 'I've been . . . outside of things. There are . . . responsibilities . . .'

A sudden fury exploded from inside of her, a rage that had been building for the last twelve months.

'Why did you do it? Didn't you love us? Didn't you think about Mama and Baba? Didn't you think about me?'

Her anger amused him. He began to giggle, his eyes forming tiny slits.

'You're laughing! You're laughing too, you donkey!' She smashed her fists against his chest.

'Stop, stop!' he protested. He grabbed her fists and held them in front of him. 'It's okay,' he whispered in her ear as she began to cry.

They walked through the olive grove for a long time. She was happy to be near him, to feel the warmth of his body and succumb to his gentle teasing. She told him everything that had happened, things she had been doing. She updated him on the neighbours, on friends and on the other kids in school. She did her impersonations of all the people they knew. She had forgotten how much he laughed at her impersonations, and it occurred to her that she hadn't done any since he died. After a while, when she had run out of sentences, they simply walked side-by-side in silence. Finally, she asked the question she had been avoiding.

'Does this mean you're back now? Or is this just a dream?'

He was quiet for a moment. He stopped walking and turned to face her. A hardness had settled in his features.

'Have you heard of the allegory of Plato's Cave?'

She shook her head.

'Never mind.'

'Why?' she insisted.

He looked up at the sky. 'Do you think a fish knows it's swimming in water?'

She shrugged.

'We live in the world like a fish in water. Just swimming, oblivious to our surroundings.' Ziad sighed, then poked her arm. 'Aya, are you not planning to ever wake up?'

She woke up. Outside her window, the birds were singing: *kereet-kereet . . . kereet*. Daylight streamed through the shutters. The olive grove returned to her. If the whole thing was just a dream, it felt more real than life.

Getting up, she snuck down the hall to Ziad's room and opened the door. The room was as it was on the day he died. His shelves still held his basketball trophies, a few stuffed toys from his childhood. In the wardrobe, his clothes were still on hangers, bearing faint traces of his smell, which seemed to weaken with each passing day. Next to his bed was a novel by Franz Kafka, with a receipt from the arcades operating as a makeshift bookmark. On his desk there was a photograph of the family taken five years ago. All four of them were having a picnic on Mount Carmel, the port of Haifa in the distance. Aya remembered that day: they had a large barbecue to celebrate the beginning of spring. That was before Mama started sleeping a lot, before the weight of things began to bear down on them.

Next to the photograph was Ziad's journal, a simple black notebook. Ziad had liked to write by hand, even though it took so much longer than just dictating thoughts to a tablet. He had said he enjoyed the material aspect of writing, the physicality of ink and the slow movement of pen on paper. He never did like technology, was always so mistrustful of it.

Her father had insisted no one was allowed to touch any of Ziad's things, as if Ziad had just gone to buy some vegetables and would soon be back. Against her better judgement, she picked up the diary and opened it to the final page. In his neat handwriting, she read the last entry, dated one day before he died:

There is an oral tradition of grandparents passing on their stories of Palestine, which helps keep Palestine alive. But is it not too much of a stretch for them to have figured out how to use these stories to imprison us? The truth of collective memories is that you can't just choose to harness the good ones. Sooner or later, the ugly ones begin to seep in too . . .

The heaviness returned, the choking sensations. She closed the diary and stumbled out of the room.

Closing the door behind her, she made her way to the bathroom. She examined her tired face in the mirror, marvelled once again at the disappearance of the large gash on her forehead. She turned on the faucet and began to brush her teeth. It took a moment to register the gritty sensation of dirt and the taste of soil on her tongue. She spat the toothpaste out. She noticed the water coming out of the tap: sandy brown, bursting out of the faucet in exhausted sputters, leaving light brown splotches on the white porcelain sink.

'Baba!' She ran out of the bathroom and into the hallway. Her father emerged from his bedroom, half-asleep. 'The water coming out of the tap is brown!'

Her father followed her into the bathroom. She had left the tap running, but now only crystal-clear water ran through.

'I swear it was brown.' She caught her father's eye. 'I swear I wasn't imagining this.'

Her father sighed and rubbed his forehead. 'Aya, what's going on?'

She took a deep breath. 'I dreamt of Ziad last night,' she confessed.

The look on her father's face unleashed a flood of tears from somewhere deep inside her.

'I miss him,' Aya said.

Her father pulled her into him. 'I know, habibti,' he whispered in her ear.

Ziad appeared in her dreams again that night. They were sitting in a clearing on top of a mountain. She recognised the view: they were in the spot where that photograph was taken, of the four of them on Mount Carmel. Ziad spoke in a slow and assured way as he picked at the blades of grass by his bare feet.

'Everything seems so still. You would never think that we are hurtling through the universe at a crazy speed.'

'What's with all these riddles?' she asked.

'All I'm saying is that things aren't always what they seem. You know what they taught us in history books. That stuff, about how we liberated Palestine, how the occupation is over now?' Aya nodded for him to go on. 'It is so advanced, the occupation. They have all these technologies . . . technologies of control and subjugation. And Gaza – our home – is like a laboratory for all that experimentation.'

'But that's all in the past . . .' She picked up a dark blue flower, cradling it in her palm. 'We're liberated now. Look around. We are free.'

Ziad snorted. 'You know how us Arabs are. We are trapped in the rose-tinted memories of our ancestors. These cached memories wrap themselves around us like a second skin.'

Ziad uprooted a blade of grass and began to break it apart into smaller pieces until the blade was nothing but a tiny stub, which he then squashed between his fingers. Aya watched him without saying a word. He appeared furious – it was a rage that far surpassed regular teenage emotions. The anger was darker, deeper than anything she had seen before. She saw it etched into his features, felt it radiate from his body.

He tossed the squashed remnants of the blade of grass behind him. Finally, he looked up at her.

'We're just another generation imprisoned by our parents' nostalgia.'

She looked at the flower in her palm. She had picked this flower off the ground only moments earlier. Now, examining it more closely in her palm, something appeared strange to her. The dark blue petals reflected the sunlight in a peculiar way. She brought her palm towards her face to get a better look.

The petals were made of hard steel, the edges jagged and sharp.

'Fragmentation bullets,' Ziad said, noticing her shocked expression. 'They blast from a gun and explode inside your body, blooming like flowers inside the flesh.'

The bullet rolled out of her palm and fell to the ground with a soft clink. The sound felt so far away. The world was spinning.

Ziad chuckled bitterly. 'Tools for murder now masquerading as life.'

She looked at him. 'What does all this mean?'

Ziad didn't hesitate. 'It means you have a decision. You can stay here, cocooned in these memories of a long-lost paradise, or you break free of this prison.'

'Is that what you did?'

'Yeah,' he nodded, looking her straight in the eye. 'That's what I did.'

Persistently, he came every night. She looked forwards to sleep, to being with him in her dreams. Her dreams began to feel more real than waking life, and infinitely more important. Through her encounters with Ziad she felt herself awakening to something, although what this was, she could not yet put into words.

In waking life her father watched her, concerned. She brushed aside his worries. She tried to play the role of a normal teenage girl. One afternoon, she overheard her father talking to someone on the phone.

'She has withdrawn,' he whispered to the mystery person on the line. 'I can hear her talking to him. I'm worried she'll do what he did . . .'

One night she woke up to find the wall of her bedroom torn down. A picnic blanket hung from the ceiling to cover the gaping hole where the wall used to be. It was the picnic blanket her father often brought to the beach. Using the blanket to cover the destroyed wall was almost comical, like a man trying to protect his modesty with a leaf. A strong gust of wind blew through the room. As the blanket blew up in the air, Aya caught a glimpse of Ziad silhouetted against the starry sky.

'It's getting harder now,' he said, stepping in from behind the blanket.

'Harder?' She sat up in bed, wrapping her duvet around her to protect herself from the wind.

'The more you know, the more the logic of the simulation breaks down.'

He motioned for her to get up. She put on her slippers and followed him through the hole in the wall.

Ziad hopped from one piece of concrete to the next,

swiftly grabbing on to the steel foundations that jutted from the concrete with the ease of a seasoned acrobat. She followed suit as best as she could, and they landed on the ground with a soft thud.

Their once picturesque Gaza City neighbourhood, with its wide leafy streets, exquisite limestone buildings, quaint cafés and vintage furniture shops, now looked like a warzone. Most of the buildings on their street were destroyed. The supermarket next door to their house had collapsed on itself. Some buildings had missing walls or half-caved in ceilings, partially covered by colourful cloth in a desperate attempt to reclaim privacy. She saw families cooking out in the open, people brushing their teeth in exposed bathrooms.

'What happened?' she gasped.

Ziad grabbed her hand and led her in the direction of the beach. They arrived at a beachfront hotel with its many layers of security. Ziad led them towards the back of the building and through a hole in a barbed-wire fence. From there, they made their way to a coffee shop in a garden overlooking the sea. There were plastic tables and chairs, and hanging plants that seemed so thirsty they looked like they might just get up and crawl to the sea.

'We're at the hotel where the media stay. It's safe here. Too many foreign journalists for them to bomb,' he said matter-of-factly.

Aya felt self-conscious, dressed in her pyjamas and slippers. Ziad ordered a Pepsi for himself and an orange juice for her. When their drinks arrived, he lit a cigarette.

'You smoke now?'

He shrugged, took a drag from the cigarette.

'Aya, the world you're living in is a simulation.'

She stared at him, speechless.

'Think about it. Only a few decades ago Israel had in its arsenal the latest in digital technology. The primary use for this technology was to shore up and further advance the occupation. How is it logical that Palestine was so easily liberated?'

'Ziad, you've lost your mind.'

'Those who keep resisting are seen as insane by those who cannot see the prison walls.'

'Where are we now?'

'This is the real Palestine,' Ziad said, gesturing at their surroundings. 'What you're living in . . . everything you think you know . . . it's all just a simulation. They've harnessed our collective memory, creating a digital image of Palestine. And that's where you live.'

She reminded herself that she was in a dream, but at that precise moment she couldn't remember when she had fallen asleep.

'Once I realised all of this . . . once I put the puzzle pieces together, I realised that I needed to get out. So I took a leap of faith.' He paused. 'When you kill yourself, you exit the simulation.'

'I don't understand.'

'You know how grown-ups always sleep,' he said, getting more animated. 'For those who weren't born in the simulation, memories return more easily. That's why grown-ups sleep a lot . . . they need to be reset. As for us . . . we are the first generation to have lived our entire lives in the simulation. We are at the frontier of a new form of colonisation. So it's up to us to develop new forms of resistance.'

'And Mama?'

Ziad hesitated. He looked like he was holding back tears. 'Mama's not sick, Aya. No matter what anyone says. She is torn: she wants to resist . . . wants to exit . . . but she also doesn't want to leave you and Baba. So she stays there, drifting in and out of consciousness. She knows that this 'right to digital return' isn't the same as the real thing . . .'

Aya felt the orange juice crawl back up her throat. Ziad noticed the expression on her face.

'What are you thinking?' he asked.

'I'm thinking that you're telling me the only way I can be free is to die.'

'You have to trust that what I'm telling you is true.'

'And if you're wrong?'

Ziad was silent for a long time. Finally, he put the cigarette out and looked at her.

'Pay attention to the song of the birds.'

Once she noticed the pattern, it became impossible to ignore.

Kereet-kereet . . . kereet.

In her head she counted: One. Two. Three. Four.

Kereet-kereet . . . kereet.

Two chirps followed by a third a few seconds later. Four seconds of silence, then the pattern repeated itself.

That morning, she spent an hour lying in bed listening to the song of the birds. The pattern repeated itself over and over again. A slow feeling of dread spread over her.

You're a woman now.

Kereet-kereet . . . kereet.

A simulation. Her brain tried to imagine it, but it was like trying to visualise what happens after the world ends, or else trying to imagine the full force of the sun. The answer felt beyond anything her brain could conceive. Trying to think about her imprisonment in a simulation was like trying to imagine her own death. It was unfathomable, the experience too all-encompassing.

Later that day, as the teaching hologram droned on and on in class, Ziad's words echoed in Aya's mind. If what he was saying was true, then all of this was just a simulation.

She pinched herself. There was pain. But was the pain real?

She grabbed her e-pen and pressed the tip of it against the soft flesh of her wrist. She felt the sharp pain as it pricked her skin. She pressed the e-pen deeper, until with a pop it pierced her skin, and a drop of blood emerged from the puncture.

Kereet-kereet . . . kereet.

Sirens sounded all around her. She looked up. The teaching hologram was shining a beam on her. The entire class turned to look at her. She glanced back at her arm, at the e-pen jabbed into her wrist.

'Urghha –' noises emerged from her mouth, but she wasn't sure whether they made any sense. The door burst open and four nurses ran in. Her wrist was burning with pain.

'I don't even know what to say,' her father said on the drive back home.

'Are we real?' Aya asked him as she sat in the passenger seat, staring out the window and absentmindedly tugging at the bandages on her wrist.

Her father stopped at a traffic light and turned to her. 'Look at me. Your name is Aya. The year is 2048. You are fourteen years old. You live in Gaza City. Your favourite colour is purple.' He paused. 'You are a real person.'

'Why do the birds have the same chirping sound?'

'What?'

'The song of the birds. It's a loop.'

Her father was quiet for a long time. Finally, he spoke.

'When I was your age, I was very close to two boys about my age. I lived in Gaza, one of the boys lived in Tunis and the other lived in Beirut. We were all Palestinians, all from Haifa, but we had been scattered around the world like shotgun pellets. Laws and borders made it impossible for us to see one another. We would sometimes wonder to each other: if our grandparents had never been run out from their homes like cockroaches, would the three of us have been neighbours? Would our personalities have been different without this weight inside our souls? What would it have felt like, to have a home and to belong to that home unquestionably?'

'Why are you telling me all of this?'

'Sometimes, home is simply a matter of changing your perspective.'

The traffic light turned from red to green and they were moving again. Aya turned to look out at the park, where young mothers normally pushed their baby carriages for exercise, and teenagers played football on the grass. Now, all she could see was a large dirt field, where a group of limbless young boys hobbled on makeshift crutches. Her breath caught in her throat.

'Aya . . .' her father began.

She started to speak but then stopped. 'Nothing.'

Her father looked at her, holding a seemingly infinite sadness in his eyes.

That evening, Aya walked into her mother's bedroom. She was asleep on her back under the covers. Aya sat down on the floor beside the bed.

'Mama, can you hear me?' she whispered.

Her mother did not stir. Aya studied her face, the way the soft hairs in her nose gently swayed with each breath. She reached under the covers and grabbed her mother's hand.

'I miss you,' she whispered.

For a moment, Aya could have sworn that her mother squeezed her hand.

One evening, Ziad came to her in a wheelchair. Both his legs were cut off at the knee, his jeans neatly tucked under his thighs.

'Ziad, what happened?' she asked, panicked. He looked thinner, his fingernails dirty, his jeans stained.

'They're creating a nation of cripples out there,' he spat the words out with a violence that surprised them both.

'Who are "they"?' she asked.

He looked at her bitterly. 'Who else?'

He pulled something out from behind his wheelchair: a

rock and a long piece of rubber. He placed the rock in the centre of the strip of rubber and stretched the rubber back, testing out the elasticity.

'This should work.' He looked at her and smiled that half-smile of his.

'What's wrong with you?' she yelled. 'Why are you doing this? Were you not happy before all of this? Even if none of this is real, it's better than the real prison.'

Ziad glared at her. 'You can keep living in a dream if you want. But I'm done. It's one thing to live in your dreams by choice, but once you realise you're a prisoner, there's no way to live without suffocation and despair.'

'But look what it's doing to you. You're a cripple.'

'My body is crippled but my mind is free. And I'm going to keep fighting until I'm completely free: body, mind and soul.'

That was the last time she saw him. Thirteen days ago. Every night she went to bed, hoping he would return, but he did not come back. Perhaps he was angry with her. She wasn't sure. If he wasn't angry then maybe there was another more sinister explanation for his absence. She tried not to think about that. Whatever the reason, there was no way she could keep living like this, not knowing what was true and what was false, what was reality and what was merely an enforced dreamland.

Without Ziad, she found herself unable to navigate between dream and waking life. She felt stuck between two radio frequencies. The two worlds were merging, and what emerged wasn't one or another but a third dimension, a nightmarish new conglomeration.

That's why she is back here. Back to where it all started, by the sea. Standing on the shore, the salty air forces its way down her throat, into her lungs. If they're right and there is nothing after death – if she has just simply lost her mind – then perhaps that's not a bad thing either. What is it that is driving her actions, she wonders? Is it a cynicism borne out of loss and betrayal, a cynicism so deep it courses in her veins? Or is it something else – a yearning to be free that exists like an itchiness under her skin?

Inching forwards until the waves kiss the tips of her toes, she stares down, teasing the waves, offering them a bit of her body. The sea and her are like two cats carefully examining one another. Slowly, she moves inside the sea's embrace. The waves reach up to her ankles, then her knees and then, as she wades in further, up to her hips. The water is cold; her skin breaks out in goose bumps. The backpack she is wearing is heavy on her shoulders.

Just when the water becomes too high to stand, she tries to swim but the stones inside the bag pull her down and her body plunges under the surface, quickly sinking to the depths of the sea. The remaining air in her lungs escapes from her mouth in sad, lonely bubbles. Her head shakes from right to left as her body tries to fight back. Her hair twists itself around her neck like the bony hands of an old woman. The roar of the sea is deafening. Her throat spasms, the pain of the constriction, tightening, overwhelming, her legs kick fiercely, trying to swim back up, but the stones are too heavy.

Notes

1. Sarah Helm, 'A Suicide in Gaza,' *The Guardian*, 18 May 2018. Available at: https://www.theguardian.com/news/2018/may/18/a-suicide-in-gaza

Sleep it Off, Dr Schott

Selma Dabbagh

I'm GOING TO SEND this on as a voice file to both of you. It is a vocal, digital letter of apology. No, it is more than that. It is a vocal, digital letter of apology with evidence. I have the recordings and I will include them. That is what I do after all. I record things. Like you two, for example.

If you've ever been in the Enclave's basement, you'll know where I am by the sounds that are being picked up. The drones are a bit more muffled down here and you can hardly hear the netting. It's just the rattle of the air-conditioning vents most of the time.

Given that this is a letter of sorts, I should possibly be more formal and present my case with specifics, as any scientist should. It's 15 June, 2048. I'm recording this in the Security Bunkers, Secular Scientific Enclave, Gaza and my name is Layla Wattan. I'm from Deir el Balah. You know Deir el Balah, the camp in the South that's spilling over into the sea. My family are from Haifa, but by that, I mean my great-grandparents lived there over a hundred years ago now.

As I said, this is an apology; a way of explaining to both of you. I couldn't explain at the time, because I couldn't speak. I still can't get your voices out of my head. It doesn't help that I keep replaying the recordings. Here's the one of

Dr Schott shouting at me when we finally met, our first and last encounter. The one where he asked who I was.

SCHOTT: *[Shouting]* Who is this girl? What are you doing? Mona, why is this woman in the corridor? Give me that!

I can tell you what Professor Kamal said after that, but I think you may prefer to listen.

KAMAL: She's a Recorder. Look at her equipment. Who gave you this?

I'd rather you didn't think of me as being a creep, or a snoop. I'm not even a proper spy. Okay, yes, I was a Recorder, but I really hadn't known what that meant when I was recruited. I am sorry for the shock I caused you both. I can hear it in your voices. Listen.

KAMAL: They can't do this to me. I was granted non-monitored status years ago. Did the General Assembly authorise this?

SCHOTT: Of course they authorised it. They make up the rules, they can do what they want. What did they tell you about us? Are you going to speak, girl? Why were you spying on us?

The short answer was that I would've sold my kidneys for a job in the Enclave. The whole of Gaza is desperate to move here. Not just because the food is guaranteed and it's about as safe as it gets; if you obey the rules that is. It was mainly because the Enclave was the type of revolutionary idea we were starving for; turning global perceptions of us on their head. I'd watched them build it from my home. The Secular

Scientific Enclave; it sounded like heaven to me. At that point, there'd been rumours about the Hyperloop, it was true, but there'd also been talk of the coming of the next Messiah, the return of our lands in '48 Palestine and compensation. I'd never believed any of it.

For decades, our building methods had consisted of little more than plastering over dirt-packed bags, so for us to see those steel frames and glass panes shoot up to create giant quartz spikes piercing the sky was like wow. Awesome. We watched them grow from our baked-in alleyways overrun with wheelchairs, chickens and petty criminals.

I should explain that the noise out there, back home, was without end or form. It was as though it grew out of the walls and expanded when released. We spoke of the Enclave's silence as a mystical force and I'd anticipated inner calm to go with it, but when I entered the walls, it wasn't like that at all. For all of us in security, accommodation was down here in the bunkers. I went for weeks without seeing any natural light. I had electricity and hot water, but after a while, I started to feel like the water, my uniform, even the walls, were all trying to bleach me inside and out.

I knew of you, Professor Kamal, since I was a young. The faces of you and your family were graffitied onto the walls of our camp. Mona Kamal; a legend. We all worshipped you, particularly the women. I knew of your construction of the first generation of Body-Bots in the underground bunker in Rafah; your ingenious use of 3D printers to create robotic limbs for the disabled, creating our own army of semi-indestructible fighters. I'd heard of how this bot army burst through the borders in 2032. I knew that your husband had been killed in the bombardments that followed, that you'd also lost your daughters to shelling.

I wanted to believe that I was protecting you, Professor Kamal. As you've probably guessed by now, part of the purpose of my mandate was to find out what the nature of your 'interpersonal relations' were with Dr Schott. The General Assembly informed me of its . . .

ROBOTIC VOICE:

> . . . concern that emotional connections are forming between the Gaza-born Professor Kamal, and one of her co-workers, the Tel Aviv-born (and Guest Visa holding) Dr Eyal Schott, in a way that will compromise their professional integrity and the security of the Economic Hyperloop or Bullet Project. Aural and sensory monitoring have detected distinctive tonal variations, all consistent with romantic empathy. Positive indicators show an 'erosion of the natural boundaries of professional camaraderie' giving rise to a danger of 'compromising national security,' as set out in the Koh' Code of Conduct Manual (2034) for the Guest Visa holders in security clearance positions. No physical rituals indicating a consummated relationship have been identified to date.

Security around the Bullet was such that even I, as a resident of the Strip, hadn't been aware that it was about to launch. It was explained to me as a . . .

ROBOTIC VOICE:

> . . . high-speed, underground shuttle link carrying goods from the Strip's economic zones to neighbouring, affiliated countries in exchange for medical, educational and infrastructural materials.

That, at least, is what the General Assembly told me it was for. My understanding is that essentially, it's frictionless transportation down a tube. I couldn't see how we could afford to undertake such an extravagant project; traditional international banking systems had been completely closed off to us for decades. The breakthrough came only, as I was told . . .

ROBOTIC VOICE:

. . . with the development of cryptocurrencies and the agreement to make block chain backed Ethocoin an official currency of the Strip, opening Gaza to new investment, from countries that felt a political solidarity. Countries as far away as Mexico, Central Africa, and China –

There were other parts of the world where people lived behind walls, it turned out. And you know how the trend goes: the more countries whose citizens' freedom of movement is restricted, the more call there is, from those countries, to only recognise Ethocoin as an international currency. The global economic balance is shifting, they say. So . . . shall I play you the first recording that I made of the two of you? It was only a month ago, but I was so new back then, so naïve. It embarrasses me now. I did try to clean out some of the background noise as much as I could, but there were a lot of drones that day and your screens seem to bleep non-stop in the lab.

LAYLA:

EXTRACT RECORDING ONE
10/6/48 10:43–10:46

SCHOTT: I couldn't sleep last night. I couldn't get this idea out of my head about hentriacontane.

KAMAL: *[Laughing]* Beeswax? We're working with a Bullet here, not a steam engine. There are no rails to rub it on, Dr Schott. Sometimes I wonder why they put you on my team.

SCHOTT: The oldest ideas are the best.

KAMAL: Is that a line from your tailor?

SCHOTT: What, you've got a problem with my pants? Corduroy is the epitome of fabric design. There was nothing left for fabric evolution to do once it hit upon corduroy.

KAMAL: Men and corduroy. RIP 2020.

SCHOTT: Where were you in 2020?

KAMAL: Well, I guess I'd just be starting as an undergraduate at MIT.

SCHOTT: Crazy. You know, I was at Harvard doing my post-doc at the time. We could have –

KAMAL: Been in the same bookclub?

SCHOTT: Sure. A geeky one on circuitry, air bearings –

KAMAL: – and waxy tracks in a vacuum for transporting pods.

SCHOTT: *[Pause]* I can kind of see you there, in the old part of Boston with dark eyeliner and a puffer jacket. I bet you hung out in that bookshop, you know the one with the great café?

KAMAL: *[Laughs]* On the square? You're right. I did go there. But you're wrong about the eyeliner. I was far too serious.

SCHOTT: Who was the man? In 2020, you said their evolution stopped. Who was the epitome of male evolution?

KAMAL *[Microphone enhancement used]* My husband, of course. We're traditional on this side. One birth, one death, one man. We grew up together and got scholarships to the States at the same time, so we could study together. We were one of the 0.1% that were lucky enough to get temporary exit visas.

[Sound of a screen being closed across a window and a vent being opened, noise of aircraft, drones]

SCHOTT: And he left us, when?

KAMAL: He . . . We should work, I think?

SCHOTT: When did you say?

KAMAL: He was killed – in 2032. There was an attack. *[Long pause, sound of messages blipping down on to the main screen]* Where were you at that time?

SCHOTT: *[Indecipherable, despite microphone enhancement]*

KAMAL: Where?

SCHOTT: I said, I was in the military.

END OF RECORDING

I *was* sent by the General Assembly, you were right about that. They wanted me to record and interpret. My expertise in such matters, they attributed to my studies in human psychology, rather than my personal experience, of which they probably knew I had pitiably little. My reports to them included comments such as the following (please excuse my rather officious tone of voice):

LAYLA: This extract shows that Prof. Kamal regrets that Schott has not been substantially modified. To share a laboratory with a Body-Bot would've been preferable. Dr Schott is actively manipulating Professor Kamal by encouraging her to speak of earlier memories, as a precursor to sexual flirtation. He is insensitive to the point of being professionally negligent about the distraction he is causing. Worst of all, Schott is clearly boasting of his previous career in the Enemy State's army.

Dr Schott, you asked what they told me about both of you. I still have the personal data recording from my induction with the General Assembly. They told me about how you had come to the Enclave after the '34 Referendum on Jewish Democracy. This is the rest of what they informed me.

ROBOTIC VOICE:
              Subject Details: Dr Eyal Schott. Guest Visa holder (b.1985). Gender: Male Fields of Expertise: Information Technology, Robotics, Vacuum Transit Circuitry. Percentage: 49.5% (of which 45% Ashkenazi, 4.5% Sephardi). Progeny: One Daughter. Karma 'Koki' Lehmer-Schott (b.2022) living. Occupation: Burlesque Club Dancer. Resident of Enemy State (DNA – 70%), Tel Aviv.

Wife: Betty Lehmer (b. 1990) (DNA – 85%) former resident of Tel Aviv, expired 'in her sleep' in 2036. Enemy State government was accused by the opposition of being instrumental in her demise based on Ms Lehmer's prior membership in the now-defunct group, Women In Black that pledged, inter alia, to 'End the Occupation' (of 1967). The couple separated in 2030. Betty Lehmer actively campaigned for the revocation of the Fifty Percent Rule prior to her ex-husband's deportation. When asked if Mrs Lehmer-Schott would accompany her ex-husband to the New Strip State she famously mocked the idea of anyone 'voluntarily wanting to live in a cage with religious maniacs,' then commenting, that it 'wasn't much different,' (in the Enemy State) 'just the cage is padded with silk and the drones use silencers.' A Betty Lehmer Memorial Fund initially worth 230 Shekcoins was closed by the Enemy State government in 2037 citing tax irregularities.

I should play yours as well, Professor Kamal, shouldn't I? They told me much that was new to me.

ROBOTIC VOICE:

Subject: Professor Mona KAMAL of Beit Hannoun (b. 2000). Gender: Female. Fields of Expertise: European Medicine (including paediatrics, orthopaedics, neuroscience). Nanorobotics DNA Percentage: Negligible (2.5% Sephardi). Progeny: Bilal and Yasmine – both deceased, having been killed during aerial bombardments of 12 of 2024 and 6 of 2032, respectively. Husband: Salah Ayyoub of Deir el Balah – killed during aerial bombardment of 6 of 2032. Dr Ayyoub was an information technology expert, who was the recipient of one of the first generation of Body-Bot 'reboots', developed by him and his wife. The couple's public work in this field has frequently been linked by commentators to the alleged underground 'Hospito-Factory', thought to have been founded in the Deir el Balah region, and blamed by the Enemy State for the 'Body-Bot army' that mounted simultaneous attacks on the Eretz and Rafah border crossings of 2032. The subsequent aerial bombing of the Deir el Balah region led to the martyring of over 1526 citizens, among them Dr Ayyoub, and his and Kamal's daughter, Yasmin.

The General Assembly weren't just nosey about you two. They're nosey about everyone. Being paranoid in the Enclave is nothing more than being streetwise: in my first interview for the role they went straight into asking me about my personal life, my family's history, and my sexual relations. Now that's the one thing they can really police in Deir el Balah. Thieves might climb through your window every night, drones circle your toothbrush, rubbish stacks up to the sky, but just think about touching a man and you'll be strung up on a phone mast by the morning. *[Pause]* My life is a solitary one. I never married. I have a negligible romantic history. Possibly this is why your interactions entranced me so much. As I told the General Assembly, I was only touched by a boy once. A boy at college. He was wily and restless and obsessed by historical statistics. You could ask him anything, how many canons were used in the battle of Waterloo or warheads in the '26 war, anything. His energy excited me. I don't think he'd even noticed me until someone told him about my crush. Then one night, he appeared in the student dorm looking for me. He'd forced his way into my room. Boys weren't allowed, of course. It was a hot day and he smelt. The smell of electricity generators, aftershave. He . . . *[Pause]* Let's listen to you two instead, shall we?

LAYLA:

EXTRACT RECORDING TWO
11/6/48 07:12–07:20

[Sound of a man stumbling and swearing in Hebrew]

KAMAL: What's going on?

SCHOTT: Are you wearing lipstick Professor Kamal? I think you are and it's the same colour as that jacket-y thing you're wearing under your lab coat. I can just see it poking out.

KAMAL: Don't touch me or my lab coat.

[Sound of a lab stool falling over]

KAMAL: Are you drunk, Dr Schott? It's 7:00 AM and you're drinking already.

SCHOTT: To say that makes it sound like there's been a break. I have not stopped being drunk. I've been on a continuum all night. But where is it leading me? Is the end in sight for this Bacchanalian night? Is it yet to come or am I there at the end point?

[Sound of belching]

KAMAL: What happened to you?

SCHOTT: A drink. Another drink and the drunk gets drunker! I found this bar – illegal no doubt – just outside the Enclave. You know, it's really not half as bad as they say it is out there. Even the bouncers with their oldy-worldy machine guns were kind of cute. They all just wanted to talk about soccer. It's not hostile like Iraq say in '28, then you could breathe in the hatred. Your state is okay when you're completely piss drunk. It's even kind of cosy.

KAMAL: I'll have to mark this in your report. It's your state too now, and it's been very good to you, Dr Schott and don't you forget it.

SCHOTT: I won't. God no. Every time I look at my fake Louis XVIth armchairs in my bot-serviced penthouse flat with my very own private air raid shelter I thank your state's Lycra socks. It was but a joke. A poor, distasteful joke of a wretched scientist at the end of time.

KAMAL: Are you ever serious?

SCHOTT: Yes, I am. I'm always serious in my work – with the one bees-waxy rail track exception – and if I am not at work, seriousness happens to me just, you know, in the moment – and it's a serene, earnest moment – it always happens right before I get extremely drunk. It always sets me off.

KAMAL: Is that what set you off last night?

SCHOTT: It was that and my daughter, Koki.

KAMAL: Koki?

SCHOTT: Karma. Koki's a nickname. A baby name.

KAMAL: You gave your daughter an Arab name?

SCHOTT: Thought you'd like that. I told you we were radicals, didn't I? Anyway, every night, religiously, I still punch in Koki's code into my tele-screen, hoping her angelic little face will pop up like it did when she was twelve, when I last spoke to her, and every night for the past fourteen years I've been dialling in and getting the same automated Hebrew message telling me that my call is prohibited, and that my ranking lacks the necessary clearances for it to be transferred to the territory in question. My ranking! They didn't complain about my ranking when I served in their army.

KAMAL: I'd rather not hear about that. Here, drink this –

[Sound of a glass being placed on a table]

SCHOTT: Water! [Smacks his lips] Cold, freshly desalinated water! Sprinkled with a touch of chlorine. Nectar of the gods. Christ that's good. Do you have more?

KAMAL: No mention of religion, remember. It's secular here. It sets off the sensors. So what happened next? I think we can be authorised five minutes to – resolve all this.

SCHOTT: Last night I got straight through. They must have changed my God damn ranking or something, but before I have time to adjust the hair over my bald patch, there she is – my darling little Koki all dressed for work in a gold lamé bikini with laser-responsive nipple tassels. Eyes zooming around like cluster bombs in the desert. Turns out she was hoping I was her dealer which is why she answered even though my number was concealed. Think I'm intoxicated? Well this is nothing compared to my baby Koki, I can tell you that. Stoned, shloned, screwed off her pretty little head on some Soma concoction.

[Voice trails off. Sound of something being repeatedly hit]

KAMAL: Dr Schott, Dr Schott, Eyal! The launch is less than three weeks away. You know what the situation will be like if the international investors don't get the results they want, not to mention the rioting that would follow if the food and medicine don't get in before the winter. This isn't some Silicon Valley vanity project of the '20s, this is a question of survival.

[Sniffing sound]

SCHOTT: Survival as what, though? The last time I felt this low was in '34 when the final DNA test came through saying I was categorically an under-50 Percenter and these maniacs on social media accused my mother of sleeping with a goy. She had a stroke. Not only was her only child about to be deported, she was also labelled some kind of Muslim–fucker.

KAMAL: Dr Schott!

SCHOTT: Sorry, Professor Kamal, Mona. Sorry. I don't know where that came from. It's not even in my vocabulary. I was paraphrasing a racist troll. Dear God. I'm becoming one of them. I'll go sleep it off. I'll be back in two hours and then we'll get that Bullet shooting down the rail like shit off a proverbial shovel.

KAMAL: And by then you'll find that it's casters, not rails.

[Sound of rattling, then of something shattering]

SCHOTT: Are they bombing again? Do they really have nothing better to do?

KAMAL: They're provoking us. They want us to test their new anti-missile Dome. They're floating shares tomorrow – a good show will push up the value.

SCHOTT: Cynical, it's all so cynical.

KAMAL: Sleep it off, Dr Schott.

LAYLA: As the ancients said, in vino veritas, and it is clear in this second recording that Schott, when inebriated, shows his true personality which clearly exhibits the following undesirable features: (1) Sexual insatiability and a desire for unwanted contact with a female member of his team. His superior, no less. (2) Alcoholism. (3) Continued attempts to contact a citizen of the Enemy State. (4) Racist language and the use of derogatory slurs.

END OF RECORDING

You can hear that I'm becoming more strident in my condemnation of you, Dr Schott. At the time, I was actually becoming less sure of everything I was doing and what I believed in, but I was not able to back out. My interview process had involved a stage that I need to explain. You see, when I arrived, the General Assembly had required me to fill out an application, including details of my romantic and sexual experience. I entered that I had none. I was then called into a meeting. It was in the Grand Chamber, which overlooked the two palms and the Moroccan mosaic fountain. There were two women with short hair and boots on the raised platform. I need you to listen to this, because I personally found it sinister.

GA OFF 1: Green tea?

LAYLA: Thank you.

GA OFF 1: Let me add some sugar for you.

LAYLA: Thank you.

GA OFF 2: I hope you are treating her well. That you stirred it in properly.

LAYLA: It's fine. Thank you.

GA OFF 2:   We want you to know that we consider your application excellent.

LAYLA: Thank you. I am very grateful –

GA OFF 2:   Pretty eyes and the same accent as my grandmother.

GA OFF 1:   Miss Wattan, we really have only one issue that we need to resolve. I just want to ask you about this question regarding romantic or sexual experience. Now that isn't really correct, is it?

LAYLA: No, really there was nothing.

GA OFF 2:   Let's show her, then shall we?

The two of them looked at each other before she pressed play on her screen. On the wall to my right the scene in my dorm appeared. It was recorded and preserved in the same way that I've recorded and preserved your voices.

LAYLA: What are you doing here? Boys aren't allowed.

[Sound of footsteps echoing]

BOY: I heard that you wanted me. What was it that you wanted me to do? This was it, wasn't it?

LAYLA: Get off me. Someone will see.

BOY: I know you want me. Why are you pretending you don't?

It was a high definition reproduction of a piece of my past I'd managed to erode from my mind. It became so vivid I could smell the boy, his breath like oil made from cigarettes. I couldn't talk after that. It didn't matter, the official did the talking for me.

GA OFF 2: Your key role, as a Recorder, will be to analyse the nature of the relations between a man and a woman and to identify the possible existence of unprofessional conduct; your truthfulness and absolute loyalty is therefore essential, do you understand?

The officer said this as she nodded to the screen, which had frozen on a frame that showed my right breast, exposed from where the boy had pulled my nightgown aside. Everyone knows how easily footage like that can spread, how simply one can be ruined. One word and they'd show it in hologram over my parents' home.

I've read that explaining the cause of a wrongdoing can elicit sympathy and forgiveness. I would not expect you to condone my behaviour. I am not sure what it is in these recordings that lulls me into listening to them again and again, but here is the last one that I have. You should have it as it belongs to you.

LAYLA:
EXTRACT RECORDING THREE
11/6/48 12:10–12:24

KAMAL: You're back. Revitalised, I hope?

SCHOTT: It took a little longer than I thought. I'm now full of remorse and repentance, of course.

KAMAL: Glad to hear it.

SCHOTT: I also took some time to find out what's been going on in the Pure State over there, why my ranking had changed and – do you know what's happened or do you totally isolate yourself from political realities down here?

KAMAL: I'm Palestinian. We're born with a news chip in our head. We don't need to read the news, we just sense it. I also have work to do.

SCHOTT: You know then, about the reversal? The Knesset decision. The liberals and the lefties have finally stopped squabbling and have got their shit together. They've overturned the 2034 Referendum. They must have finally got pissed off with those tax-evading, draft-dodging Orthodox believers for shutting down all the best bars.

[Long pause]

KAMAL: Well, what can I say? *Mabrook.* Congratulations. You can go home and get Karma off to rehab and a nunnery. I guess the charms of Elite IV won't be enough to hold you here any longer.

SCHOTT: What happened to the lipstick? You looked pretty, like Rachel Weisz in that 2D noughties film set in Africa.

KAMAL Can we continue with our work? It's really not relevant how I look or what you're going to do with your personal life either. I'll just have to re-staff if you choose to resign.

SCHOTT: You know we're way ahead of schedule. We've done so many trial runs; the Bullet's running with the fluidity of a champion ice skater. You get so anxious about these details. We've been over them again and again.

KAMAL   You think I'm, what, neurotic?

SCHOTT: 'Neurotic?' What does that mean in this dissociated world? We've all had our synapses shot to smithereens with everything going on around us. *[Pause]* But being with you, being with you, well, it . . . it adds a different dimension. A soothing one.

KAMAL: Working with me, you mean.

SCHOTT: Working with you, getting to know you, being with you. Yes, being with you. I don't know how to say this, Mona. Mona? I can call you Mona, can't I?

KAMAL: If it helps you to work with me.

[Palpitation sensor: power on]

SCHOTT: I see a possibility, being with you, that all of this, this whole fucked-up world of ours, could be manageable, could be workable. It could all be almost dream-like, if we allowed ourselves, not just to work –

[Sound of message alert pings]

KAMAL:　　But to –

SCHOTT:　　But to be together, you know, like, well, like a couple –

KAMAL:　　*[Snort of laughter]* As if that would be allowed!

SCHOTT :　　How can they forbid it? Come on – think about it, I mean this whole Enclave is set up on this much-publicised idea of non-discrimination. We could play it to our advantage, no? We could say, I mean this is, it's only – oh God, I'm fumbling like a teenager, why do we never grow up when it comes to these things?

KAMAL:　　Please don't set off the sensors with your references.

SCHOTT:　　The main thing is, Mona, you want it too. That you want to be with me. The rest we can deal with. You do want it, don't you? I know you do. I know it, but tell me anyway. I have to hear it from you.

[Palpitation sensor: rate increases]

KAMAL　　*[Very faint; detected only in the lighting cones microphones]* I do want it.

[Palpitation sensor: further rate increases]

[Sound of lab stools scraping, of a slight groan, cameras switch on in all corners, camera flashes go off capturing images]

KAMAL: They can't be! I have non-monitoring status. They're not allowed to watch me. It was one of my terms.

[Sound from the corridor]

SCHOTT: There's someone there! There's someone setting this all off.

[Sound of heavy door being thrown open]

SCHOTT: *[Shouting]* Who is this girl? What are you doing? Mona, why is this woman in the corridor? Give me that!

END OF RECORDING

N

Majd Kayyal

Translated by Thoraya El-Rayyes

The Departure

THE STREET WAS FROZEN OVER. And that sharp, nasty cold. That silent sort of cold that doesn't ride on the wind, that doesn't fall with the rain. A cold that permeates the wide town squares and the insides of coat sleeves, that sinks into the fingernails and creeps in under them. A cold that pierces the eyes and stings the lips, vibrating between teeth prised apart and worn away by the passage of time. That sort of cold that empties the streets, carefully wiping people from them so they become a giant grave for night to rest in. After the long years of heat we invented, created, contrived, lied into existence on the long nights when we lived in a void, believing in the existence of a sun. A sun we invented, created, contrived, lied into existence before it set. The sort of cold that makes a person feel lonely.

N's response today surprised me. I asked him: 'Is it cold over there?' He fidgeted, contemplating the question. When ideas move through his head, his mouth twists up along with his cheek and shoulders and he shifts around in his seat. He replied: 'People move around at night . . . a lot . . .' He swallowed the rest of the sentence and awaited my reaction to the truth he'd just divulged.

N is beautiful. The child has grown into a young man, but he still has that innocent nature. I wasn't that surprised by his reply. I already knew, of course, that their nights are unlike ours, noisy and alive with people. But the way he linked the heat to the movement of people, I didn't expect that. It raised a sharp question mark in my mind. I mean, a sharp-shaped one, a question mark resembling a fishing rod, its hook curling in, scratching my brain and stringing me up like a small fish.

I don't think I told him any of the thoughts I was having. Maybe the image travelled into his subconscious through his upbringing. It's a bitch, that thing they call an upbringing. We're only aware of the very end of its tail but its smooth slippery body stretches under our clothes and its head bites our children with poisonous memories, with images we spent a war and a lifetime trying to bury. I've done all I can to get away from the war, from the sediment it left inside me, but it keeps resurfacing. Not even our children's innocence can wash it away. N's innocence – even if it brings back memories of your voice, the warmth of your hands and your opinions on Herman Hesse – can't overcome the taste of gunpowder dust in my throat, dust transmitted from the throat of one generation to the next.

When we arrived at the Photon Transit station, N was trying to calm his nerves, to brush off the remains of his resentment and find some compassion beneath it. 'You're insane,' he said, just because I had insisted on going to the station with him in this weather. I had ignored him and reminded him to be careful with the bottle of olive oil in his bag, to make sure it didn't spill and to gram me if he was planning to visit again in the coming months so I could order a nice red grouper from Ibn al-Qalaq to eat together. These days, grouper has to be ordered a week or two in advance. He said he'd be back soon: 'Shall I bring you some Goldstar? We're allowed to bring in a six-pack,' he joked. I pretended to kick his behind and we laughed. I checked to make sure he had enough time to get to the beam chamber and hugged him goodbye.

As he walked into the station with his bag, I called out to him to make sure he hadn't forgotten his ID. So he wouldn't think I was clinging to a last chance to keep him here longer, I joked, in Hebrew: 'Do you have your ID?' He turned around, laughing and gave the reply he'd memorised by heart from all the times he'd heard me say it, even though he didn't really know where it came from: 'Where are the fish?' and walked away. Remember how much you used to love that film? Elia Suleiman . . . *The Time that Remains*. Father and son fishing at night under military surveillance. I grew to love that dialogue.

I turned around and walked until I reached the curb at the edge of Habash Highway. I sat and rolled a cigarette, watching the road and waiting for the capsule to leave the station. I watched N disappear into the tunnel leading to the beam chamber – the departure tunnel, not the arrival tunnel. There was a spectacular flash of light. It's unlike any other light I've seen, a light we don't know the source or path of, which swallows our children to over there, to the other here.

And now, this sharp nasty cold. This silent cold that pierces the eyes and stings the lips, vibrating between teeth prised apart and worn away by the passage of time. I walked along the highway towards the city. To my left, the stormy sea. How did we let the issue of the sea pass? Two weeks for a grouper. Our blind damn hearts. The cemeteries facing the sea are one of the few things that haven't changed, even though this wasn't a condition of the Israelis. We thought it would be profane, removing the graves, so we left them in the soil as is. The soil. I noticed that the municipality had planted orange trees all the way down the road, a nice idea. Speaking of nice ideas, I'd passed through Tal al-Samak and stopped to look at the rubble of the Limnology and Marine

Research Centre that you'd given the order to blow up. Funny how things came together to make its destruction necessary. At first, you'd said it was the ugliest building in the city and that the revolution should destroy the Zionists' brutalist architecture. Then you told me about the horrific memories you had of the building. After the revolution became armed, we heard the news that the place we thought was for researching frogs provided them with military support. Damn, if only I had the courage to ask N what's happened to the Tal al-Samak over there. But of course, I won't. I won't ask him anything about over there. If a single question escapes me, it would unleash a flood of others that the entire Naqab desert couldn't soak up.

I hate empty streets, hate them more than anything else in the world. But I have to admit that I like to take advantage of their emptiness to laugh out loud when I remember something funny. As I walked past Mar Gregorios church, the one that was renamed after Archbishop Hajjar, I remembered your scathing comment when you saw them raise a photo of him at one of the protests. You asked: 'Why are you carrying a photo of Léon Morin?' I've never laughed as hard as I did that day. Oh God. The church is still empty as it's always been, like a frail old man sitting by the shore. It's over a hundred years old now. I think Archbishop Hajjar had it built before he made his position clear to the Peel Commission,[1] if I'm not mistaken. No one mentions the archbishop anymore. And no one knows who Léon Morin is either. No one watches films these days. No one watches them, and the streets are empty. So I laugh alone in empty streets, chuckling into the cold night at a joke over thirty years old.

During the hour I walked, my thoughts were on fire. Fragments of memory fell like dew drops on my mind's surface. A foggy kind of regret, with images projecting from my eyes into the air before me, spilling out of me and escaping.

And once home and closing the door behind me, this place seemed small and all I wanted was to hide from the streets of Haifa. I had to swallow that loud chaos that forever urges me to talk to you.

This loneliness has become impossible to bear.

My mind was exhausted, so I escaped to the VR hoping it would distract me from my loneliness. I haven't used it for days. N had used it for a few hours while he was here, but I'd been busy. From the moment I collapsed onto my sofa in my library, and turned on the reality, an overwhelming warmth passed through the wires and headset. An incomprehensible warmth wrapped itself around the heart and body, sending it into a state of calm. N explained to me that this is purely biological, that it helps prepare the user's body to receive an accurate sensory experience and the mind to receive the data efficiently. It creates the optimal conditions for the mind to communicate directly with the internet. People are addicted to playing realities, an all-consuming obsession. If only they got something of value from this 'ultimate art', as they call it. The market is controlled by the Americans and Japanese, and they've focused all their attention on producing war and porn realities, things like that. The kinds of things people get addicted to, that keep them connected to the machine for hours and hours on end. Damn, I've turned into my father talking about iPhones all those years ago. Of course, there are some exceptions, some young people who produce their own, independent realities. N told me about the subcultures; his mind is a vast library of realities. I don't know how he finds the time to play them all. I think he'll be a good producer; he reminds me of you, with your knowledge of cinema. But these indie realities aren't as easy to find over here as they are over there.

I turned on a reality by a French-Egyptian director that N gave me for my birthday last year. I'm glad he still makes an effort to celebrate it, no one pays attention to birthdays these days. It was a historical–cultural reality about the first half of the twentieth century in Egypt. The main narrative is based around groups of artists and writers from that period who aren't very well known, in particular the Art and Liberty Group. Since it takes place pre-1947, in a time without radical political changes, the director has more freedom from the algorithm, so players have more control and the plot isn't inevitable.

He gave me this reality because I'd told him how much I love Ramses Younan and that period of Egyptian art. I'd told him how I had been surprised to find a retrospective of the Art and Liberty Group's work showing at the Centre Pompidou, when I visited Paris back in 2016. It was the first time I'd come across Ramses Younan. I hadn't known anything about him. Salem knew, he'd been with me on that trip. After we left the gallery, we walked around the city all afternoon as Salem expounded on Younan's life and his work. That was the day I bought you that Polish poster of the film *The Double Life of Veronique* that you liked. I confess that I didn't appreciate the film back then. It was Salem who chose the present and insisted that we pretend I chose it. Today, I realised that I've never mentioned Salem to N.

N says that this reality caused controversy when some users discovered that the director had removed a young Gamal Abdel Nasser from its database, so that you can't detect his presence or see him. It started a debate about the role of the director and their duty to present reality accurately, versus the freedom to manipulate it for some artistic end.

The worst part is what a rush this generation is in to be impressed and consumed by the same things older generations were, reinventing the wheel. Abdel Nasser!? Realities have tried to delete Edgar Allan Poe from history and failed. They've tried to hide George Washington too and Christopher Columbus and Napoleon and the Prophet Mohammed himself, twice. I understand that people used to debate the idea of leaving behind one's foreparents, but today? Damn.

What I've discovered, darling, from all of this, is simple. These VRs, for all of their different versions and brands, would never have worked without one key element: the isolation of the person inside the machine, their total anonymity, the complete abandonment of their memory. When a person plays their chosen reality, they are reborn, a new person with a new past. Complete isolation is the secret to eliminating the present. Isolation from the other, isolation from the self, isolation from existence. The isolation of Schrodinger's *qitt* inside the box (was it a *qitt* or *qitta*? In English, the word cat doesn't even tell you if it is male or female, that is how isolated it is). This is what we still fail to realise after the war: we accepted a life in the present, with no past. That is what the Israelis understood when they demanded Article 7 of the Agreement. That is what turned our glorious victory into a defeat.

When I connect to the VR and play different realities (my library isn't very big), I start to forget you. If I didn't, I wouldn't spend so much time in there admiring Angie Aflaton, for instance. It's you I love; I'm not interested in Cairo or Paris as much as I would like to walk with you in the streets of Hadar. We used to walk there at the beginning of the 2000s and sense the remnants of the 1990s everywhere. That was when we still used to invent the sun, before the cold flooded Haifa and everyone – Arabs and Israelis – buried themselves in the warmth of their sofas, in their different realities. Luckily for me, the VR turns itself off automatically when it registers that the user has fallen asleep. Otherwise, I would have spent a lifetime in the Cairo of 1944, looking at a Ramses Younan painting. A painting called 'Nature Loves a Vacuum'.

★

The Encounter

Ibn al-Qalaq

I don't have any grouper.

Where do you think you are? There's no grouper, it's gone . . . poof! Disappeared from what's left of the sea, eh. Where? Grouper. God forgive all of you. I do have grouper, but it's imported – frozen. But grouper from our sea? Wave goodbye. Rarer than the rarest gem. Maybe if you asked for amberjack, if you asked for mullet or seabream. It's possible, it could be possible. But grouper? I'm telling you, impossible. Not to mention that, no offence, there are only two of you and grouper is a big fish.

Try Abu Jamal. Yes, you're right, not frozen, but Abu Jamal. That son of a bitch has thirteen children, all of them raised in the sea. Not one is educated, or has formal training. They even dive with harpoons. They aren't good for anything but fishing. He's the only one who can catch a grouper from our small stretch of sea, try him. With a harpoon! The grouper that's left can only be caught with harpoons. Grouper, eh. It's a sly fish. Who's going to dive for hours to catch you one fish? Grouper. God forgive all of you. Sly? Yes, it's sly – if it senses danger or gets hooked it'll go straight to its shelter and hide, deep underground. Not to mention that it puffs itself up between the rocks so that it's hard to get it out. Or rather it did, when it was still around. Ah, that fish. Did you know that it's born female and turns male when it grows older? But it's pretty much gone forever now. They said, *Only ten kilometres into the sea are included in the Agreement*. Great. Let their ports and submarines and factories swallow everything up. Let the chlorine and excavators and dynamite burn the living and the dead in the sea. The goddamn sea. Goddamn you f . . . you cloned the country – OK, so why not clone the sea, all of it? You built a second level, you built a parallel Palestine. Fine, so clone the whole sea with it. They said *No*. Why? They said, *The neighbouring countries! The Agreement says ten kilometres, no more.* Do you have a lighter? Thanks. What is it you said your son studies over there? God protect and keep him. That's an impressive profession, but what will he do here? Haha, maybe he'll find a job in Tokyo. Reality producer, eh? Is he happy there? They say life is easier there, but I won't let my son go. His grandfather wasn't martyred in Beirut for him to live over there.

Abu Jamal. Try Abu Jamal. Do you know him? You must. Did you hear about the kid that killed his brother by accident? His son. They were playing with a fishing harpoon. Ages ago, years back, you must know the story. You don't? His eldest was fishing with a net and after a few hours, they say, he came back with a big haul of mullet. You know, those small red mullets. The younger brother came back with the harpoon and a huge grouper. A gigantic one. Abu Jamal looked at the grouper, stared and stared. He went crazy for it! 'Ah, you champion!' See, the older son got annoyed because his father wasn't paying any attention to him even though he'd caught a huge haul of mullet. So he picked up the harpoon lying on the rocks – you know what it sounds like, don't you? – WIIISSSSSSSHHHHHHTTTTT, and the arrow went into his brother's chest. He dropped down dead. Abu Jamal is a madman now, they say he went completely crazy. But try him anyway. You're only buying a fish, it's not like you're asking him to marry you. Who? Exactly, that's the guy, yes yes yes. There are a few other families that left Gaza before the genocide but his is the only one everyone knows. Poor guy, he's a simple one. He says he had a vision. He had a dream where he was surrounded by a vast whiteness and then everything around him crumbled, so he knew a catastrophe was lying in wait. When he woke up, he took his family and escaped from Gaza, two days before the bomb. For a long time, he thought he was Christ. He'd say that God had sent him a revelation because he'd been the only virtuous man in Gaza. I feel sorry for him, to be honest, he calmed down and for a while he started to get better, then that nightmare with his son happened. And still, he wants to raise his children in the sea. Bullshit. I mean, it was obvious from the beginning of the 2000s that Gaza would be wiped out. When the bomb fell, after one war then another then another then two more with two ceasefires in between then another war, the population was a quarter of what it had been in 2000. Anyway, if it wasn't for that, they would never have dreamed of signing an agreement with such a small strip of the sea. If the Gazans were around, they wouldn't have given it up. The sea is in their blood, those people, just like the Akkawis. But in Akka, they were the firewood of the revolution, not the lighters. They didn't have a say in the Agreement. But the lighters of Haifa, they didn't give a shit about fishing.

Abu Jamal, try Abu Jamal . . .

N

Are you ready? Running late? I had to play a reality and things got a little complicated. It smells good. Bull's tail? Wow. Eight hours? It smells amazing. Yes, please. Whiskey, no ice. It was a sketchy reality. Shit. I'm working on . . . on my graduation project. That novel yes, have you read it? Really? You didn't tell me that last time. Christopher Priest is excellent. But my project isn't about the novel itself, it's about language design in the 'ultimate art'. I know. I've been working on the project for three years and I still don't understand it. But basically: in most VR realities right now, there's only one language. It might be your language, say, if you're American and the reality is in English. Or it might be translated, if you're an Arab and you're watching a reality in English. No, no, I don't mean translated like in the movies . . . I mean that the database contains the information for the other language as well. But the language data is loaded as part of your character's past, so you skip having to learn the language. So I'm looking into interacting with a new language while you're in the reality itself, and the possibility that you can create an improvised language in the process, a new language. It needs a rewriting of the code so that the database expands cumulatively along different axes. It first came to me when I started to learn Hebrew.

Haha . . . it's ok, I know it's hard to get your head round. I'm not required to find the ideal solution anyway, because there isn't one. Yes please, without ice yes. Haha, no not the village elder's tail, this elder doesn't have a tail. His name is Ayman. I just remembered, his name was Ayman. If he'd had a tail, it wouldn't have been as delicious as this one. Bull's tail. Excellent, really. Cooked in beer? Really? Hm, I didn't even know you could get Guinness here. At the company where I used to work, they had a barrel of Guinness on every floor. Yes. No, Nada? No, she left the company too. She wanted . . . yes, we're still together. We're really happy, she works at another company now, she's done with university but she's setting up a big project. She wants to direct a reality based on a movie. A Palestinian movie, which is . . . I wanted to tell you about this . . . Maybe later . . .

None? Yes I remember you said something about fish last time. None at all? Hm, are they endangered? Wow. The same sea, right? I mean, apart from the ten kilometre strip, there aren't two parallel Mediterraneans like there are two lands. Yes, I thought about it when I read the Agreement. It's strange, the Agreement. This whole thing we're living in is just strange. Don't you think? Haha, yes, I know. We studied parallel universes in the time travel lectures. It's a compulsory course for all the students in the department. Even now it seems crazy, but people can get used to anything.

Yes, the war is over. That's what matters. Of course, I'm no judge. I wasn't in your place. I'm sure it was horrific. You . . . you know back there they don't comply with Article 7, I mean, not at home. No, I mean . . . what I wanted to ask is whether the reason you don't talk about it is just because of Article 7? Or because you don't want to think about what happened back there . . . ? Yes . . . no, OK, it's fine, but you know, sometimes I wonder. I've read the official reports that the Joint Committee commissioned into the history of the Agreement. But not more than that. But . . . no, of course. Of course not, I don't think anyone would dare produce a reality about the revolution. The reality that Nada is working on might have something to do with the Palestinian question, but she's going to try to focus on personal details.

What? The revolution, what do you mean what revolution? Yes, I mean the war. Sorry, but it was a revolution, wasn't it? Why not say revolution? I mean, Baba, I don't know much about it but, in general, I wasn't born yesterday. A reality? No, I don't think so. Not any time in the next few years anyway. No one would dare. Everyone feels that Article 7 is the spine that keeps the peace standing. All these people are living a trauma they can't overcome. Didn't I ever tell you, at school they taught us about the Agreement? That was the only Article they asked us to memorise. The only one. School was a funny place. I still can't recite the times tables, but I know 'Both parties shall refrain from commemorating the hostilities that occurred between them, or any part thereof. This shall include commemorations of a direct and/ or symbolic nature, as well as commemorations of celebration and/or mourning.' Hell, I know it all word for word. 'The parties shall limit activities related to the history of the hostilities between them to the field of research, under the stipulation that any such research activities must be authorised jointly by both parties.' That's it. I took twenty-seven rulers across the palm to memorise it in the seventh grade. Shit. It's not important. Empty, I'll pour another. Really? You supported that article? There's a question that's been on my mind. If you could answer it . . . who suggested the travel ban? I mean, that those born before the Agreement couldn't travel between the two worlds. Ah . . .

Any topic?

Ah, yes.

I wanted to ask you about my grandfather's house in al-Halissa, if I can live there. If the tenant doesn't mind moving out, I mean . . .

Yes. I, no of course I don't have a problem with living here with you. The opposite, actually. But I, I think I am going to move in with Nada. I told you that Nada wants to direct a reality? She . . . wants to direct it in memory of her father. She wants to direct it about a film her father used to love. Actually, that he used to love because he was in secretly love with a woman who loved that film. But she married someone else a few years before the Agreement. He was so heartbroken that he decided to stay in Israel, so that he'd never see her or her husband again. She wants to direct the reality not just in memory of her father. But . . . how can I put it, maybe in memory of all the things that were ripped apart by the Agreement. Now . . . I mean, yes you, I mean, maybe. I won't go into details – I understand that you don't want to know anything about what goes on over there – I'm sure you can imagine, the Palestinians who decided to stay there, they aren't in the best situation. I mean, there is a lot of harassment, even of . . . our generation. Nada can't stand being there any longer.

Her father disappeared a long time ago, he was . . . a fierce opposition activist. In the beginning, they said he was under administrative detention. He was detained for five years, then they released him for health reasons, and his age. I mean, he wasn't old but prison, you know, drained him . . . they found his corpse at dawn, the day after he was released, spat out by the beach next to the ruins of a concrete building destroyed in the war, by The Gregory. Yes, very sad, difficult . . . very. She is going through a lot and she wants to move here. To leave there. The Gregory. Yes, the Gregory is a nightclub, down by Ain Hayam in an old building that looks like a church. It's mostly Russians who go there. The important thing is that, Nada and I, we're thinking of moving here. So . . . I said, I thought if . . . it was possible. To move into the house in al-Halissa.

Me

Al-Qalaq didn't have the grouper I wanted. That man talks so much, it's unbearable. But he has a kind heart, he isn't underhanded. The shopkeepers in Haifa aren't too dodgy in general, since the market was never aimed at tourists. People know each other so they'd be too embarrassed to cheat one another. Another glass, please, with ice, yes. Al-Qalaq sent me to Abu Jamal, the Gazan, who lives by the sea. I walked towards him but then changed my mind. I felt a severe pang in my heart, thinking about his tragic story. That day, he became hysterical. He jumped in the water and started to swim. They found him on the shores of al-Tantoura. He imagined he was looking for his dead son. He went mad and dived into the sea to bring him back. It was pure tragedy.

I had thought of going to him. I started down from Wadi al-Nisnas Market to Laila Street, walking past a building where Ma'yan Habira used to be: a famous bar that served Eastern European food near the Seikaly building. It was brilliant, our favourite bar – your mother and I. Every time we went there, we would order the bull's tail and eat it with beer. Amazing. I don't cook it like they used to over there. When the revolution started, Ma'yan closed its doors. And when we got married in

2022, not at a church, nor with a *ma'thun,* of course. I asked her about her bride price as a joke and she asked me to learn how to cook bull's tail. Cheers! To her, my love, my heart . . . my love. Yes, please, and ice. We always used to dream about bringing back the real names of the streets, the names the Zionists changed for those 76 years. Names like al-Muluk, Iraq, Ma'moun, Saladin, al-Jabal Street. And al-Karmel Boulevard that those losers, the Cultural Liberation Movement, renamed Abu Nuwwas Street. Fuck cultural liberation. But after the victory of the . . . revolution, we found that the number of new streets the Israelis had built in Haifa since the Nakba would never have been enough for all the names of the martyrs even if the Agreement had let us use those names, so we had to use much older, traditional ones instead. In the beginning, I didn't mind. Then I remembered an old friend who used to say that the names of the young people who took the reins of the future at the barricades in Wadi al-Jemal and Stella Maris are worthier than the names of any king from an era defeated by colonialism.

This friend, Salem, a young guy. We were really close to him, your mother and I. We met him when he started working as a barman at a place we liked. We liked him because he was . . . original, weird and original. You couldn't fit his opinions into any kind of mould. No matter the topic, he had his own way of looking at it, one that wouldn't occur to anyone else. If you gave a Marxist analysis, he'd respond with Liberalism. If you said something structuralist, he'd respond with Sufism. And if you said something Sufi, he'd make everyone laugh at you. He was a central nerve in the revolution, very active and exceptionally brave. I would give him the most sensitive missions. Back then, he was also the fiercest critic of the revolution. He was a poet, obsessed with artistic, cultural and intellectual work, but at the same time an enemy of those dogs from the Cultural Liberation Movement. Their nemesis. He fought without killing. He was somehow disgusting and charming at the same time, and always arguing with your mother about cinema. Those two were like coal on a fire. As we expected, he was one of the most intense opponents of the Agreement when it was put forward. But we didn't expect he'd refuse to return with us, to the Palestine world. He decided to stay in the Israeli world. It was clear none of us would be able to travel between the worlds, only the generations born after the Agreement. So he'd decided to leave us forever. He refused. He had some strange ideas. Hard to understand. I sometimes used to think he was acting for personal reasons, especially because he'd distanced himself from us. But your mother insisted that Salem was just very principled, a radical. At one point his radicalism became more severe, especially towards me. His ideas? His ideas . . . I don't know. They weren't strange. That's not the word. Let's just say that they weren't pragmatic, not at all. We were at war, and he wanted to think about the war like someone contemplating life in Elika. Sorry, it was an old café we had back then. What wasn't possible? His reasons? His reasons. He had a lot of justifications, he's probably stuffed them up his ass by now. He used to talk about our responsibility – even if we were the victims – towards the humanity of our enemies. Fuck the humanity of our enemies, I'd say. That if we liberated ourselves without liberating the Israelis from Zionism it wasn't a liberation at all, and all that bullshit . . . that bullshit. That this victory, he thought, was essentially a hi-tech, scientific apartheid. Yes, please, no, no need for ice. My opinion? They could have what they wanted, an entire nation exclusively for their 'pure blood'. And we could have what we wanted, refugees returning to their homes in Gaza, in Nablus, in Haifa, in Jaffa, and *'God spared the faithful from the evils of war'*. What more could we want? What were we supposed to do? Put a sofa out under the shelling and open a psychotherapy clinic to cure Holocaust trauma? The goddamn Holocaust. Salem's problem was he was a coward looking for justifications. He was afraid of the future, that we'd arrived at the gates of new struggles: with Islamists, with Fatah, with the corrupt real estate companies that specialised in refugee property claims, between refugees from Lebanon and Jordan, between the Palestinians who'd been in Israel and the ones from the West Bank. Why else did he stay over there? Is that an excuse? Yesterday, I was walking down Jaffa Street, sorry, Laila Street. Honestly, Haifa today is just as beautiful as it was back then. No, I don't think we should be spiteful forever. You of all people know how persistent I am, encouraging young people to go study in the Israeli Haifa. Yes, maybe because it was the only way I could get you to live through something like what I lived through, what I couldn't talk about. You know that people from a lot of cities, especially in the Bank, criticise our Haifa, the Palestinian Haifa, for being the city that sends the most students over to their one. I think what Tamim Rabba' said makes a lot of sense, even if I disagree with him. The revolution was victorious and the refugees have returned, there's no reason to continue this obsession forever. Moving from Palestinian Haifa to Israeli Haifa, from Jaffa to Tel Aviv, from Palestinian Hebron to Israeli Hebron, from Nablus to Shakhim, it's no different from travelling to Berlin or London or Boston. But to abandon us, to stay there in order to liberate them? No way, it's absurd. Another piece? Bull's tail is good, eh? Delicious. Salem taught me how to cook bull's tail so I could marry your mother. It's a shame that he kind of changed, after we got married, but war . . . war makes people crazy.

The Return

My eyes shut. I clench my jaw. I dig my nails into the back of my neck. I remember that moment. I stand in front of the painting and stare into a vast, raging, endless sea. He was in it, a huge skeleton that looked like a shattered sailboat in front of a sea foaming at its own futility. That's how I saw the painting. Not from a distance or from close up, I saw it from the inside. It swallowed me until I felt like I'd been incarnated into the body of the nude woman standing between the boat and the sea. I don't remember where that image came from anymore. The things I've seen have become disturbingly hard to disentangle. Did it happen in the Egyptian reality in 1944? Or on that Autumn day in the Centre Pompidou in 2016? I stare at the painting. 'Nature Loves a Vacuum' – Ramses Younan battles with the phantom of Aristotle, and a sound I no longer recognise, a voice falling hesitantly into the wound of an innocent memory. Salem's voice, reading from a book he once gave us: 'I am the slave of my baptism. You, my parents, have contrived my catastrophe and your own.' I am engulfed by an intense fear.

Things have changed. I miss you even more than before. I thought my loneliness would fade when N returned. Nada is an amazing young woman, intelligent and kind, easy to let into your heart. I feel a lot of love for her. But something in N has changed. As if he's suddenly grown older, become, in a certain kind of way, a man. Now, his heart has a roughness to it – harmless but sharp. He's become more sarcastic, speaks less. But somehow more attentive, caring and worried about me, and less overwhelmed by things. I know in my heart, as a father, that he carries a heavy secret. That is how people grow old. They carry secrets that are bigger than their bodies. As for me, my body has become feeble and the secrets of the past have sniffed out the scent of prey, pouncing on me with their nightmares. And not just that, they've started to interfere with my enjoyment of VR. At night, I dream of the protests in 2020. It starts out wonderful, I'm in amongst the people, the noise, the chants, and I can feel that warmth, that heat, that burning flame. Then there is a crowding that starts to choke me and I drown beneath the protestors' feet. I suffocate in a fiery volcanic sea of people and wake up terrified and sweating. My bulging eyes light up the darkness in the room, then I am covered in a stinging cold that takes me back to the beginning.

Something else has changed in N, I see the effect studying in the Israeli world has had on him. I think, during his last visit, he tried hard not to seem influenced by Israelis. But now that he's settled down back over here, it's as if he's free from the need to prove his loyalty to this country. At first, I thought he was doing it so Nada wouldn't feel as if she were in some kind of exile. But this girl has nothing to do with Israelis. She has a beautiful authenticity, and her Arabic, maybe because she learned classical Arabic later on, has a special charm. When she speaks, she describes things almost as if she's speaking in verse. She uses striking, elegant phrases. I don't know if all the Palestinians who stayed in the Israeli world maintained their identity like this, but this Nada, she's very special. You can see a profound sadness in her that hasn't healed. It's been almost a year since they arrived, but she hasn't yet told me anything about her life over there, or her family, or her father who was found killed. Not a word. I don't ask, of course. I'd rather die of thirst than drown in unanswerable questions. But she doesn't leave space for silence, she talks lightly and distracts us from the mysteries of the past with her knowledge of beautiful things – art, realities, cinema, music. She has a good knowledge of the cinema. Not just good, great for her generation. Here, by the way, is where you can see, both in her and N – and it is sad – their longing to play uninterrupted wireless realities like they used to do in Israel. At the moment, they play five or six hours of realities a day, whereas over there they could go to work or a café or bar without being disconnected from the machine for a minute. Nada says they prefer to stay home and play realities than to go out at night. I told her that everyone in Palestine does that, that this whole generation has left the streets to bask in the warmth of their sofas, so it's OK.

It's wonderful to see life breathed into my father's house in al-Halissa. The neighbourhood has changed a lot since I was young. I would never tell Nada and N, but I would love to see a child grow up in that house. To see their steps on the same tiles I walked on. To see them dream where I dreamt, and look out the same window where I breathed in the noise of the overpass carrying cars to Haifa. But this, of course, is something I don't have a say in and it probably won't happen anytime soon. Nada is working on directing a reality and it's going to take up many years and a lot of her effort as well as N's (he is going to be a producer). I was really happy when Nada told me about the main setting of the reality; it's taken from Elie Suleiman's *The Time that Remains*. Isn't that great? N once told me about the project but I was a little drunk and I don't remember the details. He said she is directing it in memory of . . . of her . . . father?

The important thing is, this girl is very talented, very special and easy to let into your heart. I feel that N, despite everything about him that has changed, is happy. As for me, I . . . how do I say it? I feel lonely, but it's the same loneliness that old people of every generation feel. A loneliness that wraps itself around a spine of silence and tries to out-manoeuvre those predatory memories that spew poison into our children. But still, I feel happy. I would be lying if I denied that my greatest fear in life, maybe my only fear, has disappeared now. That what makes me most content about this heavy, heavy life is that N has finished his education and has come back to settle down with us, here. That the tunnel, that terrifying tunnel with its blinding light, didn't swallow him up forever.

Notes

1. The Peel Commission – a British Royal Commission of Inquiry, headed by Lord Peel, appointed in 1936 to investigate the causes of unrest in Mandatory Palestine, which was administered by Britain, following the six-month-long Arab general strike in Mandatory Palestine.

The Key

Anwar Hamed

Translated by Andrew Leber

'Daddy . . . Daaaaddy!'

I woke up groggily to the sound of Edina, our five-year-old, then jumped out of bed, closely followed by my wife Elza. When we reached her room, she was sat curled up on the bed, her face twisted in terror. Tears poured down her cheeks as she continued screaming and crying.

'Dadddyyyyy!'

She leapt from the bed as she cried out, burying herself in my arms.

'What's wrong, darling? What happened?' I asked her.

'The door!' she said, gesturing out, past her own bedroom door – which was always left open – to the entrance hall.

We didn't understand what she meant, but no matter how much we asked, her answer remained the same: the door.

I looked at my wife and she said: 'Go to the door, Moshe. Open it to check that nobody is there, just to be sure.'

Before I turned the doorknob, a thought crossed my mind and I went back to our room to grab my pistol from under the bed – better to be ready for whatever might come, I took off the safety and headed for the door, opening it carefully, my finger shaking slightly on the trigger.

I flicked on the patio lights and looked around. Nobody

there. I walked down the drive and looked up and down the road, then checked the back garden. Darkness and silence in all directions. I looked at my watch – 2:00 AM. Back at the front door, I made sure to double-lock it and check the house's alarm system: it confirmed that all windows and doors to the house were closed.

'There's nothing there, darling,' I said as I headed towards Edina's room.

As I approached the bedroom door, Elza stepped in front of me, her finger on her lips.

'She's gone back to asleep.'

We climbed into bed without exchanging a word. It had been a long, tiring day – we were out as soon as our heads hit the pillow.

★

My grandfather and a number of his friends in the United States had obsessed over the idea back then. It took up a great deal of their time and money over the course of their lives. It began as a simple effort to explore more effective ways of dealing with the Arabs. A number of politicians tried to reassure them, to brush off their concerns, but my grandfather and his friends did not share in their optimism. He was consumed by uncertainty all his life.

Their concerns turned into fear as the war drums sounded in 1967. He visited the newly-founded state several times and met with some of its leading politicians. He always went back to New York angry.

'They're asleep at the wheel!' he'd say to my grandmother.

'Aren't they in a better position to know?' she'd say. 'Relax, Akifa. Their intelligence services are strong, and they know what they're capable of – more than you do.'

Then the war came, climaxing in an explosive victory. My late grandmother couldn't help reminding Akifa that there were plenty of people looking out for the state – there was no reason for him to worry so much.

But he wasn't convinced.

'Such a small country. A slender island in an ocean of hatred!'

He guessed the victory that June wouldn't be the end of the story. And when he started reading names like Arafat and Habash in the American papers, his concern only grew.

They had to think about a solution. A *decisive* solution to this existential crisis. The state could not live under the threat of war forever. My grandfather began communicating with friends who shared his concerns and formed a loose, unnamed collective of thinkers – the nucleus of which developed a small, but well-funded set of projects, including research centres and think tanks.

At their inaugural conference they put together a plan of action divided up into several stages. My grandfather canvased the opinions of politicians, social scientists, and key intellectuals:

'There is no hope of coexistence given the differences between us . . .'

'The Arabs are convinced that we have built our nation on the ruins of theirs, and nothing we do will change that feeling . . .'

'Peace treaties and economic programs will not work. Their sense of injustice fuels the threat we face . . .'

My grandfather was not convinced that we could buy security, whether through walls or wars. He was thinking of a more innovative, unconventional solution. So he persuaded the research centres he'd funded to answer several specific questions, all of which pointed to one conclusion: the Arab citizens were not the true danger to the state.

They could sometimes get frustrated, true, but this could be absorbed with greater economic opportunities and some pragmatic policies. In fact, the findings suggested Israelis should be more concerned about their state's increasingly harsh political positions towards the Arabs, and the increasing power of an inward-looking, almost tribal political faction. 'The idiots!' he would yell, in agreement with the research. 'They're toying with the future of the state.'

'We must do something to placate the Arab citizens. Likewise, there's no reason to make an enemy out of the West Bank Arabs, just so long as we make sure of one thing: that they stay where they are. There is no objection to granting them citizenship and civil rights after the annexation of the West Bank so long as we are sure that they can't achieve any real power in the government. To remain consumers, not makers of policy. Consumers of everything! That'll keep them quiet.

'Residents of the camps in neighbouring countries are the core problem, however. They want to return to towns and villages that are no longer there. They dream of a world that no longer exists and cannot be restored, even if we agree to the idea, in principle. Even if they return, they will not find what they are looking for. But their stubbornness will not die – they pass it on to their children and grandchildren.'

My grandfather collected pictures of them clutching rusty keys to houses that no longer existed. But he wasn't mocking them, like others did. He felt a vague anxiety towards them, though he realised he was powerless to do anything about it. My grandfather feared those photographs of people holding keys more than any arms deal being signed by neighbouring countries.

My grandfather tasked all those institutions and research centres to search for a solution to these rusty keys.

By the 30th anniversary of the group's founding, my grandfather's office had seen any number of reports and proposals. Even if some recommendations beggared belief, most suggested that a solution could be found within the next 50 years – if enough money and research were deployed.

One report in particular caught my grandfather's attention. Despite his hatred of walls, and his belief that they posed no real barrier at the end of the day, he seized on one proposal for a different kind of wall: a *gravity* wall.

Only with the right 'code' could somebody physically get through the gates – these would be complex bits of code that the state would regulate, update, control. People the state wanted would be let in, and people it didn't would be kept out. We wouldn't be cutting ourselves off from the world: our drone fleets – by air or by sea – would still venture freely to all corners of the map, but only our citizens (and authorised others) would be able to enter the state.

To my grandfather's delight, the report explained that this 'wall' would not be a solid, concrete edifice, like those of the past – that would have the wrong psychological effect. Instead it would be a transparent shield, created by a subatomic 'tampering' with the gravitational field along certain geographic coordinates. Only those with the right chip (implanted in the neck of all newborns), and chips with the right code, could *really, physically* pass through at a series of gates in the wall, where the gravitational distortion was perforated.

The team behind the report provided detailed explanations, complete with illustrations and computer simulations. 'I didn't always understand the physics,' my grandfather would admit. 'All I cared about was: will the tech back it up?'

The team explained that the security precautions would be complex. All the residents of the state would carry electronic chips connected to a central computer system. The chips would be keyed to a unique code for each person based on their genome – they would be useless to any stranger who got hold of them.

'What are the risks?' my grandfather asked, as always.

'Some minor temporal feedback has been reported in

field trials,' one scientist replied, the first time he asked this question, 'but this has been fixed.' My grandfather was satisfied. This could work.

★

Some members of my grandfather's group wouldn't hear of it. 'My God!' they gasped. 'Another ghetto!'

'But what about the ghetto we live in now? International isolation? Antisemitism on the rise around the world? Should we just hide and console ourselves with stories about how the world is against us? Is that wise? Will this new isolation be any worse than the old? At least it would rid us of certain immediate threats and leave our children more secure than our own generation was.'

And so the scientists got the green light to speed up work on the project, working towards a prototype in absolute secrecy.

There was a tacit agreement not to coordinate with politicians and officials at this stage. The government could see the idea once it was ready to go.

★

The promised day arrived. They tested the idea in the lab and in the field – a complete success. The members of this once little-known collective staged a live, public demonstration. My grandfather was incredibly excited.

It took another year to build a hacker-proof encryption system, and controls for the administrators to operate the system. 'The keys to this New World will stay firmly in our hands,' my grandfather declared.

Wasn't this better than walls of cement and iron?

I was born in this New World. I did not witness the hysteria and fear that people felt in those first few years. Now that this is our reality, we live comfortable lives. We read and see TV reports about the hatred towards us in the outside world, but it just washes harmlessly against the gravity wall that separates us from their world. Even Arabs living here have a sense of belonging, and would rather be here than out in the chaos crashing against that wall.

Yesterday we celebrated the centennial of the establishment of the state. Pure, unbridled joy. My wife and I marked the occasion at a small restaurant on a beach in Tel Aviv, having left Edina at home with the Arab baby-sitter. We ordered a bottle of champagne. I clinked Elza's glass and said, 'Lachaim!'

Then we danced. When we came back to the house near midnight, we made love with an added tenderness and fell into a quiet, delicious sleep.

An hour later we woke up to Edina's terrified crying.

★

The following night, at almost the exact same time, we were once more woken by Edina's cry of terror, and rushed into her room. I tried to get an answer out of her this time – what exactly had woken her up? She sobbed that someone was trying to open the front door of the house, and that she woke up to the sound of the key turning in the lock.

Once again, I checked the door but found no one. I went outside and walked around the whole house. Returning to Edina to reassure her, I found her already fast asleep clutching her comforter. Back in our bedroom, Elza was sitting up in bed, looking agitated.

'There is nothing to worry about,' I said. 'But, to be on the safe side, I'll talk to the compound's security in the morning. We can check the CCTV.'

Elza gave me a look that did not seem reassured.

'What's wrong? Don't you believe me?'

She said nervously, 'You don't get it. Nobody has been trying to enter the building. Edina should visit a neurologist.'

I felt as though I'd been hit on the head.

'Do you think . . .'

'Yes,' she interrupted me. 'Her mind is being affected.'

We talked the subject over until morning. With the first rays of dawn, we got out of bed and woke Edina up. At 7:00 AM I called Ichilov Hospital and asked for an appointment with the mental health department. It took some doing, but in the end, we were able to get an emergency slot.

By 9:30 AM we were seated in Dr Naftali's clinic. He examined Edina and asked us some questions, then he said he could not diagnose a specific condition. Still, he wrote a prescription for some sedatives to help her sleep more soundly.

Elza objected. 'I don't want her to get addicted to sedatives and sleeping pills.'

The doctor reassured us that the dosage was quite small, with few expected side-effects.

Before Edina went to sleep that night, we made sure that she had taken the prescribed half-pill. We kissed her goodnight and went to bed. As for us, we slept poorly, waking up incessantly, with one of us going to check on Edina.

It was a difficult night, but thankfully Edina didn't wake up.

The pair of us slept better the following night, and once more Edina didn't wake up. I called the doctor with an update and to confirm how long she would have to take the pills for. He said it would depend on a number of factors but that we should check back in with him in a month. Elza was not comfortable with this solution, but at least we got some sleep.

For a while at least.

It was about three weeks after Edina had started the course. We had put her down at about 8:00 PM and had managed to get our own heads down by 10:00 PM. I was sound asleep when the screaming made me bolt upright. Not from Edina's room but from our own room. Elza was sitting up in the middle of the bed, aghast.

'Moshe, the door!'

I looked at her incredulously. 'What?'

'Moshe, they're trying the door. They've got a key!'

I tried to calm her down but she was inconsolable.

'It was not a nightmare! I heard the key turning in the door clearly, even after I made sure I was awake!'

Again, I took out my gun.

'Don't go out!' Elza quivered.

I held her, trying to calm her down.

'I want to make sure that nobody is out there, so you can relax.'

'Please don't go out! Don't leave us alone in here,' she said.

I felt trapped.

'What should I do, then?'

'Nothing – stay by my side!'

'Alright, go back to sleep.'

I went to turn off the light, only for her to snap at me: 'Don't turn off the light! I don't want to lie here in the dark.'

I kept the light on and held Elza, trying to calm her down.

'Try to sleep – tomorrow we will go back to Dr Naftali.'

She hissed back at me: 'No, I'm not crazy! There was someone trying to open the door. I don't want sleeping pills just to forget that!'

I was trying to keep it together.

'You need to talk to building security.'

I did, the next day. They checked the cameras again and assured me that there wasn't a trace of any stranger entering the building. But Elza could not relax. She said that this meant nothing – the person trying to open the door might live inside the building.

We had to inform the police. They asked for a list of names of the inhabitants of the building – not a single Arab among them. There were Arabs who frequented the building at times, including Khulood, our baby-sitter. But none of them lived in the building.

Elza refused to take any kind of medication. The next night she insisted on leaving the light on, and we wound up staying up until morning. Nothing happened.

A few days passed without Elza hearing the slightest hint of a key in the lock, so we decided to turn off the night-light, and get some rest.

What happened that night was worse than all the others.

I had been sceptical about things, sure. I chalked it all up to nerves and fatigue and wanted to try and convince Elza to make an appointment with Dr Naftali.

Then I heard the key myself. I thought I was dreaming at first, but when I opened my eyes I could clearly hear the scraping of metal on metal. I got out of bed, took out my pistol and crept towards the door. I could still hear the key fidgeting inside the lock even as I approached the door. I didn't want to take any chances, so I pointed the muzzle towards the peephole and fired.

Elza and Edina woke up and started yelling. No more key sounds, so I thought my shot had hit whoever was trying the lock. I wanted to open it to investigate, but Elza shouted:

'Don't open it!'

This was followed by a sharp scream that poured out from Edina's room.

Before I knew it, Elza was at my side, trying to drag me away.

'Call the police!'

I went back to our bedroom and dialled the emergency number. I told them what had happened – yes, they would send a patrol immediately.

I took Elza and Edina to the living room and tried to calm them down as much as possible, but I was tense myself.

It wasn't long before the doorbell rang.

'Don't open it!' Elza yelled.

'How can I not? It's the police, I called them myself!'

'How do we know they're policemen?'

'I'll look through the peephole.'

But she was not convinced, insisting that the person trying to open the door was probably disguised as a policeman.

I ignored her, going to the door and opening it. I found myself facing three policemen and invited them inside. They listened to my report on what happened.

'You say you shot through the door while this supposed person was trying to open it?'

'Yes.'

'If there were actually somebody there you would have hit them, yes?'

'Yes, I think so.'

'You couldn't have hit anyone. There was no body, and no trace of blood.'

'What do you mean? There was no one behind the door? But I heard the key! I didn't imagine this! I could hear him trying to force the door.'

Elza was convinced we should all return to Dr Naftali's clinic at Ichilov Hospital.

I tried to call the next morning to arrange an appointment, but to no avail. The number was constantly busy. I tried to book an appointment via the hospital's website, but it was impossible to load the page. There was tremendous traffic on the servers. I decided to go there myself – the matter was urgent.

I went to the secretary. She told me that the next available appointment with Dr Naftali was in five weeks – I should book immediately if I was interested. If I returned after half an hour, I might have had to wait months longer, as the number of cases under review was increasing dramatically.

Instead of booking an appointment, I decided to contact Dr Naftali after working hours, to convince him to make a special call.

★

Dr Naftali returned to his home in the evening after a long day's work. He took a hot bath, then poured himself a glass of whiskey. He sat in the hall watching an American film on television. It was barely a few minutes before the whiskey fell from his hand. He rolled over on the couch, knocking his head on the wooden edge. Opening his eyes, he reached for the remote and switched off the television.

As he left his bedroom, he heard a strange sound coming from the front door. As best he could hear, somebody was trying to open the door with a key. He rushed to his bedside cabinet and fished out his gun from the bottom drawer. He approached the door cautiously, his finger trembling on the trigger.

'Who's there?' he shouted. No answer.

He fired a bullet through the keyhole, but somebody continued to try and open the door. He panicked, emptying his gun into the lock. The key still turned on the outside.

Panicking, he ran to the storage space beneath the stairs and grabbed his old service rifle, cocked it back and returned to the door. He emptied the entire clip into the lock in one burst. He looked at the wide hole where the door's handle and lock had once been, as well as the holes sprayed across the rest of the door, and began to chuckle.

'I can sleep quietly now! There is no lock left, where will the intruder put his key?'

Digital Nation

Emad El-Din Aysha

'BUT WHO'S RESPONSIBLE?' Asa Shomer sat behind a large, cluttered desk, flanked by framed certificates, medals of honour and photographs of him shaking hands with foreign dignitaries. His pale–faced assistant paused for a moment, assuming the Director of Shabak was being rhetorical and had more to say.

'I would suggest a hacker,' the young assistant eventually replied. 'One we are not familiar with.'

'You don't say,' Shomer hissed. 'You're the tech boys. I'm the old timer here, the one who still uses Morse code and microfiche. All we have now is tech boys.' His aide continued to stand there, waiting for instructions. 'So why don't you *tech* your way to the bottom of it? Who's doing this?'

His aide continued to stand there.

'With the centenary just around the corner, we should expect more.' Shomer gestured at the virtual reality device on his desk. 'This is just the beginning.'

The headset was a typical VR console, the type used by kids everywhere to spend all their free time in parallel worlds, on faraway planets . . . anywhere but here, the promised land that Shomer had spent his entire career protecting.

'He's a terrorist,' the aide said weakly.

Shomer smiled. There hadn't been an act of good old-fashioned terrorism – a hijacking, a letter bomb, a guerrilla operation – in a long time. The word triggered some nostalgia button hidden at the back of his brain.

'But we deal with cybercrime here . . .' the aide continued, then trailed off.

His boss filled in the gaps. The Palestinians hadn't had a single state to govern for a long time. Instead they made do with a series of fragmented banana republics. Literally, they grew bananas on the slopes of Ramallah – as well as mangos in Judea and pineapples in Samaria. As such, any activity traced back to one of these glorified farmyards was no longer considered by Shabak dangerous enough to call 'terrorism'. Palestinian criminality had to be dealt with as just that – plain and simple criminality. This was a hack, so it was a cybercrime case.

'But destabilising the stock market, hijacking media outlets, hacking servers . . . these are all issues of national security,' the aide went on. 'More of the same could lead to casualties and open us up to our enemies. We need to defer this to the Ministry.'

'No, that's my call. This stays here for now.'

'Yes, sir.' The assistant saluted.

Shomer grunted, as the aide turned and left. Picking up the headset, and staring at it like it was the skull of Yorick, he muttered aloud: 'What's next? Sunglasses that make Israelis look like Palestinians?'

★

The stock market – what a joke, Shomer thought to himself, as he walked along the sea front. It was a typical Tel Aviv evening in Spring, the frothing waves looked like they were ready to bite chunks out of the promenade they were closing in on.

They were selling shares in the last remnants of what the

state once owned: schools, colleges, hospitals, bridges, even roads. Vast swathes of agricultural land were up for grabs as African consortiums made their first forays into the holy land, having lost Africa itself to the Chinese. (He had half his staff checking through the accounts of these firms to make sure there wasn't any Arab money in there). Passports were being sold for a dime a dozen to North Americans and Europeans, in an effort to beef up the country's ailing, suburban population. It wouldn't be long before they privatised the IDF and Shabak itself. Mossad was already selling its services to Colombian drug lords, if you believed the foreign exposés. It was like Rome after the sack of Carthage. There wasn't anything left worth fighting for. No wonder people wanted to 'escape' the daily grind of unbridled capitalism.

But who could believe an Arab would be capable of such ingenuity: a vision of a united Palestinian State, simmed so perfectly and in such detail, then virus-leaked into every VR console on the Israeli market – from rollerblading cyberkids to lonely housewives waiting for the Amazon delivery guy. It was uncanny. Even *he* was impressed, and his idea of a modern video game was *Fortnite*.

Shomer hated the headsets – wearing them made him feel claustrophobic though he could never admit this, so frequently did he have to wear them at work. In the privacy of his office, he would carefully put the thing on, and as his eyes focused, a series of player options bobbed up in mid-air before him:

Attorney at Arms, where you are the head of a legal team driving around in a jeep armed with a suitcase full of paperwork, allowing you to deploy UN Security Council resolutions in the field, making a decision between the '48 and '67 borders, to see which would constitute the strongest base for establishing the recently-renamed Al-Quds as the logistical capital of the Levantine economic bloc (one that by the way included a refurbished Iraq).

The Taxman, where you have to figure out how best to hide the Palestinian government's accounts from both the Israeli authorities and international auditors until such a point where you could balance your budget, finance your civil service, establish an infrastructure for law, welfare and healthcare, and build up the country's weapons stockpiles, so that, come the eventual day of independence, Palestine can simultaneously meet the West's patronising criteria for a functioning democracy, and show it has the fire-power needed to defend itself should the West fail to be satisfied.

The Horticulturalist, where Palestinian kibbutzim have turned the deserts green and stolen all the water and topsoil for themselves, and left you, a poor immigrant, to dig irrigation canals like those once imagined to have existed on Mars, crisscrossing the Middle East into a single hydraulic blob of agricultural perfection.

Catering Guy, where you run a chain of restaurants and fast food outlets, devising marketing strategies to flood the world with chickpeas and Palestinian falafel and upside-down aubergine sandwiches, breaking the back of the Israeli service sector and forcing Israelis to work as waiters, slaving away in kitchens and hand-distributing menus and flyers in newspapers to the kosher eating masses.

Cupid's Bride, where men are forced to dress up and parade themselves in front of the womenfolk, engage in sports contests or perform in poetry battles to curry the favour of the prettiest bride, in a gender-reversed world where women decide who marries whom and inheritance of land is through the female bloodlines; the way things were at the time of Musa and Yacoub.

And so on, and so on. It was the graphics that frightened him the most.

The architecture of the digital nation was influenced by the Islamic past but thoroughly modernised. The clothes –

traditional Bedouin and farmers' garments – were made out of space-age fabrics. Mosques and churches and even synagogues, side-by-side, solar-powered, energy efficient and environmentally friendly, and built out of the same rock, blending in seamlessly with the terrain. It was so 'real' you could reach out and touch it. (He almost had.) And *the people*.

Smiling, healthy and happy, but never 'content'. People expecting the best, savouring it, never taking no for an answer, and always hoping for a brighter future, no matter how good things were in the here and now. You could see it in their digitally re-mastered eyes, the energy burning away.

The game also came with an intro page that explained what the average Arab, back then, would have regarded as 'Paradise on Earth'. That is, enough to eat. Aubergine and chickpeas if you were Palestinian, just aubergine if you were Egyptian. Oh, and a woman to lay on top of, after a long day at your pointless civil service job with its pension scheme and health insurance package; a few pennies and some aspirin and Viagra to go. The 'state', for Arabs, needn't be any more elaborate than the local mukhtar. The de facto unelected mayor of a village who busied himself resolving disputes between obnoxious neighbours stepping on each other's toes.

Utopia was a dangerous thing. It had to be stamped out. Hope was contagious. Hope was 'calculating' and *calculatable*.

Something was terribly wrong. He'd stake his career on it. He'd already raised eyebrows among his younger colleagues for using four-letter words like 'West' and 'Bank' in previous conversations – habits of his youth he tried to explain. 'It was a reference to the Jordan River,' he said, but the silence was uncomfortable.

★

'They're calling him Hannibal,' the Security Minister told Shomer over the encrypted line. 'It's spread to all the social media platforms now.'

'It's a good historical analogy. Hannibal in Arabic is Hannah Baal. And Baal is the devil in scripture,' Shomer replied matter-of-factly.

'Spare me another history lesson.' Even over the garbled line, Shomer could hear the venom in the Minister's voice. 'And you're assuming it's only one hacker and not a whole online community of them. The game's world-building must have cost a fortune, and required a team of artists and coders, probably from different parts of the world.'

'That's exactly what I said,' Shomer tried to say in his defence. 'He's a counterespionage case in essence – *Hannibal*, I mean.' The name felt oddly appropriate to him, saying it out loud. Although the general was not a Utopian. He accepted Carthage for the cesspool it had become and focused his energies against Rome. The 'only' Utopian in Muslim history had been Farabi, author of *The Virtuous City*, and he got his inspiration from Plato. Something wasn't entirely right.

He lost his train of thought as the voice of the Minister came back to him.

'Then put your powers of anticipation to good use, and second-guess his . . . their, next move.'

Thinking off the top of his head, Shomer said, 'Well, if I was him, I'd program a virus to convert all online use of Hebrew into Arabic.'

★

The second stage began in a classroom, of all places. An elementary teacher in Ashdod was happily waving away in front of a virtual whiteboard – scribing intricate Hebrew letters mid-air with deft flicks of a stylus-pen for her eight-year-olds to follow – when suddenly, three lines down, a commotion started up behind her. The girls in the front two rows were laughing at her, the boys at the back muttering aggressively under their breaths. Looking back at the first line of words she'd silently etched into the hologram surface of the whiteboard, she was taken aback.

Had she been subconsciously channelling another language she barely knew?

It was Arabic. Not just the first line now, all of it.

When the kids turned to their tablets, assuming it was a malfunction with the board, they saw the same there. Frantically they began tapping, swiping, and resetting. One kid tapped so vigorously he cracked his screen. Another boy was so offended by the unfamiliar text he threw his to the floor, shouting. When the soft thud on the carpet failed to break it, he followed up with the heaviest stamp he could muster; like an act of exorcism, to smash the ghost out of it.

The teacher called her Head of Department and her Head of Department called the Principal's office. All that man could think to do was call Tech Support. By that point it had spread throughout the school. Every time one of the Tech Support guys typed in a command, the letters came out in the wrong language on their own consoles. They tried to punch in commands quickly and hit 'Return' before it was converted, but it failed, causing all the whiteboards in the school to fizzle, smoke and die.

If they had been able to phone the service provider, it wouldn't have done any good. They were having the same problems and had to watch in horror as news of the hack reached the stock exchange, sending their share price into a nosedive. The only consolation was that, shortly after, everyone else's share prices started to plunge as well – everything from telecom networks to energy providers to banks started to plummet. News of each malfunction spread through social media – ironically one service that wasn't affected so far. Then the stock exchange itself was hit. All the company names began to appear in Arabic. More money was lost that afternoon than in the run up to the 1973 war.

★

'That can't be,' Shomer protested. He was on the cipher-phone again with the Minister. 'I'm the least hackable person in this establishment. In the country!'

It was true, his metal-wire in and out trays on his desk, stacked with printouts, were entirely analogue. He insisted all reports be presented to him in hardcopy, and refused to use a tablet. He had reams of sensitive paperwork, all kept under lock and key in his one-tonne safe, with booby traps that would incinerate everything inside if they were compromised. He had the place regularly swept for bugs, and had everyone frisked for mobiles before entering his office. His office windows were made of a special non-vibrating composite that made it difficult for outside lasers to measure what was being said inside from the micro-vibrations – a precautionary measure against drones.

When his colleagues came to visit him at his place of work, they told him he looked like one of those old-time private investigators you saw on the Film Noir movie channel. The only difference being he didn't have a cute secretary in the lobby or a blonde temptress doing her best to ensnare him. He was married to the job. A very unforgiving spouse that left you suspicious of everybody and everything that came near.

That virus was a stroke of genius, Shomer had to admit. Who needed to 'liberate' Palestine if you could *convert* Israel into Palestine? You wouldn't even need to build a new world, just repaint the existing one. If only the Palestinians knew what things were like over here, they wouldn't have bothered.

'If there was a mole, it wasn't on our side,' he said a bit too forcefully.

'What are you implying? That someone in the Ministry is compromised?' the Minister barked.

'I implied no such thing, Minister. Merely that . . .' Shomer stopped for a second. The TV set in his office was turned on to the news channel, with the sound off so he could talk. He read the news crawler instead. Something about a shooting. Security guards at a bank had spotted some Arab kids on the inside, next to the vault. The guards couldn't believe it and opened fire before they even had a chance to sound the alarm.

He could see the images of the security guards being led away by the police. Each one had an identical pair of designer sunglasses on.

The Shabak chief dropped the receiver from his hand in a daze.

★

The third stage began a week later. An expat Israeli was driving down the coastline, using a bog-standard GPS to keep him on track. The roof was rolled down and the Mediterranean air was sweeping through his hair. Much of the landscape – a narrow strip of green between the greying waters of the sea and the hilly encampments, hidden behind that distant but visible wall – he was seeing for the first time.

The radio was on, blaring out the sort of tunes he suspected were popular in the remaining kibbutzes, when a brief lurch from the car took him by surprise. The radio signal crackled, then something completely alien began pouring from his speakers. He had no idea what language it was, but the genre was clear: rap.

No bother, he thought. Everyone liked rap. Perhaps he had wandered into a broadcasting zone from the occupied hills? Although he'd read somewhere that the farmers up there were only allowed to broadcast calls to prayer. He fiddled around with the knobs, searching for other channels, but to no avail. It was all foreign language rap.

He switched to a podcast, from his cloud server, but got more of the same. He shoved a flashdrive in containing some old favourites, but again, somehow, it was all in a foreign tongue. The expat then manually switched the car to autopilot so he could give his full attention to the radio, and it was at this moment that his car moved imperceptibly from what he would call a 'good' neighbourhood back in the States to a 'bad' one, where suddenly the GPS and all his other systems would start relying on local downloads, rather than satellite ones. Unable to understand the GPS, which was now talking to him in Arabic, he took wrong turn after wrong turn until he was convinced he was in occupied territory and headed for the nearest wall. On the other side, the residents – illegal migrant labourers, mostly – took his car apart piece by piece. He was lucky they didn't do the same to him.

Not everyone was so lucky that day. Traffics jams and car crashes spread from one end of the country to the other as GPS devices went haywire. If it wasn't for the old-fashioned physical street signs, people wouldn't have known what country they were living in. Virtual tour guides, eBooks and online atlases all began rewriting themselves, telling tourists they were, in fact, in Palestine, and replacing all Hebrew names with their pre-1948 Arabic ones. Even printing machines were hacked, meaning all map books came out in Arabic, branded with a Palestinian flag, still upside down in preparation for liberation day.

Soon the geostationary satellites floating up above Israel were infected, and all digital signals coming into the country came in Arabic. Record companies began going broke. The music channels started shutting down. Stereo systems, mp3 players, smartphones, all began turning themselves on, and blaring out hit singles from 1948, mixed in with contemporary Arabic grime, rap and R&B.

★

'Doctor, I think I'm losing my mind. It's like living in a play you wrote yourself. These things can't be happening. It can't all be one giant coincidence.'

'Mr Shomer, Asa, if I may. Is there a record of you predicting these developments?' The therapist spoke in a heavy Central European accent.

'No, I didn't tell anyone.' He pondered the question for a moment, thinking his doctor was making a medical inquiry. Hadn't Freud argued that the subconscious sometimes understood things better than the conscious mind?

He was about to say all this when the doctor added, 'Good. And keep it that way.'

★

'This just came in.' It was his aide.

One quick glance and Shomer sighed. 'I take it they can see what's going on over here?' The readouts were of thermal scans from Judea and Samaria, little dots of gatherings and furtive movements. The only kind of satellite imagery that could penetrate the blanket of leaves the Palestinians had to live under and subsist on.

His aide nodded.

'They've become tired of picking bananas and are finding common cause with the inmates of Gaza.' That stubborn little detention camp, Shomer thought, full of proud hotheads that refused to sink into the sea. 'Well, this is clearly a job for the Ministry now. There's evidently a level of organisation going on over there – larger than just one of their humous fests. Get this to the Minister and let's get back to our mission: Hannibal.'

His aide hesitated.

The security chief crunched his teeth. 'What now?'

'Nothing.' He turned around and left the room.

★

'Check this out!' A 14-year-old skaterboy, sitting in a San Francisco internet cafe, waved his friend over from the console opposite.

'I think I recognise that last one,' his friend said, pointing at the screen. 'I'm going with him.'

'Suit yourself,' replied the first. 'I've never heard of any of them, so I'll go with . . . er . . . that one. I like her AK47.'

Although technically Palestinians, the two boys had grown up in a variety of different countries, only really calling the virtual landscape of gaming 'home'. It didn't matter to them where, geographically speaking, any new craze or meme originated from. If it was trending, they wanted in.

And this was trending: an announcement from cyberspace, made simultaneously to every chatroom on the globe, declaring the formation of the world's first virtual government. It was a council of long-dead historical figures, apparently, that most gamers would never have heard of – Abu Ammar, Hannan Ashrawi, Ezz Il Din Al-Qasam, Abu Ali Mustafa, Mousa Al-Sadr and so on. Each had their own ministerial portfolios and the player's task was to pick one, and with them form a cabinet to address pressing economic and international challenges. What distinguished this from an elaborate version of *The Sims,* however, was the fact that real-world problems and requests were being fed into the game. Thus, real-world passports, identity cards, visa permits and driver's licences were all being sent to the players, who in order to score the highest points processed them as quickly and as fairly as they could.

Historians started appearing on late night talk shows, exclaiming how accurate and life-like the simulated political figures were: their accents, physical mannerisms and tailor-made clothes – all impossibly true to life.

The Palestinians finally had a *single* government, free floating in a digital sea, with kids around the world learning from them and grappling passionately with their historical challenges. The game infected every console in Israel, and tracked its way to every player whose medical records showed Levantine blood (dated to 1948, including Jewish and Christian players, of course). The slogan that appeared on their screens as it downloaded read, 'It's time to come home.'

★

'Whoever's doing this, he's more than smart. He's a *historian*,' Shomer said to the barren walls of his downtown apartment.

The Palestinians had tried to put together a government in exile in the wake of the Nakba, and they almost succeeded, pulling together all the notables in the Palestinian 'house' – landlords and clerics and tribal chiefs and public figures, not to forget the local village mukhtars. They were going to use Gaza as a launching pad, establishing an army, a taxation system, plans for local elections, even embassies around the world.

The problem was their own backyard, the neighbouring Arab states. They were the ones that had put it on hold indefinitely. The Jordanians weren't keen on Palestinian self-rule, which meant losing control of the 'West Bank' and with that all of the holy places. As for the dream of getting to the Mediterranean via Gaza – forget about it. King Farouk and his followers in Egypt *claimed* to be keen on it, as a check on Jordanian ambitions and as a stalking horse for their own ambitions. But then Nasser stepped in with a lot of pan-Arab bluster and ever so slowly forgot about it all. The PLO popped up in 1963. But they were always easy to control since they all got their residency permits from the host nations, and had to sell their services *to* those governments just to make ends meet.

A virtual government, a self-financing electronic parliament, didn't have that problem. They didn't have to take any crap from anybody, and they didn't even need to have physical premises for diplomatic representation.

The PLO would become an anachronism in no time at all. But that wasn't what really bothered Shomer. What kept him up at night was the realisation that the same would happen to the Knesset and the other organs of the Israeli state.

★

'We've been able to trace the hacks,' the aide said, but without the satisfied tone you'd expect with such news.

The Shabak chief sighed deeply. Progress, at last. 'Well, don't just stand there.' The aide looked pastier than usual. 'What is it?'

'You won't like this.'

'Just spit it out.'

Instead, his aide handed over the stapled-together report with the algorithmic printouts. The AI system, with its irremovable desktop image of the Dome of the Rock plastered across all its screens, used the word 'Al-Khawarizmi' when responding to the request – the one word the aide recognised.

'How could somebody hack into our defence grid? That's impossible,' the Shabak chief spat. The Turks wouldn't dare, the other Arab states wouldn't bother, and the Iranians weren't in the business of doing Arabs' work for them.

'No, it's not that. It's the defence computers.'

'What do you mean? Somebody on the inside? No Palestinian could breach it . . .'

'No, the defence *computers*. Themselves. The AI tech deployed in the war-anticipation modelling.'

'What do you mean? They've come to life?' Shomer couldn't believe the words coming out of his mouth. They sounded alien, like they were coming from someone else. He started to laugh slightly manically. *Was this a symptom of something?* he thought.

His aide nodded severely. 'Everything's online, including our own personalities,' the assistant explained. 'The defence computers, they're hacking into the national archives, the medical databases, the profiling programmes, the databases we use . . .'

'What do they want from profiling data?' He almost sighed with relief.

'The same thing our police forces want from them . . . the ability to predict everyday criminal activity.'

'Crime on our side of the fence, you mean,' the Shabak chief said. 'Why?'

'The machine is hungry for data. It needs a foe to analyse and . . .'

Oh Abraham spare me, Shomer thought to himself. It was like watching one of those old episodes of *Max Headroom* you could only find on NostalgiaTube. A machine come to life.

'But Hannibal failed,' his aide interrupted. 'With his elephants, I mean. There's hope in that, isn't there?'

'Shabak!' Shomer exclaimed suddenly without explaining himself. '*Shabaka* – it's an Arabic word you know. It means "net" or "network".' But as he looked around the room, the bookshelves seem to tilt and list, like the whole office was out at sea.

★

They had to take the defence grid offline, paralysing the country's already depleted infrastructure.

Martial law had to be declared, pitting only half the guns in the country in one direction (towards the borders) while the other half were pointed at their own people. The country was in no position to go on the offensive in an effort to keep the peace. (The Jordanians were especially happy about that, having made the same mistake in 1967, policing and 'disarming' the Palestinians to keep them in line while getting themselves into a war they'd never wanted to begin with.) The armed services had finally become what they claimed themselves to be all along – the Israeli 'Defence' Forces.

In the meantime, the virtual government of Palestine began opening up bidding rounds for contracts with foreign investors in the power and water sector, along with tourism and agribusiness, and slowly took the place of the now-defunct Israeli authorities. First in the West Bank, and then in the Arab-majority areas of Israel itself, and especially in occupied East Jerusalem.

At this rate, it wouldn't be long before the Israelis themselves signed on for their services. It was their one shot at regaining everything they'd lost over the years – including dental insurance.

★

Independence Day, 2048

The Palestinian flag was fluttering – the right way up this time – over the Dome of the Rock. Jerusalem had finally become Al-Quds again. The worshippers at the wailing wall were still there, the visiting female foreign dignitaries still had to cover their hair.

'It was you, all along, wasn't it?' the now former Shabak chief said. There was no bitterness in his voice. He was almost glad it was all over. '*Dr* Hannibal.'

'You must have me mistaken with someone else, dearest Asa,' the old man replied simply, ever the Central European gentleman.

'Only someone in your "profession" would choose such a

name. The hero you all aspire to be. A serial killer.' Shomer spat the word out.

'He ate Nazis in his early days. Can't fault him for that. I've always seen that as my job, consuming the evil within us. And we've become like the Nazis ourselves. A little cannibalism was called for. As long as it's in fiction. And fictional is another word for virtual.' The man was just here for the festivities. He was taking quite a risk, of course, hanging around on this side of the border. But that was the nature of his profession, his professionalism. You didn't have to be in the security services to put your life on the line.

'Just answer me this,' Shomer went on. 'How did you do it? I take it you aren't a hacker supreme?'

'Me, are you kidding?' The man almost laughed. 'I couldn't program my smartphone to wake me up in the morning. I'm from the old country, even older than you.'

'Then how did you . . .'

'I have patients, don't I? Arabs and Israelis alike. And, for your information, Arabs are quite gifted when it comes to computers. Steve Jobs was half-Syrian after all.'

'I had no idea.'

'I'm afraid so. Me, I was just a clearing house for their ambitions.'

'Then how did you get into the defence computer system?'

'I told you I have patients, Palestinians *and* Israelis. Do you think you are the only member of the guardian class with a troubled conscience?' he said jovially.

'A computer with a split personality. Only someone like you could have thought that up.'

'Is it so hard to imagine?' the old man went on. 'It's that mental clutter that turns Utopia to dystopia. Too many people fighting for what they think is right, and can't imagine to be wrong, blotting each other out. It was bound to catch up with us, sooner or later. We no longer speak with one voice, even in the privacy of our own homes.'

Shomer blanched.

'Don't look so glum,' the old man went on, with his heavy accent. 'You should thank the Arabs. They've finally allowed us to become ourselves again, start building anew without being afraid somebody is going to foul it all up for us when it's really us that is the problem.' The man sighed, then asked a question that had been bugging the Shabak chief himself. 'Have you ever wondered why Arabs, Muslims, don't have a utopian literature of their own?'

'At times. I had satisfied myself into thinking that it was "low" expectations. A sense of fatalism. But there was something more. I just couldn't put my finger on it.'

'How true,' the old man said, eyes fixed on the flag. 'They know the pitfalls that come with Utopia. They learned to fear themselves, the lack of humility that comes with it. They had a Utopia, of sorts, at the time of their Prophet, then it all fell apart afterwards. Everybody fighting for the promised land in his own way, turning a heaven on earth into a living hell.' A sigh, and then, 'That is what has held back the Arabs for the past century. They were never themselves in these times, unsure if they should be distrustful of their own dreams like their ancestors or should race ahead and go for broke, in emulation of us. They dithered, and dithered, and dithered. Till they came to me and opened themselves up. I had to admire that about them, how they entrusted me with their secrets. And I had to do my job, which was to help them heal themselves.'

'So, where to now?' Shomer asked, his head lowered.

'I wonder if I should retire. I've fulfilled my mission, and if all goes according to plan, there won't be any need for a shoulder to cry on anymore.'

'Or for a jackboot to run away from,' the former Shabak chief added.

Personal Hero

Abdalmuti Maqboul

Translated by Yasmine Seale

AS IF ON THE EDGE of a precipice, leaning into the world, she is alive to every movement. First the image, then a wash of sound.

Footsteps, faint among the grass and gravel. Quickening. Then nothing. The hiss of whispers circling a structure close to the ground. The wait is over. Hands take hold of the stones set in the earth and slowly prise them out. The sky's white is disturbed. Then come the howls, rippling.

Soul after soul stirs. Eyes open at the appointed time. Deep darkness. Fingers twitch and stretch into nothingness. Heads rouse themselves from their long sleep, too caught in other bodies to rise. Limbs tangle, flesh kisses flesh. Nostrils flare and the stink rushes in. Then through parted lips, a muffled cry: Where am I? Others can only moan under the weight. We're alive! Shock broken by new sounds: the clash of picks above their heads. Picks and spades. Rays steal in and brush the bundled bodies. Slowly the dust rises, and the place fills with sweet, invigorating air, like the first feast served in Paradise.

Freed, the heads lift. They are level with the ground, but from where they lie to the moon's disc nothing is visible. Crossed over them are shadows, long and thick on the rectangle's rim. A voice travels down: Ten. Nine. Eight . . . The counting stops. Shadows move across the light and raise their barrels at them, taking aim. A sight they've seen before, the dead of Kazkhana Cemetery. Shots ring around the village. Soil pours over their bodies once more.

Her own body is jacketed in cold. Frozen, helpless – not that it was possible to help, to warn or keep them safe. Only to sit in silence and watch.

The half-light of a new day breaking, maybe ending. A pale glow bathes the west side of the village. Then a red glow, then no sun at all. In other countries, people are sleepily returning to work, in time for the four o'clock bell; that's when observers start taking down names. Those who show up after three are fired: these countries value time, and hold their people dear (these are the claims of their leaders). But in our village, no one goes to work anymore, no one to the fields. They hear gunfire and run for cover, and those who stay in the open are killed.

Common to all these lands is the queer direction of time, its gears in reverse. Tank wheels, windmills, telephone dials, the springs coiled behind clock faces all run counter. Returning home at the end of a new day, people are caught in morning traffic, but arrive in time for the rooster's first call. Some will go to sleep early (at ten in the morning, say, or eleven) to wake in time for the rowdy parties at the start of the night to come. Others stay up later (until seven or earlier) and get their fill of rest. But in our village, there is no sense of time passing, only a blanket of dread.

Among it all – the fraught nerves, the trying days – a kind of joy catches at the villagers' souls. It might be hope. It is certainly mixed, with pain and fear of gunfire. The longed-for date is upon them. Today is the ninth of April, and tomorrow, the eighth, a hero will be returned to life. Nearby, the courtyards of al-Aqsa Mosque are making ready for the eminence buried in their soil; the Shadows, meanwhile, brace for a long night ringed with danger. A critical night, for those they have been coming back to kill, day after day, are simple folk, while tonight's arrival is settled in the history books: now comes a chance to remove all trace of him. Ben Gurion's orders. To send out the squads, armed to the teeth, to fan out through the squares, take up positions on hilltops and high ground, to rig the charges and – no need for picks and spades – blow up the shrine. No need to open up the famous tomb and check who lies inside.

Crouched behind their rifles under cover, some propped on their elbows, some lying down, some on their feet. Heartbeats louder than crickets. Their eyes are narrowed, their brows damp. The hours crushingly slow. One o'clock: one hour left until midnight, when souls will slip back into their bodies. Twenty minutes. Battle fury breaks the calm of night, a spray of bullets from all around and nowhere. The Shadows fall, one by one. Masked men rush ahead. As if the shots were the sky's rage, or its mercy for the people of the city. The fighters form a human shield around the tomb and five men slip between them with spades. One minute till midnight. Enough digging. The dusty national flag is lifted from the body. The spirit returns. A long breath, a swelling in the ribs. The eyes crack open, mirroring moonlight. The circle of fighters, muttering prayers, see it.

Her old eyes see it too and her heart reacts violently. This is the face she remembers.

Joy breaks over them. Tears crowd their eyes. Outside the mosque, the gunfire rises.

'Quick,' says one. 'Let's get him out before we're caught.'

Abd al-Qadir's[1] first words: 'What's happening?'

'We'll tell you later. Now hurry.'

The fighters hold out their arms to the man on his back and bring him to his feet. One by one they step out of the pit. There is a flash of the man's skin, catching the eye of the fighters waiting outside. Abd al-Qadir. It is him, of this they are sure, and their throats unlock to say that God is great, that there is no god but He. More shots: not from the Shadows but from the throngs of fighters. Rifles held high, trembling. People are massing, streaming into the streets. Thousands fill the squares. Abd al-Qadir leaves the earth; on a bed of shoulders he is brushed by palms unsteady as the guns. A smile crooks his black moustache. Snatches of talk drift up to his ears.

'We'll never leave you again.'

'Thank God we made it to you in time.'

'We are all Abd al-Qadir.'

Something stirs in his mind. A vision of his death, his burial at Bab al-Amoud. A glimpse of the final battle, his attempt to booby-trap the post at al-Qastal. His smile disappears. He freezes.

'What happened at al-Qastal?' he asks, agitated.

The crowd is silent. Then a voice speaks up: 'It falls.'

Abd al-Qadir looks down to the voice and cries out: 'The road to Jerusalem cannot fall!'

He comes down from the shoulders. He leads the crowds until they retake it, until joy returns to the eyes of its villagers. Until Operation Nachshon[2] is reversed.

In a house in al-Qastal sit the Army of the Holy War, celebrating with their leader. They tell him about the massacres, the forced departures. About the occupation of the land. They have covered only a small part of what the future brought them when the man goes into a rage. He takes from them a will he wrote himself. He postponed meeting his family in Egypt, because first he had a date with history.

On 26 March 1948, Abd al-Qadir arrives in Damascus and goes straight to meet the Secretary General of the Arab League, Abd al-Rahman Azzam. Also in attendance are the head of the Society for the Defence of Palestine, Taha al-Hashemi, and his deputy, General Ismail Safwat, as well as the Mufti, Haj Amin al-Husayni.

Abd al-Qadir kicks open the door, sending a jolt through the stone wall. Strides up to the men sitting with bowed heads. From a belt around his waist, beneath the two bandoliers that lie crossed over his chest, he fishes out his will and brings it down on the wooden table.

'What did I tell you? That you were traitors. That you were dogs. That history would record how you gave up Palestine. Well, the record is clear. And here you are, disgraced a second time. Look. Read.'

He holds up the will to them.

'To the Secretary General of the Arab League, Cairo. I hold you personally responsible for depriving my soldiers, at the peak of their triumph, of material support.'

Without a glance at their sombre faces, he disappears.

A gleeful smile. A blast of air from her nose.

His eyes lift and come to rest on the back of his speeding horse, like lovers dancing. His white scarf, pinned under the iqal, billows behind his shoulders. Birds and clouds watch him go; the earth itself thrills that he has returned to walk on it. He stiffens, head raised to the window in the side of the house. Haifa sees him and nearly breaks.

The old woman's heart beats harder as Haifa comes into view.

In disbelief she sits on the sofa, then returns to the window. Yes, he has come, at last. A difficulty presents itself: should she run to greet him on the front steps? Or stand behind the iron gate? She knows she is incapable, that her feet will not support her. His footsteps louder now, closer. Then silence. Gentle knocks on the door before it opens.

Breath rattles in her throat. Her eyes are pinned open, her heart behaving wildly. The face appears, creasing into a smile when his eyes fall on his angel. He stands his rifle against the near wall. She collects herself and rises off the sofa onto shaky legs. Her eyes shine as she looks into the high sea of his. His fingers brush her curls, her cheek, holding her to his belly as she reaches her hands around him. Abd al-Qadir is his daughter's hero; in this she is far from alone.

Though she is taller now, he carries her to the sofa and lowers himself down so she can lie in his arms.

'I told Mother you'd make it. When she said you were wounded I swore it would be like the other times, that your body would recover. I didn't believe you had died. I waited so long for you. I waited until I was old, then until I was young again. How slow the years were! I kept hearing about you, reading about you. I heard that, as a child, you bought a gun and paid for it yourself. That you ripped up your diploma as soon as you received it from the head of the American University in Cairo, in front of all the important people. I remember what you said: "I have no need of a diploma from your school, a colonial and missionary institution. I have won it, but it has not won me." Oh Baba, how long it took me to get to know you in your absence.'

His smile broadens. He takes in the face he hardly knows.

'I am not sure how it is the days are returning. Only that they have brought us together. Only how happy I am to see you.'

'When I was seventy, you were still fresh in my mind. You died before me, in your prime, just forty. I passed on your stories to my daughter. I had a life, but you were the best of it. You were my hope. And look, fate seems to have smiled on us . . .'

A smile. Tears fill her watching eyes.

A movement at the open door cuts off their talk. His life partner, his comrade in arms. And their sons, Musa and Ghazi. The family reunited. (This scene, impossible to describe, follows all resurrections, as if to compensate for the pain of parting.)

The days return for Abd al-Qadir as they once passed, full of sacrifice and protests and love of his people. Except this time there are no twists of fate; everything is known in advance. The only difference is that families hold each other closer now: a lesson they learned from death. The days pass with the same tedium. The old grow spryer and the young slip back to first beginnings. Difficult days for all the parents who have to watch their children fade before their eyes. Difficult for Abd al-Qadir, when Haifa stops talking. When his name falls from her lips for the last time: Baba. When she becomes a wailing, screaming lump of flesh between his hands. Lighter with every passing day. Until the due date: 2 April 1937. The midwife arrives on time. Wajiha, flat on her back, opens her legs and for an hour, pain squeezes her heart. The midwife asks Abd al-Qadir, waiting at the door, for warm water. She says the name of God, pulls the cord between Wajiha's thighs and ties it to Haifa's own cord with a rubber glove brought back from the future. Then she begins the difficult operation of returning a baby. (That night, the Husayni family will shrink by one.)

In the other world, the clock strikes four.

The year is 2048. On the 170th floor, high in one of the landmarks of Mountain View, the first technological experiment of its kind is unveiled. Turing's 10D, many years in the making.

Laila pulls off the headset, whose ten dimensions hold every detail of the past. Her eyes are swollen. She looks around in silence. Applause breaks the calm, rising to whoops and cheers. A young woman approaches her and helps her up. Laila takes her cane and together they slowly walk to the stage. The applause goes on for the great inventor, the visionary who never gave up her dream.

The next day, the long—awaited announcement is all over the internet. The headline jumps out: 'TURING CONVERTS ALL DATA INTO VIRTUAL REALITY'. The article expands: 'The device works by running a fully-intelligent simulation of world history in reverse, while letting players watch. Beta-testing will begin next Saturday, 8 April.' Crowds show up days before to wait their turn, all excited to meet their personal hero.

By eight in the evening, Laila is alone at home. She passes her hand over the rough wall, feeling for the switch. A corridor of light leads her to the bed. Her remaining strands of white hair are damp, as are her neck, and the legs under her bathrobe. She rests her back on the wooden headboard and takes a sip of air. Then a long breath out. She closes her eyes. Her cheeks rise with a smile. She reaches for the nightstand and picks up a framed picture. Haifa. She holds it to her chest, opens her eyes and whispers. I did it, Mama.

Notes

1. Abd al-Qadir al-Husayni (1907–1948) – a Palestinian Arab nationalist and military leader who founded the secret militant group, the Organisation for Holy Struggle (*Munathamat al-Jihad al-Muqaddas*) which he later commanded, along with Hasan Salama, as the Army of the Holy War (*Jaysh al-Jihad al-Muqaddas*) during the 1936-39 Arab Revolt and during the 1948 War.

2. Operation Nachshon – a Zionist military operation during the 1948 War (5–16 April) designed to break the Siege of Jerusalem by opening the Tel-Aviv-Jerusalem road blockaded by Palestinians.

Vengeance

Tasnim Abutabikh

AHMED'S STRIDE SLOWED. He could hear his heart pounding in his ears. In a few moments he would meet the man he blamed for everything.

A few hours earlier, Ahmed had received a phone call from a private investigator he had hired to locate the man. Yousef Abdulqader was a thirty-five-year-old widower, the detective told him, the owner of a small mechanics shop on Al Naser Street, whose main business was repairing and restoring prostheses like C-leg 500 and I-limb 350 for the local cyborgs – a trade that had gone up steeply in the last few years, the detective noted. The moment the call was finished, Ahmed's phone beeped with a link to a folder containing all Abdulqader's basic information, including his home and work address. Ahmed decided right then: he would meet this Abdulqader and get to know him. How? He hadn't thought that far ahead yet.

The street was narrow and dimly lit, as all the streets in Gaza seemed to be, maybe in all the world. As he walked along it, he thought back to the time when space had been the priority; exponential population growth – both here in the Strip and elsewhere – had forced his parents' generation to live closer together, in ever taller buildings, and ever narrower streets than his grandparents would have ever dreamt possible. But the crisis of space turned out to be only the precursor to the real emergency. Without thinking of the consequences, urban development of farmland and deforestation in other parts of the world, designed to alleviate overcrowding, ended up stripping the planet of something far more valuable: its lungs. Now the atmosphere brimmed with carbon dioxide, and the average global temperature was four degrees higher than it had been two decades earlier.

A football hit the wall next to Ahmed with a slap, bringing his thoughts back to the present. A group of children were playing air-football, their hoverboards swooshing effortlessly through the air as they passed the ball between them. Ahmed could see each player's hair was soaked with sweat behind their heavy black lifemasks. The sound of air hissing through the masks' filtering systems was audible whenever a player came close to him.

As he made his way around the children, Ahmed looked up at the illuminated sky, whose permanent cloud cover served as the backdrop for projected adverts and exhortations throughout the night. He let out a short burst of laughter at the children in one commercial – who ran in a verdant, green field, breathing clean air without aid, laughing and tackling each other to the ground as a robotic voice intoned, 'Help build a better future for your children. Unite to save the earth.' *As if breathing the fresh morning air or feeling the cool breeze tickle their skin was a privilege these kids would ever attain,* Ahmed thought. Living in idyllic, air-filtered biospheres was a luxury only developed countries possessed.

Abdulqader's profile became clearer as Ahmed drew close; he recognised the man sitting in the doorway to the shop from the picture he'd been sent. Ahmed had been expecting someone with a bleak demeanour and a sullen countenance, but what he found was a gentle-looking man tinkering with the prosthetic arm of a young girl sitting on his lap, who couldn't have been more than seven years old. Through her mask, Ahmed could see the girl's cheeks were wet with tears of laughter; her free hand clutched her stomach, and her head rocked back and forth, waving her ponytail wildly with each new joke the man told her.

Ahmed stopped a few metres short, unsure of how to approach the man. He stared at him for moment, indecisively, before being yanked out of his trance by Abdulqader's bellowing voice: '*Assalamu-alikum*, brother.' Ahmed returned his greeting hesitantly.

'How can I help you?' Abdulqader asked with an encouraging smile.

'I'm, er, looking for a job,' Ahmed said, blurting out the first thing that came to mind. 'I've been searching for something for a year now with no luck. I'm a mechanical engineer. My skills could come in handy, but I'll do anything: wipe the floors, oil your tools, even take out your rubbish. Please don't turn me down; my mother's sick and I need the money.'

Abdulqader's response was to invite him inside to talk over a glass of tea. Handing Ahmed the glass, he asked, 'So your mother is sick with . . . ?'

Ahmed's eyes twitched as he explained his mother's condition, 'A severe case of hepatitis C. She's down to one month, after which, well, you know, they'll deactivate her lifemask.'

A moment of understanding seemed to pass between them, then Abdulqader averted his eyes and cleared his throat, 'So what's your plan?'

'I sent her file to al-Hafeza Health Institute. She's eligible for an engineered liver transplant, but I need to raise the money as soon as possible.' Ahmed felt ashamed to be taking advantage of his mother's illness, but all of what he said was true; he really did need the money.

Abdulqader stood up and sighed, 'I guess I'll see you tomorrow then.'

'I'll be here at 8:00 AM sharp,' Ahmed promised.

'Wait, what is your name again?' Abdulqader asked.

'Ahmed Albardasawi.'

'And I'm Yousef Abdulqader,' he said as he patted Ahmed on the back.

'Yeah, I know,' Ahmed whispered to himself.

As he was making his way out of the shop, Ahmed heard Yousef greeting a supplier who had just arrived. The thought occurred to him that he should linger, in the narrow alley down the side of the shop, to see if he could eavesdrop on their conversation.

Before long Ahmed heard voices rising inside. 'And here I am after a month,' the supplier was shouting, 'and you still don't have my 500 shekels?'

'One more week, please!' Yousef was saying.

'And what will change in a week?' the supplier asked sarcastically.

'Maybe I'll win the lottery,' Yousef chuckled.

Suddenly the supplier's tone seemed to change: 'A week it is.'

Ahmed walked away, scratching his lifemask at how easily the man had agreed to the delay, but also smiling at the first piece of good news he'd collected: Abdulqader was broke.

Three weeks passed, and Ahmed grew attached to the routine in Yousef's shop. Each morning he would lean against the front wall waiting for Yousef to open the shutters; children waited eagerly on the shop's doorstep, anticipating the man's ready supply of cookies and jokes. Every other day, he knew to expect another outburst from Abu Mohammed, the butcher, as he hobbled across the street carrying his rusty

I-limb 350 – insisting he didn't need a new model, just an adjustment. Ahmed was especially fond of Roaa, the semi-enhanced girl he'd seen the first day he came to the shop, particularly her daily speeches about teachers, friends and living with diabetes. When sunset came, on every day except Fridays, Yousef retreated to his private room at the back, hidden behind a false wall made out of a set of shelves stacked with unread books. No one else was allowed in this back room, not even Ahmed. And when the two closed the shop for the Friday prayers, Ahmed was sent home, always wondering what Yousef did with the rest of his day.

On his fourth Friday on the job, Ahmed decided it was time to find out, before he lost all sight of why he was there. After being hastily dismissed by Yousef, he stepped into the narrow alley again, and waited until his boss emerged onto the street with a small box in his hands. Ahmed felt adrenaline course through his veins as he began to follow Yousef at a safe distance.

Keeping at least 50 yards behind him at all times, Ahmed pursued Yousef down dark, quiet streets which seemed to get darker and quieter with every turn. Eventually he found himself on Habash Street, more a back alley than a street, flanked on both sides by decrepit looking warehouses. In front of one of the warehouse doors, Ahmed saw his boss stop, suddenly, and knock twice. Ducking behind an old vending kiosk, Ahmed managed to make out the figure of the man who greeted him – tall, well-built, wearing a long leather coat – before they both closed the door behind them. Ahmed couldn't stand the thought of not knowing what Yousef was up to. He circled the warehouse, searching for a chink in its armour, eventually finding a window that offered a perfect view of the two men in profile.

Although Ahmed couldn't quite make out the men's faces, he could see the tall man flailing his arms angrily. Yousef placed a hand on the man's shoulder, then handed him the box he had been carrying. Tentatively, Yousef lifted out its contents: a lifemask.

Ahmed's eyes widened and he took a step back. He had never seen an unworn mask before. Each citizen received one at birth, which adapted, expanded and even changed colour as they got older. Sometimes they needed repairing but never replacing. Smuggling unassigned lifemasks into the country was a well-known offence, as criminals were known to use them to evade identification. Yet here was his boss, handing one over to a well-built man in a long coat, in an otherwise abandoned warehouse. At that moment, there was a rustle behind Ahmed, and the muscle-bound man turned to the window. For a second, before he managed to duck out of sight, Ahmed glimpsed a face he recognised. This was the only man who, when he visited the shop, was allowed into Yousef's secret backroom, presumably to discuss business, as loudly hurled abuse was generally heard the moment they closed the door behind them. *That was too close*, Ahmed thought, and resolved to snap a few photos of the two men, using his lifemask's smart-glasses, and leave as quietly as he could.

On the walk home, Ahmed tried to clear his head. When he arrived, his mother, Feryal, greeted him at the door with a smile and a warm hug. 'How are you, my son?' Ahmed never liked lying to his mother, so he deflected with a question of his own, 'What's for dinner today? I've been daydreaming about your trademark cheese and olive sandwich,' he said, squeezing her hands, his eyes smiling sadly.

'Right away! You only had to ask,' she responded cheerfully. 'You know nothing makes a mother happier than feeding her child.'

Ahmed grabbed her other hand as she was turning to leave, forcing her to face him. 'The real question is how are you feeling, Mother?'

'Like yesterday and the day before,' she answered. 'I thank God regardless. '

'Sure, you do,' he said, taking a seat at the table. She was the strongest woman he knew and seeing her wither day by day only made him weaker too.

Watching her in this frail state, excited by the prospect of making him a sandwich, he decided he would do the right thing. For his people, but most of all for her. He would turn Yousef in. Tomorrow, he would go to the Israeli authorities and hand over the photos he had taken in exchange for an extension of his mother's deactivation date.

The next day, with his head hung low, Ahmed left the police station. He felt like he had relinquished the last piece of his identity, as he handed over those photos and described what he'd seen to the Israeli security officer.

Ahmed approached the shop with glazed eyes and ringing ears. When he reached the shop, he barely registered Yousef's hand on his back when he heard the words, 'Is it your mother, boy? Is she having a hard time again?'

Ahmed averted his eyes, leaving him with no answer.

'Come,' Yousef said, 'I think it's time to show you this.' He moved to the back of the shop and, with a little effort, slid the shelves aside. Behind it appeared a door, which he opened, and stepped through, signalling Ahmed to follow.

'For the last couple of weeks,' Yousef said, shutting the door behind him, 'I've been working on something.' He made his way around his desk and opened a small drawer.

'This is for your mother,' he said as he lifted a large, pale blue lifemask out of the draw. 'As you know, pale blue is the colour for healthy adults, with no criminal records, classed as no threat by the IDF,' Yousef explained. 'I know she's only got one week left. This should buy her more time.' Then he handed Ahmed an envelope. 'And this is an early paycheck.

I hope it will hurry the paperwork at the institute so she can get the treatment she needs.'

Ahmed's heart pounded. 'You're telling me you were working here all this time, trying to save my mother, while I conspired against you?! No, no! You're supposed to be the villain,' he sputtered.

'Conspired against me? Villain?' Yousef's eyebrows knotted.

'I know about you and your family!' Ahmed responded harshly, clinging to the reasons he hated Yousef in the first place. 'And of course, you are. You help criminals evade the law. I followed you yesterday and saw your secretive exchange with that gang member.'

'You followed me?' Yousef gasped. 'What gang member? That was Roaa's father. Her deactivation date was yesterday because her health was deteriorating so I made her a mask for the same reason I made your mother one, to buy her more time. Also it was black, you should've recognised that it was for a child, not an adult gang member. And what does my family have to do with this?'

Ahmed's hard expression melted at the mention of the girl's name. It was true. He had seen the girl deteriorate steadily over the last few visits. Yousef was right; she should've been dead by now.

'What does my family have to do with this, Ahmed?' Yousef asked again, his tone rising.

Ahmed's eyes found Yousef's, filling with fury, 'What do you think my primary motive to work for you was?' he asked. 'I came here seeking vengeance.'

This is the story he had memorised: There was a farm labourer once, who kept his wife and two sons fed by looking after fields and animals that belonged to a wealthy Palestinian. People regarded this rich landowner as the bedrock of the village, someone everyone else could come to for advice and help.

One summer night, the youngest son fell asleep in the farm's stables, something he often did as it was cooler in there than in the house. At some point in the night, he woke up suffocating. Looking around wildly, he could only see smoke and burning hay. The horses were frantic, rearing and kicking, their neighs filling the night air. Immediately the boy realised that the rumours of the last few days – of villages being burned to the ground – were now coming true here. They had thought they were safe under the protection of their landowner, but they were wrong.

The son looked around for a piece of cloth to cover his mouth and nose before squeezing his small frame out through one of the stable's windows. He stood there for a minute, looking at the raging fire before he remembered his family. He raced back to his parents' house, but his pace slowed as he drew closer to the sight of it being set alight by soldiers. Within moments, flames started to lick the window panes, and the memories of many generations seemed to be rising into the air with the smoke.

He immediately spotted his parents and his older brother. They were standing in the backyard with their hands in the air as three soldiers trained their rifles on them. The boy wanted to get to them but his legs wouldn't move, leaving him helpless, cowering behind a low wall. The son would always remember what his mother was wearing that day – a white dress with red embroidery, her eyes never leaving the face of her older son who, in turn, was eyeing the barrels of the rifles.

One of the soldiers seized the mother; her screams mixed with her husband's and older son's cries. When another soldier cocked his rifle, the boy couldn't hide anymore and stepped forwards at the same time his brother lunged towards his mother. The older boy only covered a few feet before he was cut down by a bullet. As was his mother, mid-scream, the red in her white dress spreading in the deafening silence that followed. His father didn't wait for the bullets to find him; he collapsed to the ground clutching his chest.

Years later the truth would be revealed. The landowner, on whom the boy's father had leaned for support, had sold the property to Zionists, betraying both his family and his countrymen. He had sold them all for money. And from the day he fled, the boy swore he would avenge his family's murders one day, however long it took.

'The landowner was your great-great-grandfather,' Ahmed concluded. 'The boy was my great-grandfather.'

Yousef stared at Ahmed for a moment as his words sank in. Then he looked him in the eye, 'Where did you hear this?'

'The story of the stable fire and the soldiers was told to me almost every night as a child,' Ahmed explained with clenched fists. 'It was my inheritance. The rest has come out recently; there was a book based on the diaries of the man your great-great-grandfather sold the land to. His name was Yahya Saleh.'

'Don't tell me what his name was! You think I don't know his name?' Yousef snapped. 'My great-great-grandfather was a patriot; he never would have sold his land to the enemy. In fact, he tried to do the exact opposite. When his mother fell ill and needed medical attention in Cairo, he accepted an offer from someone he thought was a friend: this man whose name you've just discovered. Yahya Saleh offered to keep the land safe from invaders. His said it would be easier to protect the land if the owner was present, so he suggested transferring the deeds to him, on a temporary basis. His friend promised he would return them when my great-great-grandfather was able to return. He even signed a separate contract to this effect. But a week after he left, this friend turned out to be a Zionist in disguise, and betrayed the farm's employees to the militias.'

Yousef explained that Zionist settlers used many schemes to seize control, and justify possession of Palestinian land.

Zionists with Arabic-sounding names who spoke the language fluently often travelled undercover as businessmen, making offers to landowners. Some people, according to rumours spread by everyone but Palestinians, actually said yes. But this story was deliberately spread and exaggerated to delegitimise the Palestinian cause. If land was sold at all, Yousef insisted, it would have been because owners were panicked by the attacks and sold without thinking. But it was extremely rare. In most cases it was taken by deceit, or just straight theft. 'But who cares about history anymore?' Yousef asked. 'Real history, that is. Even *our* school books are published in Jordan.' In the case of his great-great-grandfather, no money could have bought that piece of his country, Yousef explained. So, they leveraged it through his love for his sick mother and took it by deceit.

Yousef reached for a box on the bookshelves and retrieved an old folder of documents. 'Here, look at this,' he said, handing Ahmed a single sheet of paper, brown with age. 'This is a written agreement between my great-great-grandfather and Yahya Saleh outlining the terms that he then broke. No Israeli court would deign to look at such a document though.'

Yousef leaned on the desk, the air of the room suddenly weighing on him, 'Can't you see? I'm not your enemy; we only have one enemy, you and I, the same one: the people who turned us against each other and now control every inch of our lives down to the oxygen we breathe.'

Ahmed felt as if he had received a heavy blow. He had just destroyed a man without any cause. He fell to his knees, his eyes unable to meet Yousef's. 'But the damage is done; they're coming for you,' he spluttered.

'What did you do, Ahmed?'

'I turned you in to the Israeli authorities! I handed them pictures of the exchange that you made yesterday,' Ahmed confessed.

Yousef snatched Ahmed's arm and pulled him to his feet, 'We need to get out now! Hide your mother's mask.'

The moment they had replaced all of the shelves to the fake wall, hiding the workshop, they heard sirens blaring in the distance. Yousef turned to Ahmed and whispered urgently, 'You're one of the brightest people I know. You have a good heart; I've seen it in the way you are with Roaa. You can't help if you've been misled. So I trust you, Ahmed. I trust you with my work. Carry on what I started, my boy.'

Yousef held Ahmed's face between his hands, determined to make his point sink in, 'Do you hear me? Do you understand?'

'Yes,' said Ahmed, tears sliding down his face. 'Yes. I promise.'

Seconds later, a fleet of small, hovering drones blocked the entrance to the shop. Israeli soldiers barged in with taser guns aimed at Yousef. They shouted at him to put his hands behind his head while they pushed him out onto the street with the butt ends of their rifles. The circle of onlookers grew wider, as the lieutenant in charge of the platoon pointed at Yousef and addressed the bystanders in a loud voice.

'You're about to witness the fate of a man who disobeyed the law and disrupted the order we try so hard to enforce,' he boomed. He turned to his deputy and commanded lazily, 'Deactivate the mask.'

The heavily armoured deputy stepped forwards and, after first swiping an identity card past the side of Yousef's head, then flipped a switch just behind his left ear. Yousef remained calm for an entire minute while the onlookers held their breath. Then his knees buckled and he fell to the ground, his hands clutching his neck as he started to choke. His face turned purple and by the third minute, he had stopped thrashing. The soldier knelt down to check his pulse, then signalled that there was none. The platoon quickly boarded their vehicles and left the body sprawled on the ground for all to see.

The next day, the news hit every corner of the city, and the public nature of his termination had the opposite effect to what was intended. Instead of spreading fear it lit a fuse. Hundreds of people attended Yousef's funeral that night – families of people he had saved (including his supplier) and relatives of others who hadn't survived but who had at least been given hope by Yousef's efforts. Others came just to hear the man's story: how his own daughter had been sentenced to deactivation at the age of two due to a congenital heart disease, putting her on a 'high cost' list, and how this had been why he dedicated his life to helping others sentenced to lifemask termination.

Three days later, Ahmed sat beside his mother at the subsequent memorial service for Yousef. That morning, he had handed her Yousef's final piece of handiwork, the pale blue mask. It was also the first time he had managed to look at himself in a mirror since that day. His eyes were bloodshot from lack of sleep, and beneath them dark circles had appeared; his hair was dishevelled. For three days he hadn't left his desk, which was already piled high with schematics, blueprints and sketches. Most of the sketches were Yousef's, of course, but already Ahmed had started scribbling some of his own ideas down, exploring ways of improving the efficiency of his boss' design, and even thinking about locally sourced products, as a way of making them more affordable.

As everyone stood up to leave, Ahmed stayed behind. He made his way to the room at the back of the mosque where Yousef's hologram was positioned. He reluctantly lifted his head to gaze at Yousef's bright smile. Seeing him in this form, without his own mask, was a revelation. But he wished the real person was standing before him; he wished he could hear the man laugh again and, through the glass visor of the mask, see those laughter lines spread across his face.

Ahmed ran his hands through his hair and held his head. He let out a shaky sigh as Yousef's image became blurry from the tears in his eyes. He wiped them away and set his jaw as he made his promise: 'I will dedicate the rest of my life to redeeming myself, Yousef. I swear. I will honour your vision. We shall reclaim the air we breathe, if not the land we stand on, one mask at a time.'

Application 39

Ahmed Masoud

SMOKE DRIFTED OUT OF Rayyan's mouth as he dropped his jaw, turning it into soft, concentric circles. Poking his index finger through the middle of them, he turned to his friend, smiling: 'It's going to be OK, *wallah*, trust me.' His eyes beamed with excitement. Not knowing how else to convince his friend, he leaned forwards and embraced him, ignoring his lack of reaction.

'Relax, man. Trust me,' he tried again as they began climbing the marble steps of the Gaza City Municipality Building, pausing half way to look back at the three lemon trees in the square below them. Their leaves looked so dry under that thin layer of dust it could have been autumn. But this was the *khamaseen* season, late-spring when the Sinai's sand yellowed the city sky as it passed overhead, carried by the southern wind. At the top of the steps, a large, olive-wood door greeted them. Rayyan pressed a button and a red laser flickered across his face, before turning green. The door opened and he entered. Ismael, still looking perplexed, followed him just in time before the door purred shut behind them.

Inside the high-vaulted foyer, three long corridors stretched out in different directions. In the first, to their right, video screens lined the walls on both sides evidently showing live feeds from all over the city. Each screen had a tag: J1 and J2 fed from Jabalia Camp; G1 through G4 covered the major squares of Gaza City. And so on.

The middle corridor seemed to only contain a long series of lifts, with no buttons, just numbers above each one. These, Ismael was familiar with. He loved the faint quiver of excitement they sent through you whenever one of them opened its doors, knowing you had chosen it from the micro-movements you made yards before. The moment you stepped through, you were moving, plummeting downwards at a speed given on a small screen on the left-hand wall: usually 10 metres per second, before slowing and then surging sideways at 10, 20, 30. Lift-tunnels like these spider-webbed deep beneath the old city and beyond, spanning all of what was once called 'the Strip', and linking with another network of tunnels under what they used to call 'the Bank'. If you had the correct entry visa, the lifts would speed you to your destination in minutes. This network had been the collective pride and joy of the independent republics who had pledged to build them in the so-called 'New Dawn' that followed the collapse of the Oslo Accord and the 2025 invasions, when each major Palestinian city had been forced to declare itself an independent state.

The third corridor ran alongside a series of small meeting rooms. As he walked past, Ismael could see each one was filled with men with moustaches or women with headscarves surrounded by news screens, typing frantically at their desks with each new development. In one room, a hologram of an Indian man in a border control uniform was giving a presentation on new software that could identify illegal immigrants through facial expressions.

By the time Rayyan reached the room at the end of the corridor, Ismael had caught up with him. They stood still for a moment as a small, hovering drone-cam emerged from the wall and performed a retinal scan, before the big olive-wood door slid open. The room was crowded; men in suits jostled with others in *jellabiya* and traditional dress. A young woman in a long, flowery skirt and reading glasses that wrapped around her entire head was looking down as they entered. The murmur in the room suddenly stopped.

'Please be seated,' the woman said, gesturing towards the bench in front of her. The two of them sat down in silence.

'My name is Lamma El-Rayyes and I am chairing this emergency session,' she began. 'Gentlemen, your actions have had considerable consequences across the state, so, if I may, I would like to start by asking you to tell us the facts, as you understand them. We are not interested in the whys of the situation, just in what happened. First, which one of you submitted the application form?'

'I did,' Rayyan answered without a moment's hesitation.

'Well, actually, it was my idea,' Ismael quickly added.

'As I said, Mr Ismael, I am not interested in ideas. I just want to establish the facts. I will then report my findings to his excellency, the President of Gaza City, who will talk with his counterparts, the presidents of Khan Younis, Nusairat and the others . . .' Lamma waved her hand in the air and a large display screen appeared on the wall behind her. She played around with the bright green buttons on her control pad and a document appeared.

'Is that your signature at the bottom of the page?' she asked, looking at neither of them.

Rayyan and Ismael looked a little bit confused.

'No, of course not,' Rayyan started. 'This is the signature of our great leader, Mr Hamad Hamoud, as you know.'

'Is this a trick question?' Ismael asked.

'No, it is not,' Lamma fired back, fixing her stern gaze on them, 'This is not an authentic signature. One of you has forged it.'

A murmur of disbelief spread through the room and a couple of men started heckling.

'This is going to break the peace deal completely,' someone muttered.

'We're doomed!' shouted another. 'We're heading straight back to the rule of Hamas and Fateh.'

'The Israelis won't be happy either,' observed an elderly man at the back.

Lamma cleared her throat and the whole room fell silent again. She had an air of natural authority that commanded the room's respect, to the extent that Ismael found himself wondering how far her obvious ambitions might end up taking her.

She raised both hands in the air and continued, 'I have to hand it to you; you are a couple of tricksters, it seems.' She turned again to the facsimile looming large on the wall display. 'So, you forge a document, purporting to be from our leader, apply to the International Olympic Committee for the State of Gaza to . . . host the 39th Summer Olympic Games in 2048.'

She turned to face them, and the room. 'Now, let me ask you,' she said, pausing for effect. 'Are you out of your minds? This is only eight years from now.'

She stared at them for what felt like an eternity. Hearing the contents of the document being read out loud felt even more ridiculous than they had anticipated. They both knew the seriousness of the matter, of course. They could be hanged for treason, and the fire in Lamma's eyes seemed to confirm they should expect nothing less. They both fell silent, not knowing what to say. They looked at each other, as if realising, for the first time, the reality of what they'd done.

The air of confidence that had filled Rayyan on the steps of the building just a few minutes earlier had entirely disappeared, replaced by a sheepish, apologetic look. Ismael's mind wandered from the room, back to a time when they'd both been kids studying together at the UN refugee school. They were only ten years old when the war broke out in 2025. He didn't remember much about how it all started, but he remembered the day the school was bombed as if it were yesterday. Smoke rose in all directions, shrouding the playground like a hood. Ambulance sirens filled the city, as he stood there watching everything unravel around him: all he wanted to do was run back home to his parents' house in Beach Camp. But he was frozen. He wished his father was there to pluck him out of the chaos, people screaming and running in all directions. He wished his teacher was there to shout at him, and scare him into snapping out of it and running. But nothing happened: he just froze. The smoke got thicker and closer, until he could see nothing at all, and just as he closed his eyes, Rayyan grabbed him by the wrist and dragged him away.

They ended up in the El Ansar District in Gaza City. Israeli soldiers had already landed by sea, docking their heavily armoured ships at El Mina, Gaza's only port. They were also bombing from the air, using advanced high-speed drones.

The two boys roamed the city for days before eventually settling on a bombed-out residential block on El-Farra Street as their shelter. To their delight, in one of the apartments, they found cans of sardines, humous and fava beans, which sustained them for a week until an old woman, a former resident, came looking for her belongings and found them. She brought them back to her new abode in a less bombed-out part of town, where she, her son and her daughter-in-law raised them as their own. They couldn't return to their families in Beach Camp; the IDF had installed checkpoints everywhere, surrounding and besieging every city, town and village in the Strip, just as they had done in the Bank. Realising there was little hope of ever returning to their parents, Rayyan and Ismael stayed with their new adopted family. From then on, they were brothers.

The Palestinian cities, unable to physically connect with each other anymore, declared themselves independent states. Israel had taken control of all the roads between them, and air travel had not be possible since the end of the twentieth century, so the city-states had put everything into tunnelling back into contact with each other – starting with shabby old holes Hamas had first dug during its rule – holes that had proved utterly useless in thwarting the invasion when it came.

With time, the city-states grew apart, in outlook and habits, and ever stricter immigration policies were gradually introduced. On several occasions, tensions slid into open military confrontation, and warring Palestinian cities fired homemade rockets that flew high over the heads of Israeli soldiers, usually landing in the empty fields that acted as buffer zones around each city. The hostilities persisted until a peace deal between the states was signed in 2030, acknowledging the independence of each city-state and the integrity of its borders, even though these borders were very much still under Israeli control, a fact nobody seemed too keen to dwell upon.

★

'We could be looking at another war, here.' Lamma's voice brought Ismael back with a jolt. 'Either with Khan Younis, or Rafah, or even Ramallah. Their presidents will all think we didn't consult them in this decision; that the Republic of Gaza City wanted to do this on its own, to steal the limelight. And don't forget Israel! They will no doubt accuse us of breaking our agreements with them on this. Bombs will probably start raining on us because of this; not only on us but on all the other states. Where will this end?'

All Ismael wanted was to be out of that windowless room and in the open, enjoying the sandstorm. He looked at his friend, then mirrored him, staring back down at the floor. It felt like the whole room was watching him. But when Ismael eventually looked up again and caught the eye of one old man sitting at the back, his smile seemed genuine.

The truth of the matter was it had all been a joke, a game of dare which neither party had expected would go this far. Ismael was the first to suggest it and called it 'Operation Application 39'. Rayyan said he would look after the paperwork and that was that. They submitted it online; not expecting it would even be read. The two men's day jobs were in the municipality's IT department, positions which gave them enough free time to develop a series of elaborate hacking schemes to entertain themselves in the long hours between reboot requests. At first, these consisted largely of hacking into local celebrities' social media accounts, and playing practical jokes on their celebrity friends. But they grew bored of this, wanting something more challenging to pass the time. The International Olympic Committee's computer system offered the perfect challenge, and hacking into it even allowed them to look at rival applications from other cities. 'Just for research, you understand,' Ismael, the better of the two hackers, giggled at the time. 'So we don't look like complete fools.'

The IOC's reply, dated 12 January 2040, came addressed to the president and read: 'The International Olympic Committee feels that the application is very strong and that by hosting the 36th Summer Olympic Games, Gaza City would be able to celebrate and further cement the peace deal signed ten years ago.'

'I am sorry, Ms Lamma, it was just a bit of fun, we didn't think it would actually lead to anything . . .' Rayyan said with pleading eyes. Ismael looked at him with pity, all-too aware of how difficult it was for his friend to admit their mistake.

'What do we do now?' interjected someone from across the room.

'We turn it down, of course,' another answered.

A woman, who looked in her sixties, stood up. She was smartly dressed and wore a shawl around her shoulders.

'Excuse me, Ms Lamma. I realise this is a reckless violation by two obviously irresponsible individuals, but we are here now and, I think, instead of wasting time revisiting how this was allowed to happen, we should instead be thinking of how we could make it work for us, how we can seize it as an opportunity for the whole republic – a chance to show the world how civilised we are. We may actually be able to get the other states to agree . . .'

The room erupted into a cacophony of agreement and dissent. One of the men in suits said the old woman was clearly crazy. 'Show some respect, you ignoramus!' a younger woman shouted at him. Rayyan leant towards Ismael and nodded towards her: 'Asmaa Shawwa – she served in the Abbas government in the early 2000s.'

'Enough!' shouted Lamma, slamming her fist on the table; the room promptly fell silent. All eyes were now on her.

'I think this is a decision for the president, not us. As I said, I just wanted to establish the facts and now that I am confident this was not an act of deliberate sabotage, I will take the matter to him and see what he says. Mr Hamoud will surely have the wisdom to see through this. We will adjourn the meeting and reconvene tomorrow morning. You two are coming to the president's office now, with me.'

Rayyan and Ismael stared at each, terrified. They had never met a senator before, let alone a president; they were just two IT clerks at the municipality.

'Do we have to?' Ismael muttered but didn't wait for an answer.

The room started to empty in silence, people walked out of the main door, each throwing a parting glance towards the two men.

In a soft, slightly robotic voice, Lamma ordered the

room's computer to shut down, and as they stepped outside the three of them were met by a small crowd of people waiting in the corridor for their lifts to arrive. A robotic assistant, with a painted-on suit, rolled towards Lamma, taking her bag and ushering the three of them towards an opening lift. Inside, there was only one button on the wall, which read 'The Office of President Hamad Hamoud'. Lamma pressed it and within an instant the doors were shut, leaving the boy standing outside.

The lift plunged downwards and, after a minute or so of sideways acceleration, started ascending again. When the bell rang indicating it had arrived at its destination, a computerised female voice welcomed them to 'The Office of President Hamad Hamoud'. 'If you are carrying a weapon,' it added, 'you will be neutralised immediately.'

'If only we had time for you to hack this motherfucker and de-smug her?' Rayyan muttered, as they stepped out, into the bewildering light of a penthouse office.

As they entered, President Hamad Hamoud was busy going through a pile of paperwork behind a huge desk. He looked very tall even though he was sitting down. The two friends felt deeply intimidated by the surroundings and avoided direct eye contact as the president lifted his head up and greeted Lamma.

'*Ahlan*, Lamma, how did the meeting go?' the president smiled, before glancing back down at his papers.

'Well, these two idiots are the ones who submitted the application and forged your signature . . .'

'Can you hack her too?' Rayyan whispered. 'She's rude . . .' Ismael concentrated on keeping a straight face.

The president stopped reading and looked at the two of them. He stood up and removed his small glasses, placing them carefully on his desk, then stared once more at the two men still refusing to make eye contact.

'I believe you understand the seriousness of your actions?' he asked as he approached them.

'Yes, sir,' they answered in unison.

'So, what shall I do with you now? Have you hanged for treason?'

The silence that followed was unbearable. They still couldn't look the president in the eye. They were expecting soldiers to barge through the doors at any moment. Ismael's hands were shaking, and Rayyan could see it.

'Well, Lamma, we are where we are. I have been thinking a lot about this and I believe we should go ahead and host these games. These two goons might have actually brought us a gift –'

'But, sir . . .' Lamma interrupted.

'Let me finish first, please . . .' Mr Hamoud's tone was serious. 'The Republic of Gaza is a thoroughly modern city these days, both in terms of technology and infrastructure. Besides, this could be an opportunity to unite all the Palestinians states together.'

'But sir, it could bring about war again, with everyone!' Lamma responded sharply.

'So be it, we will be ready for it . . .' The president's authoritative tone signalled the end of the conversation. He went back to his desk and paperwork. Lamma indicated to Rayyan and Ismael to follow her and, within seconds, they were out the door.

They followed her in silence as she marched back to the lift. The door was already open and, stepping inside, they found themselves instantly transported back to the municipality building, where they were ushered into a small meeting room followed by Lamma's personal assistant, a small robot that glided along on two big wheels.

'It's the 30th of March 2040, this meeting will be recorded and minutes will be sent out directly to you half an hour after it's finished. Please refrain from using offensive language, anything you say will go on your HR profile.'

'*Shukran,* Tamir,' Lamma addressed the robot which had moved to her side, and started scanning both Rayyan and Ismael.

'OK, well . . . You are very lucky to be here right now despite the havoc you have caused. I am sure Mr Hamoud has made a huge mistake, but he is the president and his wishes must be followed. So . . . tell me, when you submitted this application, did you have the faintest clue how Gaza would actually be able to host these Games? How are we going to host a marathon, for instance, when the city's only six kilometres wide? Or the water sports – rowing, sailing, long-distance swimming – when we only have a two-mile long stretch of coast?'

Lamma didn't sound genuinely angry, more frustrated. She seemed to have accepted the decision, but she looked away as she reeled off her questions, not expecting an answer.

'We could dig more tunnels,' Ismael said.

'What?' she snapped.

'The Israelis control all the land between our states, they control the airspace and the sea; only the earth beneath us remains unoccupied. We could build tunnels that circle the city deep underground – 2R – that gives us 31.42 kilometres, one and a third laps and you have a marathon!' Ismael said enthusiastically. 'We could build football pitches, velodromes . . . whatever we want down there!'

'What about water sports, smart alec?' Lamma cut him off.

'Well, we have two miles of coast. We can do all the swimming stuff in there, set up lanes going along the coast, backwards and forwards; all we need to work out is how to stop the waves. I am sure a few rocks will do it. For diving, we can dig under the sea too. Make the seabed deeper. For water polo, we could use one the new water-tanks the World Bank donated to the camps. Why not?'

'So basically what you are saying is that more tunnels and a few rocks in the sea are all we need?' Rayyan asked sarcastically.

'Yes, we know how to dig them, alright! We've been building them since the 90s, so why not now?' Ismael had rediscovered his self-belief.

Lamma watched the two young men and wondered where they would have been if the situation was different, if the war never happened. Her own father had been killed defending Gaza City during the Israeli invasion fifteen years earlier. She'd been sixteen at the time. The day her father never came back was the day she decided to study politics and begin her long, remarkable pursuit of a political career. A lot of people admired her; several unlikely men had even proposed to her, apparently, but to Ismael she looked like someone too smart to jeopardise a career by allowing herself a private life.

★

Thus it was announced that Gaza City was to be the first Arab city to ever host an Olympic Games. Rayyan and Ismael walked out of the municipality building that day feeling elated. They didn't say a word to each other as they walked through the long corridor towards the exit. But as they stepped down onto the street, surrounded by honking cars, the buzzing of delivery drones, the flickering of advertising screens, they began to laugh. Looking at each other, their laughter grew and for a moment they struggled to catch their breath.

They were through-the-looking-glass now; what had started as a joke had become a new reality, one with the potential to change the whole city's future. After a century of being cut off from the world, now, suddenly, the world was going to come to them. *To pay a visit to this prison*, Ismael thought; *its first ever, in order to watch people running, jumping and throwing things!*

Neither Ismael nor Rayyan had ever set foot outside of
Gaza City. Even getting into other coastal states within the
Palestinian federation needed a visa and a string of transit
permits which neither of them had ever succeeded in applying
for. What they knew of the other states they had all learned
from their grandparents. As teenagers, they'd dreamt of visiting
the Republics of Ramallah and Nablus in the Bank, or to one
day hike across the gentle hills of old Palestine, to breathe its
fresh air, to take in the scent of olives in the groves that
stretched, in their minds, all the way from Bethlehem to
Jerusalem.

Collecting themselves from their momentary hysterics,
Rayyan and Ismael set off down the hill towards Talatini
Street, in the direction of home. As they passed Al Ahli
Hospital, an Israeli drone flew low over their heads and landed
nearby, only to then transform into a bipedal robot. With its
oddly dog-like face, it began scanning the streets with its dark,
translucent eyes, as pedestrians looked away.

The dog-robot then scanned Rayyan and Ismael, who
knew to stand completely still and stare directly at it. Looking
away would only get them tasered. On each side of its long,
pointed face, just below each camera-eye, a screen flashed into
life and began scrolling through the two men's vital information:
dates of birth, addresses, bank account numbers, professions,
etc. Across its chest stretched the blue and white Israeli flag.
Ismael wanted to punch it in its solar plexus, knowing it
probably didn't have one. Reading his friend's thoughts,
Rayyan put his arm around Ismael's shoulder: 'Look it's one of
your favourite breeds!' he laughed, awkwardly. 'Oh, but it's
been scrapping with other poodles,' he added, noticing a
horizontal scratch across the blue of its chest.

After a pause, the robot retransformed itself back into a
drone and they both sighed with relief to see it fly away.
Usually, when a robot stopped people like this in the street,

someone was either tasered and arrested, or worse. The two men laughed at the day they were having. As they walked in the direction of the Rimal neighbourhood, a strange sense of invincibility lightened their steps.

★

Over the following four years, preparations got under way across the city for the vast infrastructure necessary to host such a colossal international event. Ismael's idea of building most of the facilities underground was eventually accepted, and thanks to the unique expertise of Gazan builders in all things subterranean, the work was completed ahead of schedule. Most of the facilities were built within three years. The main challenge was how to build the athletes' village, given that there wasn't enough space left aboveground in the republic. The solution came from an expert in the United Kingdom of Saudi (which, since 2036, had assimilated all the other Gulf countries). A Dubai-based architect proposed using the rubble excavated from the tunnels to build a man-made island in the sea, just off the Gaza City shoreline.

Rayyan and Ismael were on the planning committee, chaired by Lamma, their original indiscretion long-since forgotten about. All members reported directly to the president who was, despite his old age, very keen to follow up on all the details. Mr Hamoud was also forever receiving delegations from the other Palestinian republics. Indeed every planning meeting had envoys from the other states in attendance; despite their fury in the early days for not having been consulted – in some cases even threatening war – now they pored over each decision in detail to make sure every shekel allocated by the Olympic Committee could be seen to be benefiting the federation as a whole.

One state had never forgiven Gaza, however. Salah

Zourob, the president of Rafah, had been so furious about the application, he severed all diplomatic relations with Hamoud's government, and closed down the lift-tunnel between the two states. It had been four years since any goods or individuals had travelled between them. Indeed recent noises heard travelling down that particular tunnel had been interpreted by military experts as the sound of troops gathering at the Rafah end.

The party that was most upset by it all was, of course, Israel. Tel Aviv had been trying to host the Olympic Games for decades. The Knesset contested the results, and took the International Olympic Committee to court, initially alleging corruption, but later changing their stance, claiming the bid had been an elaborate attempt to hoodwink the international community into unwittingly funding a new era of military tunnelling: what lobbyists called 'the terror from beneath'. Unexpectedly these appeals failed to reverse the decision, although Israel, Russia and the Confederate States of America all declared they would boycott the Games the moment the appeal was overturned. Despite this, the Israeli government still took it upon itself to make sure the preparations for the Games failed, instructing all security agencies to gather more intelligence about the planning, and sending in a new swarm of microscopic drones to infiltrate each of the development sites. Aware of this, Mr Hamoud demanded the utmost secrecy, and only discussed plans through encrypted messaging systems. For some reason, he tasked Rayyan and Ismael with monitoring security protocols and attempted intelligence breaches by Israel directly. Israel, in turn, encouraged the president of Rafah to attack Gaza, giving President Zourob the intel, weapons and temporary access to what used to be called Salah Eldein Street – the now overgrown thoroughfare which once ran the entire length of the Strip.

With four years left to go, war loomed, and the dream of

hosting the Games 'without mishap' grew ever more unlikely. After one particularly long day, the two friends sat down for a shisha-vape, in a café in El Rimal Park, near what used to be the Unknown Soldier Statue. The two men never needed much encouragement to reminisce about life at school before the devastation of April '25, but these days every time they started to, their talk stuttered to a halt, both thinking about the further devastation that awaited them. Their conversations were increasingly given over to these long pauses, so much so that Ismael was relieved when today's silence was broken by the sound of a large drone landing just a few feet away and transforming into a bipedal dog-headed robot. As it conducted its usual retinal scan and screen scroll of their vital information, Ismael noticed a horizontal scratch across its chest.

This time there was something different to the process. Both screens lit up and a pair of bulky metallic antennas extended from the machine's shoulders, arcing round towards the two men, each holding a pair of self-locking handcuffs. 'In accordance with Israeli Law,' its dog-mouth intoned, 'I am placing you both under arrest. Any attempt to escape will put your lives in danger.' The two friends were wise enough to stretch their hands out willingly as the self-locking handcuffs flew to their wrists, snapping their hands together, before yanking them both to the ground. The dog-robot began its transformation back into a drone, ready to airlift Rayyan and Ismael into Ashkelon Prison, where they would no doubt be held indefinitely under 'administrative detention' laws.

But as the drone prepared to leave, its muzzle started to flinch oddly, its left leg suddenly jerked upwards, kneeing itself in the chest. Orders began to issue from its dog-mouth in an array of different languages: English, French, Chinese, and others the men didn't recognise. Its cheek-screens scrolled through all kinds of images: schematics of missile launchers, satellite photography, maps of what appeared to be the location of Israeli troops just outside of the city's perimeter fence. One screen froze on this last map, while the other continued scrolling through the names and mug shots of high ranking Gazans under the title 'Assets'. Suddenly, smoke started rising from the dog-robot's head until it stuttered to a complete standstill. The handcuffs sprung open.

Rayyan started running down the street. But his friend couldn't tear his eyes away from the slumped head of the machine in front of him.

'Come on, what are you waiting for?' Rayyan yelled, stopping to turn round. Ismael didn't move.

'Did you see that?'

'See what?' Rayyan shouted, now running back towards him.

'I didn't just jam it,' he said holding up a battered-looking handset he'd been clutching all along in his pocket. 'It spilled its guts for me.'

'As I always say, you're a genius Ismael, and we need to mass market those things,' Rayyan replied, physically grabbing Ismael by the upper arm. 'But come on.'

'Listen. The IDs it just scrolled through – that was its most valuable information. This little device' – Ismael waved the handset again – 'gave it a psychic stomach bug, and what it threw up was the most classified information it had access to. Don't you see what this means, bro?' Rayyan looked lost. 'The AIs have a subconscious! It chose to share this, to confess *this*. It could have shared a million other data sets, but this was the one it was least comfortable with.'

'It's a trap,' Rayyan said, without looking at his friend. 'And even if it isn't, what can we do with it. Drones are tracked; if we drag it off somewhere to download all that, the whole Israeli army will be knocking at our door . . .'

'Not if we take it underground,' Ismael replied still staring at his keypad. 'It will lose its GPS signal. Look, this is a gift; we can't just pass it up. Besides, they know about us already, clearly. They'll just send another drone soon, and then what? Do you want us to keep running forever? Let's just take this one; we have nothing to lose . . .'

Ismael pleaded with his friend, who just stood there trying to think. Rayyan knew that Ismael was right: there was no point in just running; they needed to go into hiding and they needed any advantage they could get. He didn't relish the prospect of returning to a life on the streets, again, on the run.

'OK, OK,' Rayyan conceded, helping his friend to lift the robot's heavy carcass into the back seat of his self-drive, parked across the street from the cafe. They instructed the car to travel at top speed. Ismael had long since hacked into its limiters, so they watched with some apprehension as the self-drive swerved round kids playing hologram football in the street and pedestrians on motorised skateboards. Five minutes later they were frantically carrying the machine up the steps of the municipality building and bundling it into the nearest lift. After taking a second lift a few moments later, they felt they were plunging deeper than they ever had gone before. Ismael had been the one choosing the lifts and the destinations. Every few minutes or so he would link his handset to the lift's computer and name a new destination – usually the name of some long-lost village, that his grandmother had told him tales about – coupled with the phrase 'but don't alight'. This, he explained to Rayyan, was his way of making a longer journey, which combined with his handset's masking hack, would make the journey untraceable in the lift's records.

'All those permit applications they rejected!' Rayyan said, in awe. 'We could have hacked our way out of Gaza all along.'

When the doors eventually opened, they came out into a platform marked 'Amman Tunnel'. They had crossed the entirety of Palestine and now appeared to be in a different country altogether. The tunnel, Rayyan explained to Ismael, was strictly for emergencies, and for use by the president and his diplomats only.

'What do we do now?' Rayyan asked, contemplating the lifeless dog-robot on the floor of the platform beside them.

'Well, now we reboot it and find out what it was trying to share with us. Believe me, I was born for this hack. Hey why don't you go get us some food and coffee, and I'll get started.' Without even looking at his companion, Ismael started unzipping his backpack, opened up his laptop and patched it into the robot. Meanwhile, Rayyan headed up a flight of old-fashioned stairs to ground level. On their way here, he had shown Ismael the schematic of where the lift would come out, slap bang in the heart of Amman, opposite the Third Circle, not far from Rainbow Street. They had both heard stories about how crowded Amman was, being the only reliably peaceful country in the whole region. With the exception of the United Kingdom of Saudi, it was also the only country in the region that hadn't been divided up into various states. When he returned an hour later, laden with falafel sandwiches and bottles of Coca-Cola, he couldn't stop talking about what he'd seen: billboards advertising gadgets he'd never heard of, Israelis, Jordanians and Pal-refs laughing and joking with each other in the shops – clearly living side-by-side! Shops accepting shekels. So full was he with his own news, he barely noticed the beaming grin on his friend's face, the lights pulsing behind the robot's eyes, and the data streaming down the laptop's screen.

'Look at this!' Ismael screeched.

'Hey, what did I call you? Oh yes, "Balfour"! Hey Balfour, dance for us!' The robot started twirling around, playing Hebrew music and gyrating the way you might expect a bipedal robot with a dog-shaped head to gyrate.

'What the hell?'

'It's mine now – my own little pet. I have overridden all the IDF protocols and I can make it do whatever I want!'

'This is dangerous,' Rayyan muttered.

'More dangerous than what we've done already? Why?'

'Well, we get it to do anything we like? Any crime we want, any retaliation; it will make us invincible.'

'Damn right!' Ismael interjected. 'The information it's shared alone is game-changing. Man, I have details of President Zourob's imminent attack against us. I have the names of people leading the forces, the names of Israeli officials supporting it. But, above all, this damn thing is somehow connected to the central database in Israel and, guess what, I have access to everyone's details, including phone numbers in Palestine, Israel, Jordan and Egypt. I can send all of them a text message right now if I want to . . .'

'What?' the plastic bag with falafel sandwiches fell from Rayyan's hands. 'Wait, we need to take this back to the president. We need to let him know . . .'

Without thinking, Rayyan bundled the three of them back into the lift and hit a button on his handset. Their stomachs grumbled as they tunnelled sideways through the Judean mountain crust. Ismael in particular lamented over the image of the plastic bag, containing his falafel, abandoned on the platform. Eventually they arrived at the Gaza Municipality Building, and switched into the lift marked with what Ismael now recognised as the president's seal. Lamma was already in the office, having received their message insisting on her attendance. She couldn't believe her eyes when the two of them walked through the door, carrying the robot.

'What the hell?' she said, looking at Rayyan, and immediately called for her personal assistant to come in and apprehend the two visitors. 'Are you Israeli agents now?' she asked bluntly. Mr Hamoud side-stepped towards his desk, with thoughts of the panic button written all over his face.

'No, wait . . . please don't, Mr President, we can explain,' Ismael did all the talking. Rayyan simply stood still, at first frozen with fear, but, after a moment, a little smile flickered across his face.

'This machine came to arrest us this morning but it malfunctioned and we managed to hack it. It reports to me now, it does anything I want it to. Watch. Balfour become a drone!' The machine instantly folded up its limbs, extended its antenna and began hovering towards the ceiling. 'Balfour, tell Lamma who your master is and who your enemies are!'

'My name is Balfour and my master is Mr Ismael. My enemies are the enemies of the Republic of Gaza City.'

Rayyan and Ismael explained everything about the leaked attack plans, the informants' IDs, and most of all the databases.

'Sir, this thing is tracked,' Lamma interrupted. 'We have to destroy it immediately. It could be relaying this conversation, and our location, to the Israelis right now.'

'Don't worry,' Ismael smiled. 'I've disabled that too. We're safe – well, not Rayyan and me, because we're still on their list – but you are.'

'OK, you two need to be taken to a safe house,' the president answered firmly. 'I need to think about what I am going to do with this. Once more, it seems, you two bozos have brought us another gift without fully understanding it. Lamma, will you get me Senator Shawwa.'

★

Ms Shawwa was sweating as she re-read the final draft of the message that was going to be sent out to all citizens – over three hundred million people – across the entire region.

'Mr President. It's ready. Would you like to press the send button?'

Mr Hamoud stared over her shoulder, reading for what felt like the millionth time.

> To all those who believe in justice, to those who still believe in the future, I, Mr Hamad Hamoud, President of the Republic of Gaza City, appeal to you to stand with us. When we won the privilege of hosting the Olympic Games, we saw it as an opportunity to redress decades of separation and a century of fighting – to come together as humans, no matter what our differences. However, it has recently come to our attention that the Israelis and the President of Rafah are planning to attack us with the express purpose of cancelling the Games. I appeal to you to rise tomorrow at midday, to come out in the streets, walk with your leaders, and declare your opposition to this. Let us make this a show of solidarity and a rejection of any further wars. Thank you, and may Allah bless you all.

Mr Hammoud cross-checked the Hebrew translation and then pressed the button. For a moment everyone stared at the floor in silence. Lamma eventually broke the spell by walking towards Ismael and Rayyan and patting them heartily on the shoulders. 'You two brought so much trouble to this city, why couldn't you be like everyone else and just live your lives?'

'We chose none of this,' Rayyan was quick to answer.

Lamma approached the president, who looked tired and anxious. 'My fellow Palestinians,' he addressed those in the room. 'We've done what we can. Let's see what happens. I am tired now. I need a rest. Tomorrow we will either wake up with peace or further trouble. Whichever it is, things will never be the same again. These two idiots may be what we've all been waiting for, for better or worse. Good night, Lamma. I hope you can lead this nation to peace after I'm gone.'

★

At 11:00 AM the following morning, the president, Lamma, Rayyan, Ismael, Ms Asmaa and the entire municipality building staff stood outside the president's office. A TV crew was recording the scene as Mr Hamoud declared the start of his 'March for Peace'. Knowing that half of the city now surrounded the building, he spoke directly to the camera, asking the rest of Gaza's citizens, those not yet out in the square, to walk with him, from here up to the northern most border point, then down to the southernmost, from the gates of Erez to the gates of Nusairat. 'I believe that our fellow Palestinians will join us.'

As they started to march from the president's office, whoever remained in their homes or offices came out and joined the throng. As the president's march passed by El Wihda Street, the momentum was visibly gathering. People started closing their shops; others came out of the mosques to join in. By the time they reached El Jalaa Street, the march was already two hundred thousand strong, all chanting and calling for peace.

The march continued through El Saha, then upwards onto Omar El Mukhtar Street. By the time they got to Shujaia, the numbers had reached over three hundred thousand. The scene was overwhelming for Rayyan, who chanted louder and more excitedly at every new corner.

Everyone was marching peacefully until they reached the Sheikh Ejleen area by the beach, very close to the border with Nusairat. An Israeli drone appeared, transforming into a bipedal robot as it landed, effectively blocking the path of the march. It extended its shoulder-antenna and crossed them resolutely, staring at the advancing crowd.

'Mr Hamoud,' it announced, in its monotone, 'it has been deemed that you are contravening Article 48A of the 2026 Peace Accord; I am hereby placing you under arrest.'

The crowd fell silent, as hundreds at the front tried their

best to casually look away, look up or down, so the robot couldn't scan them. The president, by contrast, walked straight up to the drone and stared directly into its lifeless eyes. He gave it a kick with his foot, and everyone cheered again.

'Security unit under attack: engage now,' the robot intoned, then fired a round of bullets directly between the president's eyes.

The president's body fell backwards sending up a small cloud of dust as it hit the ground. The cheering ceased and everyone stared dumbstruck at the pool of dusty blood spreading slowly from the back of their leader's head. People started to scream and run towards the robot presumably to attack it. Metres before reaching it, they all found themselves fragmenting, midair, as the TV cameras automatically powered down.

More drones appeared in the sky and before too long, an army of metallic robots had assembled to face the angry protestors, who were undeterred and started running towards them. The robots opened fire across the promenade where the president had been shot, as well as across the beach where many protestors had fled. They continued to scour the area, spraying bullets in all directions, for a further forty-five minutes. When they eventually stopped, the air was thick with dark smoke. Waves lapped the shore with blood.

Thousands more, many of whom were at the rear of the march, managed to run away in all directions. Ismael was on the ground, crouching behind a vape kiosk. He had been shot in the knee, but, once the bullets had stopped, Ismael started hobbling back along the promenade to look for Rayyan. There was no sign of him.

His legs gave way and he collapsed, to his knees first, then his hands caught the ground before it slammed into his chest. All was silent, the whole city lay lifeless – only Ismael's heavy breathing and the sound of waves could be heard. After a few moments, he tried crawling on all fours, then, slowly gathering strength, he got up, and began limping across a terrain strewn with corpses, dark gouts of blood crusting on the yellow sand. Ismael kept walking until he reached the border. He wanted the robots to come back, to shoot him. Two crows came into view and started cawing loudly as they circled the corpse of a woman. Ismael wondered whose body it was; she looked in her twenties, lying to her side with one hand clutching her stomach where the bullet had hit. He thought of the woman's family and whether they were waiting for her at home or if they too were lying dead somewhere nearby. Ismael shut his eyes.

He woke up three days later in Al Ahli Hospital, his leg bandaged and his head spinning from the medication. Through blurred eyes, he tried to focus on the TV screen on the other side of the room. One headline declared the International Criminal Court would conduct an investigation into what had happened. Then another headline ran along the bottom of the screen about an emergency meeting that the IOC was holding in Zurich to determine whether to go ahead with the 39th Games in a new location or, for the first time in the modern era, to let the torch go out.

The Association

Samir El-Youssef

Translated by Raph Cormack

ACCORDING TO MOST REPORTS, the victim was just an obscure historian. Professor Omar Hijazi, 68 years old, found dead in his study, from a single laser wound to the forehead.

The story was that he had been killed by accident. Thieves had snuck in to burgle his house but the historian had appeared and surprised them, so they killed him. That was the line the morning broadsheets went with, buried in the local news sections, but for Zaid, still finding his feet as a junior reporter on the *Daily Diwan*'s crime desk, this was a chance to cut his teeth. Perhaps it was the victim's wife's insistence that her husband had been the victim of a political assassination that drew him to this particular case. In a social media clip that rose up on his feed, the woman – Mariam – could be seen ranting about death threats and a state cover-up. He had been killed to bring an end to his research, she said, a study into extremist organisations. And there was evidence to support this claim; nothing had been stolen from the house except three years' worth of notes that he had been making on the subject – now gone without a trace. She had also found a piece of paper lying next to the body with a small circle drawn on it. A symbol which she said, on the video that had played again and again, she was all too familiar with.

The police refused to assign any significance to a little drawing like this, but Zaid began to the entertain the idea that this might be the first of a series of assassinations, and this circle might be the calling card for the 'terror organisation' Mariam had ranted about. The first question he had to answer though was: who would want to kill a historian in a country where historians were all out of work, obsolete, unable to publish, and no longer enjoyed any degree of public recognition that could make them of interest to anyone?

The criminal investigation quickly ruled out the initial media reports that the murder had been committed during a burglary – but they were not very enthusiastic about the political assassination theory either. Zaid tried to look at the case from the police's perspective and he had to admit one unavoidable fact: despite all the talk about extremists working to destroy the peace that had reigned in the country for twenty years, not one political assassination had ever been committed. In fact, no politicians had been the target of an attack of any kind. So why bother with historians, and an obscure one at that?

Since the 2028 Agreement, the people of the country – all the different sects and religions, Muslim, Christian and Jewish – had decided that forgetting was the best way to live in peace. The study of the past was forbidden. Some historians, who had managed to acquire a decent share of fame before the agreement, argued in vain that an objective reading of history was the way to avoid returning to the woes of the Eighty Year War (as that dark period in our country's history had become known). The government issued a decree, as part of the Agreement, which banned anyone going back over the past by writing, speculating or in any way publishing about it. The law was well-received by an exhausted, war-weary people.

'Don't talk about what happened before.'

This was the phrase everyone repeated, in Jerusalem and other cities, whenever someone tried to talk about the days before the 2028 Agreement. The 'past' came to mean only the last few years, the immediate peaceful past, which had to be preserved so that a peaceful future could be guaranteed for the generations to come.

But if it had not been a political assassination and he had not died defending his house from thieves, then why had the historian been killed?

Who were the most probable suspects? Zaid asked himself. The wife? Unlikely from the beginning, as she had an alibi: she'd been visiting her family in Acre on the day of the incident. His wife's lover? This was the theory that the police were pursuing. Although there was little evidence she even had a lover.

When he talked to his sources down at the precinct, it seemed this is what the police were putting all their efforts into. While they were distracted, Zaid decided to revisit the wife's theory and see if anything was missed.

Zaid started to hang around in bars and cafes that his sources at the precinct claimed were hangouts for extremists. According to rumour, there were dozens of different extremists groups: the Jozoor who fought to preserve the history of the land reclamations, the demolition of houses for alleged security reasons; the Jidar who harboured evidence of the effects of the near twenty-year blockade of Gaza; the Mathaf who secretly preserved evidence of the atrocities of Occupation; the Harb faction, and so on. They varied in extremism, Zaid's sources claimed. The Harb faction merely called for the number of casualties from operations referred to mysteriously as 'Cast Lead' or 'Protective Edge' to be agreed and to go on the public record. Others were more militant, calling for a complete reversal of certain aspects of the Peace Agreement. They all met at their own venues too: the Jozoor's met at Cafe

Sammak on Shohada Street; the Jidar's met at Bar Mokhtar in Jondi Square. The characters who frequented these clubs did not disappoint. Through casual conversations, and pretending to be a lonely drunk, Zaid began to meet people whose existence he had only ever heard of before.

'Peace agreement? Peace agreement, my foot!' said one man in his fifties.

'This agreement was made by the heads of the different sects and religions and has nothing to do with us,' added a young man whose hands bore the marks of a manual worker, probably a builder, Zaid thought.

'There are lots of people just looking for the right chance to end this government –'

'– end the state itself,' interrupted the builder.

'But why?' asked Zaid, amazed to be hearing these views.

'Like we said, the Agreement is not for us,' answered the young worker.

'But that would mean sending the country back into a time of war,' implored Zaid.

'So be it! War is better than the lies that they call peace,' said the man in his fifties.

The journalist was very taken aback by what he heard in the hours he spent frequenting these joints. He wondered how the security services could be unaware of these groups. And, moreover, why they were so desperate to claim that these kinds of groups did not exist.

At this point, Zaid got in touch with an official spokesperson from the security services, chief inspector Rashad Sadek, who had a good relationship with the media and was always appearing on TV downplaying one story or another. At first, the inspector repeated the things he had already been quoted on in various public forums. As for the people Zaid had met in those funny bars and cafés, he, and the wider security services, were well aware of them, but considered them of little importance. They were just individuals – racists and extremists, yes – but not an organised group; their activities were limited to spouting tirades in bars.

Zaid tried to interrupt the chief inspector and tell him that he hadn't just met people with these views in dodgy bars. They could also be found in public libraries and fancy theatres and opera houses – reputable places! The chief inspector waved his hand in the air to dismiss Zaid's concerns. He said that the extended calm of the past twenty years was clear proof that those so-called extremists were insignificant, and it was best not to pay any attention to them as long as they were not actually committing any crimes.

'But what about the murder of the historian?' interrupted the young journalist.

'What about it? Do you have the slightest proof that any such group was responsible?' replied the chief inspector, getting a little annoyed. 'Indeed, give me one piece of evidence that proves these supposed 'groups' have done anything illegal at all, let alone anything in connection to the Hijazi case, and you'll see how willing I am to deal with the matter.'

Zaid was helpless before this simple challenge. He would have to conduct a lot more research into these groups before he could substantiate any link between them and the Hijazi case. So he went back to solitary drinking in Bar Mokhtar on Jondi Square, pretending to be nursing a broken heart after a divorce, occasionally drinking faster than he should for someone technically at work. This time, when he talked to the regulars, he tried to provoke them to go further than what had gone before. He asked directly about the murder of the historian, spurred on by an occasional remark they'd let slip about how he got what he deserved. When encouraged, some had gone so far as to say he was a traitor even to the old discipline of history – that once noble, now illegal study of the past – because he did not write objectively about it and was happy to depict it as though it all resembled nothing more than the barbarism of the Middle Ages, as other historians in the late 20s had begun too. 'Hijazi's work was detached but at the same time, highly judgemental,' a railway worker with half of one ear missing explained to Zaid.

'But why is he so different from those historians of the late 20s, people like Dawood, whose writing had laid the foundations for the 2028 Agreement?'

The answer to the journalist's question came straight away.

'Precisely *because* he was just an obscure historian,' the railway worker said emphatically. 'He was out of the spotlight, there was no heat on him. He was free to tell our history as it really happened, instead of just repeating the fake, official version that became the basis of the state since that accursed Agreement. He was a renegade, but he wrote like a secret government stooge!'

On one particularly long night in Bar Mokhtar, an old man, evidently overhearing Zaid's conversation, approached the group and, without saying a word, slipped a folded napkin into Zaid's hand. Before he could unfold it, the man had left the bar. There was nothing on it, of course, but a small, hand-drawn circle. Zaid tried to follow the old man out onto the street, but he'd disappeared.

Zaid threw himself into a frenzy of new research, investigating previous uses of circles and symbols of unrest or secret societies in European archives, as well as visiting illegal backroom speakeasies that his new friends in Bar Mokhtar on Jondi Square had recommended. Some people took against the kinds of questions he was now asking and started giving him funny looks. Perhaps it was too obvious what he was trying to accomplish – establishing a link between the symbol and the crime. People started to grow wary of him. Even the regulars became hostile and refused to talk. And so, despite the new pieces of information he'd gleaned, he still had nothing close to hard evidence that tied members of any of these groups to the murder.

But he didn't give up. The more people he spoke to, the more negative opinions he gathered about the late historian, but nothing he could use in a court room. In the end, the only thing he could do was retreat from this giant dead-end of a case, and get back to his career.

This he did, returning to unexciting stories about corruption and mismanagement in the public sector, until three weeks later, a strange, handwritten note appeared in his in-tray at work. No one in the office could offer an explanation as to how it got there. No circle this time, but an invitation from a Dr Tariq Salama — a prominent surgeon it turned out, formally expressing his desire to help. How could a man of his position help him? Zaid wondered. The whole thing felt odd, but having already given up on ever getting a break with the case, he was ready to accept any offer, no matter how unusual.

'The way I can help you,' explained the doctor, sitting in a high-backed chair in the office of his private surgery, browsing what seemed to be a scalpel inventory on a tablet screen, 'is by disburdening you of a number of misapprehensions. You seem to be pursuing this case as if there are several different underground groups. That is, of course, a cover story, for the police, who publically won't admit there are any at all. The Jozoor cell, the Jidar faction, they're all fake, Mr Zaid.' He put down the tablet, after tapping a few options. 'I came up with the names myself,' he added with a degree of pride. 'There is just one group that knows their rights and is slandered by those who deny it.'

'What rights are you talking about?' asked Zaid.

'The right to remember!'

'You mean the Eighty Year War? The dark past?'

'The dark past! This is what you and the rest of the country call it. But we in the Association know that the past was not dark, it was honourable. It was a time of struggle, when people fought nobly in the service of ideals.'

'Can you really say these things?'

'Yes, I can and so do many others,' the doctor proclaimed as if he was addressing an unseen crowd. 'In a country like this, to forget is a sin. To forget is a sign of deep-rooted corruption. The people of this country decided to forget to preserve the stupid Agreement, but no one has the right to forget the past.'

'But the people *did* forget, and they are happy for it. It has been a success for twenty years.'

'They will have to remember one day.'

'And who is going to remind them? The historians?' the journalist replied sarcastically, though he was actually trying to find a way to bring up his questions about the murdered historian.

'No, not the historians . . .'

'Tell me then, is this Association, as you call it, linked to the murder of the historian?' Zaid went straight to the question, hoping to get an answer that would help his investigation.

'Not in the way that you mean, not in any legal sense. We just cleared the path for it to happen . . .'

'How?' the journalist interrupted.

'You won't believe how, so I won't tell you.'

'Try me!'

'No, no. You won't be able to believe it because you have no faith in the right to memory over forgetfulness. This is what we believe in. We have faith that memory will prevail in the end. Whoever believes this doesn't need anyone to tell him who murdered the historian.'

'What if I wrote down everything that you have told me and published it in a newspaper?' Zaid challenged him.

'Who would publish that? Which newspaper? And who would believe it? Have you forgotten that we live in a country of forgetfulness and everything that contradicts that damn Peace Agreement fades away before this government of amnesia?' As the doctor said this, he drew a circle in the air with his finger.

'What is that?' Zaid flinched, looking at the doctor for an explanation. But the doctor simply declared the meeting over.

The doctor was right and Zaid knew it. No one would publish an article like that because no one wanted to believe it. No one would believe who had killed the historian or that a prominent surgeon was the apparent leader of an extremist organisation – even that extremist organisations exist at all.

Suddenly Zaid saw it: the meaning of the circle the doctor had drawn in the air, the circle on the napkin pressed into his hand in Bar Mokhtar, the circle drawn on the piece of paper beside the dead body of the historian. It represented the extent of what was currently understood in this country, or what the Peace Agreement allowed them to understand. It really was a very small circle. The journalist realised the task now at hand was not to find the historian's murderer but to expand this circle, to expand the minds currently bound by the government's need to forget.

Zaid felt no relief at this discovery. In fact, he felt depressed and suffocated. Such a task would be next to impossible.

Commonplace

Rawan Yaghi

IT WAS A NIGHTMARE. Or so he would have assumed if it weren't for the shaking of his bed and the quivering of the window above him. His left leg rose and paused for a moment, mid-air, waiting for the next explosion. Hesitating to jump out of bed before the next rattling quake, he waited to see whether, when it struck, it would sound further away.

'Fuck.'

He got up, still thinking about the intensity of the last explosion and trying to calculate its distance compared to the one before that. He was never right about this. Often the explosions seemed closer than they were. On his way to the bathroom, his heart sank at the sight of the battered backpack in the hallway: today was the day. Adam's eyes were half-open as urine trickled down the shining porcelain in the pale dawn light. He had been lucky with this place, he thought, finding an apartment block with enough empty space beside it to let sunshine and moonlight in through its eastern windows. There it was again: his head spinning as if the ground beneath his feet were the deck of a boat, listing back and forth with the waves. He squeezed his eyes shut.

Outside, the light was still merciful as seven hundred hours drew near. His steps carried him soberly across the neighbourhood – a small district, in which buildings jostled together without order, till their outline against the sky resembled a jagged line of rubble. Rooftops rose and fell unpredictably, each segment marked by a different colour, or style of window. Adam headed to his usual post on the usual corner, and upon reaching it retrieved from his backpack a crate of what they euphemistically called 'grapes', which he'd bought from a smuggler on the southern border. His rates were reasonable by most standards: 50 dollars a pack was a good price for an item so dearly cherished in this part of the city.

Sitting on the outskirts of this precipice of a town, the neighbourhood was continually on edge, bracing itself for another swarming attack from over the wall. The last time this happened was when a group of young men, unknown to everyone else in the city, were caught digging a tunnel from a deserted house on the edge of the buffer zone, out towards the wall and the green land beyond. This green swathe of pasture was visible to anyone who dared look out their eastern or northern windows, and whether they looked or not, its existence occupied everyone's minds.

When the swarm came it was methodical. It went straight to the house in question, circling it and darkening the sky around it. Some kids tried shooting at the machines with slingshots, but those were the ones who, come the next day, had disappeared along with a few other children whose mothers swore had been at home at the time. The drones placed an explosive device on the roof of the house, hovered upwards, to about four metres above, and paused with their robot arms dangling like wet, dead spider legs. A moment of pressure and then the roof of the house was transformed into a million tiny fragments that fell to the ground in unison. A hail of bullets and it was all over. We weren't even sure the walls were going to keep standing because of how many bullets were fired into the interior. Everyone remembers the blood seeping out of the half-collapsed front door and onto the pavement in the street out front; the slowly forming puddle, the edge of which crept towards the onlookers, inching backwards.

Adam's customers were no different from the rest of the unfortunate inhabitants of the neighbourhood. Their need for sedatives was a product of their location and the things they'd witnessed in this wretched place. It was the same crowd each morning: Abu Ahmed – tall, with messy hair and brown eyes that looked smaller than they were behind his thick glasses – was a shopkeeper at a nearby boutique (he had originally trained, and graduated with distinction, as a civil engineer, but his father was sensible enough to keep a tidy business downtown); Rami, the bright, high school kid who obviously stole his money from his father, would time his visits to coincide with the moment his beautiful long-haired neighbour walked past each morning, indifferent to his wide-mouthed stares; the bright-eyed, hyperactive Hala, whose parents seemed too embarrassed to pay for her grapes themselves; and Basel, the pale-skinned, slightly overweight NGO director, who complained about it being too hot all the time, and bought his 'grapes' by the pack, not the roll-up. Adam exchanged small-talk with all of them, but never smiled. A sturdy look fixed itself resolutely on his face as the merchandise and money changed hands; his facial expression, the grip of his handshake, his eye contact, everything needed to be kept in check.

'Are you going to watch the game tonight?' Mohammed, a childhood friend that Adam grew to find intolerable, shouted, from across the street.

Adam hesitated. 'I might have to work late tonight,' he shouted back. He worried about whether his hesitation was picked up by any of the monitors.

'Oh, come on. You said that yesterday. Give yourself a break,' his neighbour begged.

Adam nodded and continued along the sidewalk towards his spot, avoiding a number of goods spread chaotically on the ground for trade. An old, deflated football caught Adam's attention, half-hidden between pots and various items of clothes. His eyes landed on it as he passed by, but he didn't slow his pace. Reaching his usual position, his eyelids suddenly became heavier and he automatically rested his back against the wall behind him.

Adam had this habit of always imagining how he might appear from a three-metre distance, knowing that somewhere, someone was watching a video of him from that kind of vantage, following every move he made, every customer he spoke to, every penny that went into his pocket. He knew someone, or something, was always there though he couldn't quite place it. He would flatten himself against the wall lest whatever might be watching him went behind his back. The idea of it being behind him bugged him. Even when the midday sun burned the back of his neck he refused to move. He loathed the fact that it had to be this wall with this mural he pinned himself against. Every day, as he headed out for the corner, he hoped someone had painted over the image during the night. It ascended two metres above him, on a wall that shielded the house of a man said to have made a fortune smuggling drugs into the city. Behind it was one of the few houses that remained unattached to others, with the rare luxury of a garden around it. The mural's red and black colours entwined in a delicate composition of Arabic letters, forming the contours and outlines of a boy's face whose eye sockets had been hollowed out.

His sister, Rahaf, had been a year older than him. He often woke up to her round, olive-brown face, her eyes dark as cinnamon, staring down at him as if she had been trying to open them by mere force of will, then smiling to herself when it worked. Even at the age of fifteen, it seemed to others that she was still, in her heart, a toddler discovering the world for the first time, asking questions insistently about everything.

She had been a habitual collector of antique oddities from the sidewalk trade piles – objects that, to her at least, spoke of a different age. She would buy them in return for food they grew in their apartment's many window-boxes. 'This is the best quality wool you will find anywhere in the city,' she declared to her brother as she put on an oversized coat. 'Oh my God! I look like Sherlock!' she added in amazement. It made him laugh. Standing by the wall, now, he could have sworn the coat was Sherlock's own, and that somewhere in one of these sidewalk piles he could find the deerstalker to match it. She looked at him in the mirror, as she imitated the detective firing out deductions at incomprehensible speed. She would run around the room and pretend to find the answer to the mystery in an old suitcase, or under a bed, then present it in triumph to her little brother. Eyes sharp and eager, she would stare down at him, her chest heaving to catch a breath, and with her nostrils flaring, declare: 'Valetudinarian!'

'Sociopath!' he would respond.

'Ratiocination!' she would giggle back.

'Axiomatic!'

Walking home from school one day at the age of fourteen, Adam had discovered Rahaf's body dumped on the doorstep of their apartment block. Her face was bloodied and her eyelids blue, sunken back into the hollow sockets behind them. Nobody had touched her since her body had been dumped there. He knew everyone was afraid to come near. Were it not for her distinct green dress he would not have recognised her at first. That's all he remembered from that day, seeing her and thinking she was dead. She wasn't, however, there was still breath in her body. But no matter how many times he visited her in the Centre for Hope, a medical facility established exclusively for cases like hers, no matter how long he spent watching her chest rise and fall artificially, watching the scars around her padded eyes slowly darken, the image of her green and bloodied body couldn't be shaken from every thought he had of her. After each visit, he would climb back into his bed and sob, wishing he had been around to stop her before she was taken that December day. His neighbour, Abu Rami, told him, energetically, how she must have wandered into the Eastern Land looking for empty tins. 'She asked us if we had any that she could trade for some potatoes. I told her she wouldn't find them anywhere in the city. That stupid son of a bitch, Maher, told her she would be able to find things like that near the Eastern Land. And poor thing, she believed him. Trust me, son, I told her not to go there. I did. I warned her.'

Abu Rami's words rang in his head whenever he thought about his own, much-planned journey. 'She went in day light. Poor thing. She was so beautiful. May Allah grant you patience.' Adam cursed him every time he saw him. When he got older, and his body was strong enough to get into fights, he tracked Maher down, pinned him to the ground and punched him repeatedly until he broke his jaw. No one stopped him.

As it neared twenty-one hundred hours, the air cooled, and the sun's oppressiveness gave way to darker skies. His arms felt lighter by his side and his heart pounded faster with anticipation. The streets fell quiet, except for a few last-minute customers. He waited a moment after the hour struck, then proceeded back to his apartment, noticing for the first time the navy-blue colour of the evening dying the walls, sidewalks and sentry points as he passed.

By now, his head buzzed as if a tiny drone were hovering about his earlobes. With his bounty deep in his backpack, and his hands on the shoulder straps, he stood, somewhat hunchbacked, peering at a gigantic strip of concrete bathed in the orange of the floodlights, less than a kilometre away. The first 300 metres into the 'No-Soul Area' were strewn with randomly built walls of no particular design or apparent purpose. A wall would stand two metres long and five metres high. Just a few metres away, another stood five metres long and two metres high. The wall beside Adam was the last one before a completely desolate stretch of land, nearly a kilometre deep. A maze of unseen mines now stood between him and the final wall with its orange lights. Just a few metres from where he stood, Rahaf had been taken by a drone. He imagined the machine shooting a tranquiliser dart at her as she dodged between the peculiar walls, scooping her up in its spider arms, and taking her behind the great orange wall. The last of the odd-shaped walls was 300 metres into the No-Soul Area. This was significant. He rested his back against it and closed his eyes. The memory of the bed's shaking that morning resurfaced and, for a moment, Adam imagined he was back there, half-asleep, having one of those dreams where you try to walk through each step of your plan, but each step frustratingly takes you no nearer to where you want to be, until you wake up in panic. He squeezed his eyelids down hard to pull himself back into the buffer zone that stretched in front of him.

He was calm now. No rocking floor, no shaking bed. He smiled, his eyes slowly tracing the crack in the orange concrete all the way to the wall's top, where old-fashioned barbed wire spooled out a jagged horizon. He began to climb. His gloves proved effective for the first few metres but as he reached the top and punched the barbed wire clear, it cut through to his knuckles. In the space he'd cleared, he perched for a moment. Already half a dozen red laser targets were swarming across his chest. He smiled as he followed their thin red trails back through the night air, upwards left and right, to their sources.

He could never decide on how far away they were. One minute the trails seemed to go up half a mile or so into the starless sky, the next they ended abruptly just a few feet from his face. He saw many other lights, white torch beams, scanning across the wall, looking for other possible intruders. Beneath him, on the far side of the great wall, he could see that the ground was studded with shards of glass, all pointing upwards, glittering in the moonlight. He wondered why he hadn't been shot yet. Clearing more space for himself, his hands now bloodied and numb, he lay down. His smile persisted, just as the memory of Rahaf trying to will his eyes open persisted. Then, he felt like he was already down below, penetrated by the shards on the Eastern Side that moments before had looked so tempting to touch.

She laughs at her reflection in the mirror, in the Holmes coat, sleeves too long for her arms, dangling as she lifts them. She runs back to him, pokes him, then flees before his lips curl up in fury at being caught off guard before he can get to his feet and catch her.

The image of her swarmed around him, like the embrace of barbed wire. His smile persisted, looking up at her, looking down at him.

Final Warning

Talal Abu Shawish

Translated by Mohamed Ghalaieny

HIGH UPON THE HILLS surrounding Ramallah, the city's residents, together with the settlers of the Modi'in Illit colony, would cleanse their eyes each morning in the streams of light that cascaded at daybreak. The sun would rise gingerly until fully round, announcing itself above the peaks in an act, which once complete, marked the beginning of daily life.

The solitary balcony in Rahel's flat overlooked these hills, so hardly a day passed when she didn't enjoy this recurring spectacle. This morning was no different. As soon as her sons had left the house, she slunk back to the balcony to enjoy her sugary coffee.

Sheikh Hassaan, the Imaam of Ramallah's main mosque, was beginning to feel tired. Four hours had gone by as he sat reading from the Quran in the mosque's courtyard. He often led the people in the *Fajr* prayer and would then pass the time in devotion till the sun rose before returning to his home in the centre of Ramallah.

It seems as if I have been awaiting sunrise for ages, he thought to himself as he gazed over the mosque's dome towards the hills. They appeared to him as black trees surrounding the sleeping city. It was the middle of May, the sky was as clear as a mirror suspended above the sea. The sun had set the day before, just as it always had, rolling down to the west of the city, giving no hint that this time it would not return.

He felt a tightness in his chest that grew into anxiety and then panic.

Rahel reached for her smartphone to check what time it was, and was surprised to be greeted by a black screen. She tried switching it on, assuming she must have shut it down the night before, but the screen remained black. Putting it down, she hurried inside. The brass pendulum of her great-great-grandfather's clock caught her eye. It wasn't moving; it hadn't moved, apparently, since 5 o'clock that morning. Rahel felt herself begin to panic, she reached for the landline receiver but could hear no dial tone. Her fear drove her up to her study, to check the security monitors, but to her dismay they were all switched off too; only black screens stared back at her.

She collapsed on a sofa and stared at the dark hills, blinking.

Sheikh Hassaan felt suffocated. With great effort, he got to his feet to turn on the mosque's air-conditioning, but as he did so he noticed that all the lights were off. Trying to switch them on had no result. Grabbing his phone from the pocket of his jalabiya, with the intention of calling the electricity company, his eyes were only met with a neutral black screen. At this, he went straight to the mosque's windows that faced the hills, turning frantically from window to window. The cascade of light he had become accustomed to every morning wasn't there.

Before anyone could stop him, the sheikh was running out onto the main road leading to Al-Manara Square, shaking and frothing as he cited verses from the Quran.

From her bedroom window, Rahel noticed that a large number of the colony's settlers were out on the street, walking towards Sha'ar ha-Melekh St and the Synagogue, as it had the best views of the hills. In her panic she decided to follow them. But her fear wasn't abated when she heard the neighbours' conversation about what had happened that morning. One neighbour, Itzik, was saying he had been online when the internet dropped out, then shortly after the TV stations had followed, and after that the electricity went, leaving every device in the house black, even battery-powered items. He had rushed to his safe to retrieve his most precious documents before he left the house.

Another neighbour, Zahava, spoke more fearfully, 'I put a cheese pastry in the microwave, and before I could get it out I felt some sort of electric shock. When I got it out it was charred, as black as night.'

'I woke my husband Rehva'am,' she went on, 'and he went around the house with his Uzi on the kill setting to check we weren't being attacked or anything, then we put on the first clothes we could find and came to join you guys.'

Rahel wished she could just get in her car and speed off over the hills, onto the highway leading to the capital, but she didn't want to be seen as the first to flee this mysterious black-tinged day.

At the centre of Ramallah, Sheikh Hassaan found Al-Manara Square filled with the city's residents, all fretfully extolling the name of God and nervously repeating verses from the Quran.

Approaching the square from the other side, a Christian congregation was surrounding the city's priest, Father Yohanna, although the lit candles he bore solemnly as he walked did little to take the edge off the darkness that enveloped everything.

'Sheikh, what's happening?!' The questions rained down on Hassaan from every direction.

'It's all over,' he said, unable to hide how fearful he was.

'What are you saying? Please explain!'

'Allah's wrath is upon us, this is the end. It is Al-Qiyaaamah, Judgement Day.'

Someone in the crowd reacted promptly to this, seeming calmer and more collected than most:

'Stop this ridiculous talk. You are spreading panic with this nonsense.'

Sheikh Hassaan gave the man the filthiest of looks. He knew him all too well, there was a running feud between them. As far as Sheikh Hassaan was concerned, he was the Imaam and guardian of religion, as for Isaam, he was an atheist kafir; he posed more of a threat to the city than anything, even this.

Isaam's mind was ticking like a computer microprocessor. As soon as he realised that what was happening was no nightmare, nor was it a scene from a movie like that one starring Michael Renie almost a century ago, he had started piecing the morning's events together, and reviewing them like a film critic.

The houses of Ramallah vomited forth their contents: men, women, children, grandparents, even their owner's animals – cats and dogs and donkeys! All making their way towards Al-Manara Square, some running in panic, as if only the centre could explain the happenings of that mysterious morning when the sun broke its daily promise.

Things were no different in Modi'in Illit, the Jewish settlement. The streets were teeming with people and the houses were all empty. Everyone had wanted to get in their cars and flee with their families to their 'capital', but the engines lay silent and unresponsive as well, so they had no option but to stand rooted to the western end of the colony and simply observe what was about to appear from behind Ramallah's hills.

The speed at which the colossal white limbs of the creature rose above the horizon was so gradual, so calm, observers initially thought that they were just part of the horizon. The white line rose gradually until there could be no mistaking it – this wasn't the horizon or even the sun – at which point its approach sped up. To Isaam, it looked like a cosmic whale riding a tsunami-sized wave towards them.

The folk in Al-Manara Square fell to their in knees at the sight of it, their faces transfixed, their arms raised to the sky in surrender, repeating tearful prayers.

'More of the Shahaadats,'[1] shouted Sheikh Hassaan in a frenzy of fear, "Keep repeating it! We are about to meet God.'

'Shut up you fool, this is a flying saucer come to visit us,' Isaam shouted at the sheikh, but he continued his feverish calls. Isaam had with him his retractable telescope and was marvelling at the size of the vessel.

Everyone started shielding their eyes from the sun, trying to make out the object as well as Isaam was, not used to straining the naked eye so much. One of the other things they did see clearly though was the sight of a long parade of settlers, from Modi'in Illit, heading towards Ramallah on foot. As the Palestinians around him panicked at the prospect of all-out war with the settlers, the priest simply nodded in serene acknowledgement and continued his incantations.

Back in Modi'in Illit, outside his synagogue, Rabbi Weiss had ascended a small platform and roared at his people, 'When the catastrophes are upon us and death is inevitable, we must leave our material possessions, leave everything and disperse. Retreat and take shelter with our neighbours. Yahweh will not forsake us. This mythical creature has blocked the road to the capital, so let us go east towards Ramallah, I am sure *Allah* will protect his *Ram*.[2] This is Yahweh's will and what he has ordered me to tell you.'

Within three hours, the entire population of Modi'in Illit had arrived in Ramallah, bearing no arms and offering gestures of peace. They had been able to walk all the way to Al-Manara because the city's border guards had, like everyone else, fled to the centre.

Amidst the widespread panic and general conviction that the end was indeed nigh as the colossal many-limbed, many-mouthed spaceship homed in on the skies above Ramallah, Sheikh Hassaan and Father Yohanna approached Rabbi Weiss who was at the front of the crowd that had just arrived. As if following some script, the three figureheads solemnly joined hands and began chanting in a single tongue. Nobody could understand a word of it.

Rahel sat down beside Isaam on one of the benches opposite the square's famous lions, and, unable to stop shivering, instinctively snuggled up to him. 'Keep it together,' Isaam tried to reassure her. 'Everything will end peacefully.'

'My children, how will I get hold of them? Nothing is working. Are we all going to die today?'

Isaam patted her shoulder. 'It's a matter for the cosmos. But fear not. There will be some resolution to this dark assault. There always is. The history of science fiction tells us: nobody comes this far without either a fight that they never win, or to teach us something about ourselves that we desperately need to learn. My theory is the latter. In fact it's happening already. Can you not see how trivial our differences are in the face of such a momentous event?!'

Ten or so metres away, the sock seller Hakeem – or 'The Balloon' as the city folk liked to call him – was standing frozen to the spot. The sight of the strange visitor above had held him in a trance all morning. Suddenly he snapped out of it, and out came his usual, booming laugh. For a moment, he couldn't stop laughing and it seemed as if he had gone completely mad. Then he calmed down and started looking at Rahel; he recognised her as the manager of the farm he used to work at. He'd worked there for years before the Israeli authorities barred him, following the completion of the Apartheid Wall and the comprehensive regulation of labourers' movements that followed. A crazy idea took hold in Hakeem's head as he passed his gaze over the hordes of people cramming into the square, all united by dread.

Half a mile away, in the courtyard of the security centre, known as Al-Muqata'a, local leaders were gathering. Fumbling with their smartphones and bluetooth headsets out of sheer habit, knowing they had all gone silent, the politicians paced from one huddle to another, utterly impotent. Senior officers, standing at the windows above them, scanned the crowds outside, looking for their junior officers and soldiers. One of them cupped his hands together, and bellowed commands to soldiers outside, insisting they report to duty.

As for the guard at the Eastern cemetery, when the terrifying object had first appeared, he'd thrown down his hose, stopped watering the plants and started running towards Al-Manara. Now he knelt in front of the flowerbeds saying: 'I swear I heard them calling. The dead were calling me to them. Oh God be merciful.'

Suddenly, over all this chaos and noise, over the screaming of the crowd, the chanting of the religious leaders, even over the soft voice of Isaam calmly reassuring the whimpering Rahel, a serene voice spoke in everyone's ears. Silence reigned. It was a whistle at first, a long haunted wail that seemed to come from all of the spaceship's many orifices at once, and was followed by a shrill, robotic voice that translated the whistles into Hebrew and Arabic.

'Our leadership has delegated me the task of visiting your

world to deliver a first and final message. Cut it out. We are blessed with superior technology, weaponry and war craft. The destruction of this sector of your world's surface would be instantaneous. However, we will refrain in order to give you one last chance to rectify your behaviour.'

'Told you,' whispered Isaam, still stroking Rahel's hair.

A massive wave twitched among the crowds, hearts rose in people's chests. Then there was silence, calm and anticipation.

'Your struggles in this tiny sector of the planet's surface have, for more than a hundred of your planet's orbits, caused more tension and conflict, directly and indirectly, beyond its borders than any other area of its size in the known universe. Your conflict acts as a symbol, a case study, a metaphor, a lightning rod, a red rag for conflicts across the entire planet's surface. By continuing to threaten the planet's stability as a whole, you also threaten the wider galaxy's stability . . .'

'This is word for word, isn't it?' scoffed Isaam.

'Your petty squabbles can no longer go unchecked,' the visitor continued. 'So, with this visit we have deactivated all your electron-based technologies, as well as paused your planet's rotation. Your highest civilisations are but collections of stunted, primitive, myopic life to us. No defence, however sophisticated, can hope to withstand this censure!'

Isaam's mind began to wander. He smiled to himself, 'What we need to do here is Jeff Goldblum the situation. Give them a cold. But wait, no, that only works in David versus Goliath plots. *War of the Worlds.* This is no independence battle; this is a call for ceasefire. Hmmm . . . Michael Rennie again.'

The voice went on with its message, 'However, we promise you, this energy curfew will end the moment you commit to what we want. All we request is justice. If you consent, we will redraw the borders correctly and depart from this world immediately. We will continue to monitor your world from afar but our interference with this world will be over. Do not misunderstand us, our interference today is only to protect the wider galaxy from your nihilism; it was evident that you were incapable of achieving peace on your own. So we were forced to impose this solution. Your futile conflicts must end today.'

A terrified silence fell on the crowd. After this last instalment of whistles and monotone translation, the whole crowd seemed to stop breathing all together. Their eyes began to follow the gentle movement of the giant saucer towards the hills to the west. All of a sudden, a searing light dazzled the crowd. The edge of the sun appeared in the distance, to the east, like a frowning, lipsticked mouth that slowly grew bigger till it shone as a whole disc high over the hills.

A cacophony of ringtones, music and engine sounds erupted in the square and spread out across the city at great speed. Everybody had somebody to call and reassure. Indoors, an orchestra of electronic devices announced their return in every house, apartment and office. Music resumed, news readers' faces appeared, pornographic films started up again where they had left off, Quranic verses alongside Christian hymns and Jewish zemirot all started again mid-sentence. Modern life returned, as instantaneously as it had ceased.

The strange, gigantic visitor faded into the horizon. When it was no longer visible, people lowered their heads, pensively pondering the message it had given them and the peculiarities of the translation. Some walked in the direction of the western hills, following it, as if to delay the mysterious visitor's disappearance over the horizon. The rest crawled towards their homes. The only people left in Al-Marana Square were Sheikh Hassaan, Father Yohanna and the Rabbi Weiss, still holding each other's hands and chanting, ever softer to each other. Isaam made his way to Al-Tireh, and found a spot under the Mandela statue with the best view.

Taking out his telescope, he tried to make out the figure of Rahel amongst the throngs of settlers walking back to Modi'in Illit. When he saw the settlers' way blocked by a colossal new wall that hadn't been there before, he couldn't help but laugh.

Notes

1. Muslim proclamation of faith: There is no god but God and Mohammed is His messenger.
2. Hill or height. Ramallah is sometimes referred to as Allah's hill.

The Curse of the Mud Ball Kid

Mazen Maarouf

Translated by Jonathan Wright

1

The Dead Guy

I'VE ALWAYS WANTED TO be a superhero. I didn't want to save the world, or even save all the children of Falasta. I just wanted to save my sister when they came to steal her imagination. If you had asked me then what kind of superhero I wanted to be, I would have said an extremely small creature, one that tracks down germs and bacteria in the bodies of children and destroys it. 'Robomicrobe', I'd call myself. I'd say all this because I was always sure that when my sister lost her imagination, she'd end up the same as all the other children around us. However much she ate she'd still feel hungry until she died. When children in my neighbourhood had their imaginations stolen from them it caused brain defects. It made the brain stimulate the stomach into feeling hungry all the time. The Aharon Kibbutz Institute didn't need the imaginations of Falasta's children, particularly. But the institute director, Ben Moshe the Elder, had devised a way of putting these imaginations to good use. Just mentioning his name here was enough to inspire dread. The stolen imaginations were gathered together inside an artificial satellite that orbited directly above us, they called the Dabraya Star, taking its name from 'the angel of death'. We couldn't tell it apart from the thousands of other satellites and stars in the night sky, but the Dabraya Star had the ability to beam the children's imaginations back into the past, where they took shape in the form of 3D games in front of other children – hungry, naked children with shaved heads who are said to be held in camps. Without warning, whenever they climbed into bed, holograms flashed in front of them and continued to morph and evolve until they dozed off. The next night new images took shape for them to play with. And so on. Their mothers told them, 'This is why you were put here. Because you have nicer games than any other children in the world.' But the Dabraya Star above us scared the children back in my neighbourhood. It made them afraid to look at the sky at night, or drove them to throw stones up into the sky when they became desperate from always being under siege. Unlike them, I wasn't scared by objects in the night sky. In fact, I prayed every day to become Robomicrobe, so that I could plant a part of my imagination into the cells of my sister's brain. That's because I have more than enough imagination to go round, you see. 'O Lord, make me a superhero when my sister falls ill,' I would pray. 'Only when she's ill. Turn me into Robomicrobe. So that I can cure her. After that restore me to my normal state.' But I realised that it was only by experience that you ever knew you qualified to be a superhero. So sometimes I would go to the Samra butcher's shop and try to pick up the sheep that was tied up at the back ready for slaughter. I'd try to lift it a little off the ground and run a few yards with it. Or, for example, I would stand at the hospital gate, next to the beggars and the peddlers. Whenever I saw a boy or a girl going into the hospital with their mother or father, I would ask them enthusiastically, 'Are you ill?' If they didn't answer

I would walk behind them repeating the question in various forms: 'You're ill, aren't you?', 'My sister's going to be ill too but I'm going to save her. If you have any brothers or sisters, maybe you'll survive.' Most of the children would shake their heads in fear and, triumphantly and with a smile, I would say, 'I knew you were ill!' This made their mothers angry and they would start insulting me. I was willing to do anything to prove to God that I had all the right qualities to be a superhero. On one occasion I jumped on a thin old man wearing thick glasses. He used to pass in front of our house every day on his way home and trip over the stump of an iron post my grandmother had planted in the ground to mark the boundary between our house and his, next door. I didn't realise he was doing this deliberately, to force my grandmother to pull the post out. I waited for him. When he fell, he did so little by little, as if in slow motion. He went down on his hands. I thought that if I could pounce on him from behind as soon as he tripped and then twist his body around before it reached the ground, then I would save him. That meant I would be on my way to becoming a superhero. I waited for him outside the house. As soon as he went past, I came up behind him and then, as soon as he stumbled, I pounced on him. But this caused a fracture in one of the old man's ribs and, to cover the old man's medical expenses, my grandmother had to mortgage Mukhtar the bull, which was lame because it was missing one knee. My grandmother told me off sharply at the time, but I looked at my sister and hugged her. I told her I wouldn't give up. Until that incident at school. We were in geography class. Suddenly I started imagining that my sister had fallen ill. I left the classroom and headed to the tank of drinking water. I plunged my head into the opening of the tank and tried to hold my breath under the water for as long as possible while imagining I was speaking to my sister. 'I'll save you. I'll save you. You're not

going to die. You're not going to die,' I told her. But I fainted
and my body slumped into the tank. The school kids and
teachers looked for me everywhere and at last they found
me. I was fished out of the tank but from then on no one
wanted to drink water from it, although they rinsed it out
twice. After that the other kids called me 'the dead guy'. 'The
dead guy's come, the dead guy's gone, the dead guy's fallen
in the tank again,' they said. And that was because I had, as
they put it, passed away for a few minutes until my heart
spontaneously sprang back to life. Even my grandmother
called me 'the dead guy'. I repeated my performance:
whenever I imagined my sister had died, I went and stuck
my head in the water tank. Everyone complained about me,
except my sister. She never called me 'the dead guy'. She
didn't like this new name. I wasn't bothered, except that the
headmaster decided to expel me for causing trouble. I told
my grandmother I preferred to be close to my sister at all
times. So I started waiting for her outside the school gates,
and as soon as she came out, I would ask her immediately if
she was well. Grandmother would wring her hands in
exasperation. I told her I was behaving that way because my
sister was going to fall ill soon and would die if I didn't do
something about it; I was getting ready to save her. I didn't
know how I was going to do it. But I kept praying to God
to make me a superhero. I thought God would answer my
prayers so long as I always behaved like a superhero. I wanted
to show him how serious I was about it, show him that I
wasn't just behaving like a stupid kid. But my sister died, and
I didn't become a superhero. In fact I ended up in a glass
cube. Grandmother isn't around any longer either, or the
butcher, his sheep, or Mukhtar or even the old man who, it
turned out, had actually been my grandfather until he
divorced Grandmother and moved into the house next door.
No one. I am the last Palestinian, and that guy driving the

motorbike is Ze'ev. He drives it slowly and warily, like the leader of a gang – 'in case someone tries to shoot me', he says. But if he needs to be wary of anyone, he'd do best to be wary of himself, because no one else has ever opened fire on him. Also Ze'ev has another reason: he's not just worried someone will shoot him dead, he's also worried they'll set about shooting me and then be ordained 'the hero' instead of Ze'ev (even though the only person who's ever had a motive for killing Ze'ev is Ezer Banana, and he's dead).

Eli

Ze'ev's motorbike has three wheels – a rare model. It is one of those with a sidecar for an extra passenger. But Ze'ev has disconnected the sidecar and, on the base, carries the glass cube that I now live in. The cube has two layers of thick glass, with insulating gel between them. Ze'ev takes the motorbike out of the garage once a month. The motorbike trip is what I most look forwards to, because every time, whatever our destination, I know we'll go past the wall and I'll see the guava tree that once belonged to my grandmother. Ze'ev knows that people might make fun of him. So he's tense and he always grips his pistol tight. His pistol is a Luger that his great-great-grandfather looted from a German officer in a detention camp at the end of the Second World War. His great-great-grandfather was called Eli. Ze'ev sees him as a superhero. 'Given that he was naked, starving and weak, how on earth did he manage to overcome that officer?' The German was massive, Ze'ev claims; he must have been the most formidable officer in the camp. Eli is said to have felled him with a bullet between the eyes, followed by another upwards under the chin. Then he despatched the seven other soldiers around him. Four of them were less than twenty years old. The sight of their formidable officer, swimming in his own blood with his face torn to shreds, so alarmed the other soldiers they trembled in their boots. After that, Eli headed to the women and children's hut and let all the children out into the forest, firing shots in all directions. Everyone waited till he ran out of ammunition, but the magazine in his pistol didn't run out. It automatically reloaded with new bullets. After 59 children had run off into the forest, he came back to the camp. He was planning to release the rest of the prisoners, but he stopped at the door and fell to the ground. The Luger was no longer in his hand and he had spent the last ounce of his strength. Ze'ev would even wear a T-shirt with a picture of Eli's face on it and some words referring to his heroism. 'And this pistol! If I tell you it reloads itself, you'd better believe me,' he once told Ezer Banana. He wanted to send him a message – the pistol could fire, not forty or a hundred bullets but until it was so hot you couldn't hold it any longer. He was so attached to his pistol you might say he breathed through its muzzle.

An Advertisement

Every week we go to a primary school in a kibbutz or a town we haven't visited before. Ze'ev puts me on display in front of the schoolkids in the playground for half an hour. None of them have ever seen a Palestinian before. They look at me, walk around the cube and touch it. Some of the kids ask, 'Are you the last Palestinian?' or 'Are you the guy who killed Ezer Banana?' But I don't respond. Shortly after I was put in the cube, they injected me with a liquid that made me lose all control of my body. It focused my memory on one scene, so much that it made me shiver constantly, which in turn paralysed me. The whole process turned my teeth into a soft, bendy material, like the rubber in erasers, making my teeth loosen in their gums painlessly and drop out into my mouth.

They were extremely hot, which made me spit them out immediately. After that there was no longer any point in talking. If I tried to speak my mouth would heat up. My gums would turn into a kind of gooey paste and stick together. They could tear too. Similarly, if I tried to do any activity, like turning into little mud balls, for example, my body would turn sticky. All this so that I couldn't turn my robomicrobe idea into a reality.

Ze'ev and I have been friends since our time at the orphanage. That's what he tells me anyway. I don't remember anything about it. I mean, Ze'ev has never shown me anything to remind me of it. When I lost my teeth, I lost all sense of myself. I shouted, wept and snarled like an animal. I punched and kicked the door of the glass cube. But the glass absorbed every blow and I collapsed on the floor. Then Ze'ev didn't want to look at me. But the next day he said, 'I'll show you something that will ease your pain.' He showed me the footage of a toothpaste advert I had taken part in, though it was never broadcast. A toothpaste advert you've taken part in isn't much fun when you've lost all your teeth the previous day, unless someone you once loved very much appears alongside you in the advert.

My Sister

As soon as I saw the footage, which had remained unedited, I remembered that I once had a sister. A little sister. She was more than five years older than me, but she always seemed like a little sister. The afternoon before she died, an NGO van arrived to take me to film the advert for the toothpaste, which was called 'Hope'. The aim wasn't to promote the toothpaste so much as to inspire people with the knowledge that there was at least one Palestinian child out there who was still in good health. In the studio I asked if my sister could appear in the advert alongside me. But the producer said my sister wasn't right for the ad. Her teeth were yellow, and her face was pale and miserable. If she appeared in the advert, it would remind people of their own children who had died, having shown similar symptoms themselves. I said she had been hungry, eaten some guavas and fallen sick, but she would recover.

I lived with my sister and my grandmother in the last house in the village. The other houses were behind us and a few yards ahead was the wall. My grandmother was emotional all the time. She swore at Amir, the watchman at the kibbutz next to our village, and Amir swore back at her. They hadn't actually seen each other since they were children, but they exchanged insults all the time over the wall, whether it was raining, windy or hot. Every morning my grandmother would go up to the wall and shout, 'Amir, you fake-Arab thief!'

Amir would wait for her to finish, before shouting back, 'At your service. And thanks for the guava tree. A lovely present. I'll take care of it for the rest of my life.'

Then my grandmother would shout, 'A thief just like the rest of them!' Grandmother had been insulting Amir ever since the wall was built between our house and theirs. That was in 1982, two decades before they started building the official Apartheid Wall. It was just a small wall. For about half a century the pair of them never failed to carry out this ritual. At one point, Amir disappeared and, for three weeks, my grandmother lost all her composure. She would go to the wall several times a day and shout, 'Hey Amir, you fake-Arab thief, where are you? What are you doing with the tree? Don't you dare to reply?' Then she would come into the house and say, 'The poor guy seems to be ill or maybe he's passed away.' As soon as he came back three weeks later, Amir started to dig around the guava tree. When she heard the sound of digging, my grandmother rushed to the wall and said, 'That guava tree's been left alone for three whole weeks! Thieves without consciences! You stole the tree: now look after it.' That was her way of luring him into explaining why he had been absent. Amir didn't tell her that the retinas of both his eyes had suddenly come detached and he had lost his sight. He told her he had been in hospital with gout. Grandmother said, 'Ha, that's the tree's doing!'

Sometimes she'd throw stones at him from behind the wall, and in return he'd throw guavas at her, which made her fume with rage. Amir would tell her that he owned the land like any Palestinian. 'If you were Palestinian, as you say, you would move here. But you prefer to stay in the kibbutz. Don't pick the guavas till they're ripe. The tree will feel cold and die. If it dies good things won't happen to you. It's not your tree anyway, so why are you looking after it?'

'If I could give the tree back to you I would. That would spare me your shouting,' he replied. Deep down, Grandmother knew that Amir was Palestinian but probably wasn't allowed to move from the kibbutz to the village. Amir did in fact look after the tree and he only pelted Grandmother with fruit that had fallen. Just to annoy her.

In her last days, when Amir felt tired and couldn't water the tree so energetically, Grandmother's body started to dry out. Whenever a drop of water in her body dried up an identical droplet appeared in the veins of the tree. All the water Grandmother asked for, and that the villagers gave her to drink, went in the end to the guava tree behind the wall. But before she died, Grandmother's body turned into a material rather like the bark of trees and it was easy to carry her. In the end, one day, the wind blew her clean out of the window. I ran outside and jumped up to catch her, then tried to pull her back to the ground by her dress, but the wind lifted us both up into the air, higher even than the wall. I saw the guava tree that day, and Amir as well. I recognised him even though I'd never seen him before. He was digging up the soil around the trunk of the tree with his hands, then smelling the soil. He looked up and sniffed the air. But he didn't see us because he was blind. I wanted my sister to see the guava tree with me, but she was inside lying on the straw mat. I tried to get Grandmother down so that I could fetch my sister. But my hands slipped and I fell. Grandmother twirled in the air like a leaf and disappeared from sight.

When I told the neighbours what had happened to Grandmother, they said, 'Everything's possible!' and looked at the sky. 'If she flew off, she's bound to come back some day,' one of them added. But Grandmother didn't come back, and my sister kept feeling more and more hungry each day. She wasn't hungry because her imagination had been stolen. It was hunger of a more familiar kind. The guava tree was ours, but the wall cut in front of it so it was counted as belonging to the nearby kibbutz. The wall was thick and high. I grew tired of seeing my sister hungry. One night I lifted her onto my back and headed out to the wall. Instinctively I grabbed a piece of the wall with my hand and it came away as if it were a sponge. 'Did you see what I just did?' I whispered. Above us, a camera moved and an automatic machine gun started emitting red tracking beams, but otherwise didn't react. Once through the wall, I climbed the tree and picked three guavas, for my sister to eat. We went to the tree every night, like this, climbing through an opening in the wall I had made with my bare hands, so my sister could eat from the tree. A few nights later, though, she developed a stomach ache when we got back home. Then she started vomiting in her sleep until she was too exhausted to raise her hand to wipe her face, which I had to clean with my sleeve. The next morning she woke up hungry again.

On the last day of her life, my sister was so weak she couldn't even wrap her arms around my neck for me to carry her. So

I left her at home, went to the tree and brought back her guavas. I emptied my pockets and said, 'Look, four big guavas. You won't be hungry for two days now.' But my sister said she no longer felt hungry and just wanted to sleep. 'Don't sleep,' I said. She nodded, and for my sake she kept her eyes half-open like a doll.

Then the NGO woman arrived and said, 'Would you like to act in a toothpaste advert?' In the end they had my sister stand next to me in the advert. With what strength she had left, she put her arm around my neck and leaned her head on my shoulder with tired eyes. When she got back home she closed them.

To encourage her, I said, 'Since you no longer feel hungry, that means you're cured. Like me. Your teeth will turn bright white and you'll no longer have any ribs protruding in your chest. It'll be like your belly button has turn inwards again.' Neither I nor my sister knew that Amir had sprayed the guava tree with carcinogenic pesticides.

Simon

Amir's family were Palestinian Jews, but they were forced to live in the kibbutz. His father had built a house away from all the settlers' houses and close to our village. But they were forced to build the wall between us and them. That was because Simon, a resident of the neighbouring kibbutz, had gone to south Lebanon as a soldier in 1996 and when he came back he was disturbed. He had almost lost his mind. His wife asked for a divorce. Even though he was mentally unfit, the court had ruled that Simon and his relatives should have custody of their son. He would wake up at night, take his son out of his bed and walk past the houses till he came to Amir's house. He would walk past Amir's house and then come straight to our house and knock on the door stammering. When Grandmother's father answered the door, he'd say, 'This is my child. Kill him. I killed a child exactly his age and this is my atonement.' Then he'd go home by himself. In the morning Grandmother's father would ask Amir's mother to take the boy back to Simon's family. It was Grandmother's father and Amir's mother who started the war of insults between the two families, and Amir as a boy would come and collect the child from Grandmother's father without speaking to Grandmother, who was just a child like him at the time. They exchanged hateful looks. Amir took the boy back to Simon's house but Simon couldn't remember anything about what had happened. So a simple wall was built in the middle of the path between our house and Amir's house.

Now that Simon's path to our house was blocked, he would turn like a robot and retrace his steps. The wall later became part of the Apartheid Wall and it cut us off from the guava tree forever. Amir and Grandmother never saw each other again. But some months after the wall was built Simon became a peace activist. They eventually found he had killed himself with a bullet to the head, and beside him they found his son, who'd had a heart attack from the shock of hearing the shot. Before she died, my sister told me that Grandmother and Amir secretly loved each other. Once she had heard him say to her over the wall, 'Marry me and the guava tree can be your bride price! Say "yes" and I'll dig it up and bring it over and we can live together.' Apparently that day Grandmother came back inside with tears in her eyes, and she was still upset when she closed them to go to sleep that night. We knew by this point that Grandfather had treated her cruelly from the time when his bull had died to the time they divorced. He lived in the house next door. Amir sprayed the guava tree with carcinogenic pesticides to protect the tree, as he had promised Grandmother he would.

After she died, he kept saying every day, in a voice that grew increasingly frail, 'Aren't you going to marry me?' When I heard this myself, I shouted back that Grandmother had died. If he had been interested in my sister I would have said, 'And my sister too!' From then on, he never came to dig around the guava tree and the tree withered. As for my sister, when she eventually succumbed to the poison, I was sitting beside her. 'Wish for something, anything, and shut your eyes,' I said. 'Then open them.' I felt I could bring about any wish for my sister in her last moments. As I was saying this, my body transformed into very small balls of mud. I didn't know I could do this but for some reason it didn't surprise me. I put some of the balls into her hand and my sister shut her eyes as I had told her to do, then she clenched her fist. I waited but her eyes didn't open. Ever since my right eye has had a faint blue glint to it.

Mukhtar

I was like my sister. I had also died once. Or rather that was the case for a time. I used to shout 'Why don't the dead ever really die here?' and would find myself all agitated. But this was before Grandfather went to the wall to fetch his bull, Mukhtar. That's what he called him. Grandmother would tether the bull to the wall between us and Amir. She would whip it with an electric wire every day, and say to Grandfather, 'I'm going to leave it here until it drags the wall down.' She gave Mukhtar hay, and hoped that he would pull the wall down or even remove a chunk of it so that she would be able to see the guava tree, if only for one last time. 'Ignorant woman,' Grandfather muttered. 'She wants to see Amir, not the guava tree.' But one morning, when we went to fetch Mukhtar, we found that the wall's automatic machine gun had shot him in the knee during the night. The bullets had completely destroyed his knee. A part of the wall had moved a little and Grandfather said the poor bull had been in such pain that he got up and pulled the wall a few inches. Now he was crouched on the ground, leaning against the wall, exhausted. He was in so much pain that an uncontrolled stream of shit came out of his arse. When Grandfather saw him, he massaged the creature's neck and started crying and slobbering all over himself. He cursed Grandmother and Amir.

I was with him at this point. I said, 'Let's go inside, Grampa.' I told him I was afraid the machine gun might shoot me in the knee as well. But Grandfather said, 'I wish it would! It would probably be for the best,' and then he started stuffing mud into his mouth. I thought Grandfather was doing this to protect himself from the machine gun's bullets, so I did the same. I swallowed as much mud as I could. My throat and stomach hurt like hell, and I shut my eyes. After a while I heard Grandmother and my sister crying and saying I had died and Grandmother was arguing with Grandfather, but their shouting annoyed me, so I opened my eyes and came back to life. And since then I haven't felt hungry.

2

South Falasta / Greater Israel

After my sister died, I was moved from the South Falasta sector, which was miserably poor, to Greater Israel, to a place near Wonderland. The country is now in two parts and, between them, a wall passes by Gaza and then Beersheba in a diagonal line as straight as the trajectory of a billiard ball, until it hits the Egyptian border, at Taba. The wall is equipped with highly sensitive detectors and nothing can get across it. Even a mosquito, if it tried to cross into Greater Israel, would receive an electric shock that would extract all its energy and leave it stone cold dead. That's how the detectors worked. Then there is the gravity wind emitted by the Dabraya Star, made from graviton particles. The wind blows every night and extracts from the children of Falasta everything they have imagined during the day. All of that is then drawn up to Dabraya and stored there. The most developed material, if it is not sent back in time, is inserted into the minds of children in Greater Israel as and when they need it. I didn't realise I had thought about the robomicrobe so much that it was deeply embedded in my mind and the graviton wind couldn't steal it from me. I had imagined the robomicrobe so often that the idea had acquired a powerful immunity. In fact, it was the only thing that survived in my head after I fell into the water tank and later swallowed the mud. Because the idea was still alive in me, I came back from the dead twice. So I was moved to the Elvin Orphanage to have the idea extracted from my head and developed into a real robomicrobe that could help the Israeli population to live forever. There I met some Jewish children who had damaged imaginations. They were seven girls and three boys, all the complete opposite of me. Their minds were blocked and couldn't take in anything anyone else had imagined. Except for Ze'ev, whose mind suddenly started to produce a flood of images from the life of Eli, his great-great-grandfather, despite the fact that no one had ever spoken to him about the man. Before long, he not only insisted Eli really existed but told us stories about him every day. 'I can get the Luger back for you,' I told him. 'Wish for it and you'll find it in your hand.'

'And how long will I be able to keep it?' he asked.

'Until you fall asleep!' I said.

'But I want to keep the Luger forever,' he replied. 'Don't worry. Once I've convinced them Eli really existed, I'll be released from this place.' Waiting for this day, however, exhausted Ze'ev and sometimes he cried at night like a little child, although he was seven years older than the rest of us. The other children cried like him too. Once a week, scraps from the imaginations of South Falasta children were pumped into their heads. But this only made them feel like they were trapped in the imagination of some other, unfamiliar kid, which would make them freak out. When this happened, I stood in front of them, saying 'Look!' and I'd turn into small mud balls. The children would come up to me and each of them would scoop up a handful of the mud. It tickled when they did this and I would laugh. 'Shut your eyes,' I would say to them, 'and clear your heads of all the images you don't want to think about.' When they did this, the mud balls emitted radiation, and when they opened their eyes again the claustrophobic chaos of the unfamiliar children's imaginations would be resolved into calming holographic 3-D images: a pen writing with light in the air, for instance, or galaxies expanding slowly across the universe, or even a wooden car that can melt into a tree and then re-emerge as a car on the other side. These were all things that have been taken from the imaginations of children from Falasta.

Ben Moshe the Elder

Jacob Moshe, the manager of the Elvin Orphanage, would take pictures of me with a camera implanted in the pupil of his eye whenever he interviewed me. I didn't know it at the time, but he distributed these images to the brain-interfaces of his family members. His son, Ben Moshe 'the Elder' was CEO of the Aharon Kibbutz Institute, a secret astronomical and biological research centre, where his brother-in-law, who had imitated him in everything ever since he was a child, also worked as his assistant. The day he received the photographs, Ben Moshe 'the Elder' had a phone call from his father's wife, Abela. 'Jacob is in the garden' she said, 'staring at the soil and talking nonsense.' When Ben arrived, he heard Jacob saying, 'The soil, it's moving. It's slipping. The Palestinians are stealing the soil. They're clawing it back. They're preparing a giant made out of mud balls that will roll on top of us and bury us alive. This is a sample!' He took some mud balls from his pockets. Ben Moshe 'the Elder' didn't have any brothers. He acquired the title 'the Elder' when he was at school, because he was such a bully. But he was also top of the class. His brother-in-law-to-be copied him, even his bullying and his specialisation in nuclear physics. He married Ben Moshe's sister just to be his relative. Even when he slept with her he followed her brother's style of fucking.

Ben Moshe took the mud balls from his father in an attempt to calm him down. 'Father, they're no longer called Palestinians. We've moved them all to the south, out of Tel Aviv, Haifa, Acre, Galilee and everywhere. We've evacuated the settlements in Beersheba. And now we call them the Falasta. Don't you remember how we went bowling to celebrate it, and you had to apologise for what you did to Mother. Are you going to repeat that with Abela?'

Jacob held his son's hands and burst into tears. 'Abela?' he said in a trembling voice. 'She's the seed of hope in my life. If only you knew how much I love her. But the soil is slipping. This is all there is!'

Those were hard times, back then. Ben's mother had been struggling with cancer in hospital, and his father had just started an affair with Abela, the nurse taking care of her. Ben was involved in fights at school daily. In the end he had fractures in his jaw and had to have screws put in his mouth on both sides. His brother-in-law stayed loyal to him. He did everything he could to have his own jaw broken, in turn, and have screws planted in them. He argued with taxi drivers and the police until he got what he wanted.

Ben put his ear to the soil. Then he shouted excitedly: 'Damn! My father's right. The soil is slipping!'

'Do something, please,' said Jacob.

When he was only nineteen, Jacob had been part of the elite force that had stormed the Jenin camp in 2002. 'This isn't an end fit for a hero,' Ben told his brother-in-law, as they headed back to the institute that night. 'But I'll sort it out tomorrow!' When Abela called the information desk at the institute, Ben and his brother-in-law were in the middle of gathering signatures from colleagues for a decision that had already been made, and offering mud balls in small plastic bags in return.

'There's something I don't understand about your family,' Abela said over the phone. 'Your madness!!' She had packed her bags and had decided to leave the following morning.

'In an hour's time, you'll discover it's a madness that you like,' Ben replied.

Abela was sixteen years younger than Jacob. She was a former fashion model and the old man was enamoured of her as much as his son was (and his son-in-law, of course). When the massive explosion took place, Jacob was still sitting in the garden. In fact he hadn't budged an inch. He probed the soil with his hand and smiled. Then he stood up and went into the house. Abela was sitting in the kitchen smoking. Jacob hugged her and said, 'Our most beautiful dream has just come true!'

Ezer Banana

At 11:15 PM on Thursday 5 March, 2037, a biological warfare munition that had never been tested before was launched into South Falasta. It contained smart bacteria or, to be more precise, a payload of microscopic robots programmed to identify the Falasta wherever they were, inside or outside the region. These nanobots fed on uranium and produced poisonous polonium in people's bodies. Within three weeks there wasn't a single Falasti still alive except for me. But during those three weeks my body glowed in a surprising way, as if it were being constantly injected with a dose of radiation. This added to the panic among the Jewish kids in the orphanage, so I was moved this time to the Aharon research laboratory. After doing all kinds of nuclear and other tests, Ben realised the terrible truth: my cells glowed immediately after the death of every Falasti and the reason was simple. Whenever a Falasti died, as they breathed their last, their cells were turned into pure energy that was transferred to me and stored within me. The Falastis were doing this in revenge for all the children whose imaginations had been stolen over the years by the Dabraya Star. This meant that, on my death, I would release massive amounts of energy. A secret report on the subject said: 'There won't be an explosion, but a silent gust of wind that will turn everything into dust. Stealing the robomicrobe from his imagination is no longer a priority.' From that moment on, I was put in the glass cube, which was designed to absorb the energy I emitted when it touched the sides of the cube. Whenever this happens, I feel electricity coursing through me and fall to the ground.

Around about the same time, Ze'ev got some good news: 'Congratulations. We've established that Eli really did exist.'

'You owe me an apology,' he replied.

'So it's been decided that the Luger will be returned to you and left in your care,' they told him. But this was on condition that he should keep me company at all times.

'That's easy, since we're friends,' Ze'ev said. He was forbidden to tell me the real reason why I was being put in the glass cube. As soon as he arrived into Room 803, he said, 'You're being pursued by a bacterial robot and you have to stay in this cube. If you die it means we all die. In other words, I will die. And anyway, you're the last Falasti!' As he was saying this, I was curled up in the corner like a sticky lump of mud, exhausted and sad. It was me who had always wanted to be a robomicrobe, and now I found myself pursued by one.

They put me in a steel-plated room on the eighth floor below ground level. But my constant shivering exhausted Ze'ev. It was a shivering that made you understand how lonely I was. One morning, he woke up tense, as if from a nightmare, and said, 'No one could put up with this!' In full view of the monitoring cameras he pointed the Luger at me and shouted, 'Either we move from here or everything's over.' I couldn't move. My nervous system was wholly focused on shivering. I couldn't budge one inch from where I was. Half an hour later, the door of the room opened and Ezer Banana joined us, with a pistol in his hand. Ze'ev hadn't expected to see him. 'They sent you to take my place, didn't they?' he said. But Ezer tried to reassure him. He said it wasn't a military pistol but contained a shot of adrenaline to shoot at me if I was in imminent danger of suddenly dying. 'We're still friends!' Ezer said. But Ze'ev spat and said, 'Sudden death? Friends? Is that what you were told to say? Even our friendship was part of their plan, wasn't it?' They argued a lot that day, Ze'ev denying everything Ezer told him. 'Sure,' Ezer said, 'and my pistol doesn't really contain an adrenaline shot, just as much as your Luger isn't the one that Eli used.'

Two Backgrounds

Ze'ev is an orphan like me. His story is that his grandmother stabbed his grandfather in the back and killed him four years into their marriage, and then his mother killed his father in the same way, also after four years of marriage. Yehuda, Ze'ev's father, had also lived in an orphanage for a while, just like him. Because of his family history, Ze'ev was wary of girls after he moved to the orphanage. He preferred girls who didn't show any interest in him, because he felt it was safe to hang out with them. As for girls who fancied him, they terrified him. For years he slept with a metal shield on his back and a kitchen knife under his pillow. That was until he met Ezer Banana in the carpentry workshop where he worked, in the evenings, before returning to the orphanage at night.

Ezer acquired the 'Banana' name because his spine was so bent. He had worked as a hitman for eleven years when Ze'ev met him. Everyone agreed that he was the luckiest killer in history. He managed to kill forty-three people and was caught red-handed seven times. But the court acquitted him on each occasion. Every time they found him lying unconscious alongside the victim, his body dripping with sweat. That was because he had diabetic attacks while he was completing each mission. He felt an ecstatic surge course through his body when committing murders and the sugar level in his blood spiked. But the unlikelihood of this fainting bystander also being the perpetrator wasn't the only reason the court acquitted him, it was also because his seven victims were the most hated people imaginable. No one liked them – neither relatives nor acquaintances – so much so that Ezer was regarded as a godsend. His reputation spread as far as Queens in New York, Tijuana and Bogota. Some fellow hitmen even sent him letters of congratulations. That's how Ze'ev met him. Ezer brought the bundle of letters to Ze'ev's carpentry workshop saying, 'I want you to make me some frames for these letters.' Ze'ev read them and was amazed. He thought Ezer could also be a godsend for him as well. He made the frames for him for nothing: 'These are on me. Consider them a gift,' he said. Ezer hung them up at home as testimony that the world's most hardened criminals recognised the uniqueness of his style. From then on, he and Ezer became firm friends. Ze'ev no longer had to keep the knife in his pillow when he slept or wear the metal shield. Whenever a girl aroused his suspicions, even if she wasn't pursuing him, he would send Ezer Banana to bring her to an understanding. Ezer wouldn't say much to the girl. He would just ask her, 'Have you heard of a hitman called Ezer Banana?' She would understand who he was immediately, because you didn't need to see his picture to recognise him. Just looking at his posture, you couldn't help but think of bananas. Eventually no girls dared approach Ze'ev. 'The stories that happen in this place don't happen anywhere else,' Ze'ev once told me. 'Here you need a hitman to make your life better.'

Porno

Ezer Banana would always bring Ze'ev porn films for them to watch together. On his twenty-second birthday, as he inserted the memory chip into the 3-D film projector, Ezer said, 'It's one of the ten best porn films of the year. Sophia is the star, but I'm not going to watch it with you. This isn't your birthday present, you see. You'll get that when the film's over.' And indeed, at the last scene in the film, Ze'ev found the star opening the door and coming into the room. She was wearing a bathrobe, and underneath the robe the same lingerie made of candy that she'd been wearing in the film. Ze'ev stood up and quickly pulled up his pants. But before he could say a word, she beat him to it. 'I'm sure you've come already,' she said, 'but I'll make you come two more times.' That was her famous line in all her films. Ezer waited outside the room. In fact, he left the Aharon Kibbutz Institute completely and went for a short walk. But first he tried to reassure Ze'ev. He told him it was Sophia in flesh and blood and she wouldn't do him any harm. This didn't make Ze'ev any less tense, because he had never slept with a woman before and he had no more trust in Ezer Banana than in any other hitman. So as the star began to undress, he pulled out the Luger and came up to my glass cube, and whispered, 'I'll keep the gun aimed at you, just to frighten her.' But he refused to taste the underwear for fear the candy was poisoned. Sophia said, 'Don't worry. It's not in my interest to have one of my lovers die.' Sophia's dream was to become the world's top porn star, and although she was young, her reputation had spread online across the world. In fact, Ze'ev couldn't resist her. He kept hold of the Luger as she crouched between his thighs like a cat and licked his cock. He put the muzzle of the gun to her head from above, massaged her head with his other hand, and said, 'Nothing personal. It's just a matter of family history.' When he ejaculated she was on top of him. He couldn't control himself. He pulled the trigger of the Luger and it fired a bullet, up towards the steel-plate ceiling, just missing Sophia's right breast in the process, which made her angry. It had frightened her. 'You bastard, don't you know how hard I've worked to make my breasts this shape?' she said. She put on her robe and left the room.

'You promised to make me come twice, you tease!' Ze'ev called after her, chuckling. 'If you want to be a porn star you have to put up with a variety of pressures.'

'You'll pay the price for this! We'll all pay the price,' she shouted from the corridor. As it happened, Sophia Porno didn't know why she had said, 'We'll all pay the price.' But she felt certain that this was what would happen. At first, she attributed her fear to the fact that the Luger bullet had only just missed her breast. But when she thought about it, she was only really frightened when she looked at me. What no one noticed was that the bullet, after just missing her breast, changed course and hit one of the top corners of the cube, sending a small crack through it. But none of that would have happened if it hadn't been for the magnetic surge inside me that caused the extraordinary acceleration in the bullet that changed its course. This surprised me, and alarmed me too. I was being pursued by a bacterial robot, and the crack in the corner of the glass cube meant that the robot might now be able to get to me. Then I realised that the energy stored inside me was waiting for any opportunity to escape, regardless of whether I lived or died. That made me sad.

Ze'ev didn't notice anything. He was still lying as Sophia had left him, staring at the ceiling and finding it hard to believe that he had finally got to fuck someone. Then he turned to me. When he saw me curled up in the corner, breathing heavily and trembling, he said mockingly, 'Don't act like you're the one who got to fuck!' I wasn't surprised at his hostility. Since Ezer had arrived, Ze'ev had become a different person. I stayed like that till nightfall. Ezer was still sitting outside the room. As soon as he came in, he hugged Ze'ev limply and said, 'I hope we can be friends again like before.' But Ze'ev didn't say anything and they both went off to bed. Minutes later I had my first real sense of the end. My body emitted an orb of white energy, which leaked out of the crack in the cube and assumed the ghost-like appearance of a young man I'd never seen before in the middle of the room. It was followed by two more orbs that left my body in the same way. The three ghost-like young men, who were clearly brothers, then disappeared through the walls of the room, without looking back.

After that I slept for a whole month. I was exhausted, like someone who had literally given up the ghost three times in as many minutes. Eventually I woke up to a putrid smell coming from my own body. Ze'ev was sitting close to the cube. He stood up, came over to me and said, 'We thought you were in a coma.' After less than half an hour, a medical team came into the room to examine me. They were dressed in plastic overalls and Miriam was with them. That was the first time Ze'ev had set eyes on her. As for Sophia, after the Luger incident she became 'pornophobic'. She no longer trusted any of the actors she worked with. She would scream and suddenly put her hand on her right breast as if a Luger bullet had gone right through it. Eventually she became known as the actress who made the male actors around her tense and whatever she did to her co-star's cock, he couldn't get an erection. She would suck it and stroke it and pull it, and nothing would happen. Her last film ended with a scene in which she breaks down and weeps bitterly. After that she retired and worked in whiskey ads. But when she raised her glass to her mouth in the advert and smiled affectedly, she couldn't stop herself from cursing Ze'ev in a snarl that was almost inaudible. When he first saw the advert, Ze'ev shouted like a madman, 'She's insulting me, the whore, she's insulting me!'

3

A Jar

Ezer and Ze'ev went on watching Sophia's porn films. Ezer didn't want to do it but Ze'ev insisted because Sophia had insulted him in the whiskey ads. He would say, 'Let's have a little laugh.' Ezer got used to it with time, but he did his best not to look at Sophia on the screen. He made do with listening to her fake moans. He saw no problem in that. Her voice evoked old images and feelings. The reality was that Ze'ev masturbated with complete concentration, while Ezer masturbated with his eyes to the ground, as if he were thinking of something valuable he had lost five minutes earlier. When they finished, Ze'ev would freeze the picture at her right breast and shout, 'Bingo! You should have seen her face! It was the only time it looked like a real human face. All the time I was fucking her, she put on that animal face. Some bullets, when they miss you, make you human.' Ezer listened, staring at the ground or looking at me anxiously and sometimes asking Ze'ev, 'Do you think he's okay?' 'He's like a time bomb,' Ze'ev replied coldly. 'If he stops shaking, all we can do is pray! There's enough energy in him to wipe us all out in the blink of an eye. What do you say, shall we put Sophia Porno in with him? Hey, you! Don't you want to fuck? It would be her greatest film. Sophia Porno has a nuclear fuck!'

In the orphanage, Ze'ev had always behaved like a friend, a true friend. But as soon as he saw that I'd become just a body shaking in a glass cube, he said, as if he were seeing me for the first time, 'How can I be friends with a body that does nothing but shake in a glass case all day? You can't talk to him or touch him. I'm not even sure he feels anything. He's been dead since his people died. Or rather he was dead the first day he came to the orphanage.' Ze'ev was puzzled now whenever he looked at me. Although Ezer Banana had joined Room 803, Ze'ev no longer trusted anyone, especially as Ezer hadn't previously been known to have friends. Ze'ev was the only person to ever do Ezer a favour, when he framed those letters for him for free. But since he received the Luger, he felt his fate was to become a hero like Eli, and not to have his reputation tarnished by friendship with some hitman.

Ezer was no less disturbed by me than Ze'ev. After Sophia Porno's visit, he started coming up to the glass cube and whispering, 'We're both killers, but we will never be friends,' implying his only friend was Ze'ev, even though he now had other opinions on the matter. Ze'ev felt there was some trick being played, because we were trapped in a steel-plated room eight floors underground, which meant that if I died, there wouldn't be any victims other than him and Ezer. 'They might put what's left of our ashes in neighbouring holes in the ground. Indeed why bother with two holes? A small jar would serve the purpose. The ashes of Eli's grandson, mixed with the ashes of a hitman whose career was cut short by bouts of diabetes. What an honour!' All that made Room 803 more tense and depressing. Ze'ev's hostility didn't provoke Ezer. On the contrary, it merely made him sad. Ezer was still confident, though, that all these measures were just temporary and that things between him and Ze'ev would go back to how they used to be as soon as the institute developed an antidote to bacterial robots and invented energy absorption suits that would allow us to relocate to a room above ground. Until then though, Ezer would continue to experience loneliness – the loneliness he had felt all his life – whereas Ze'ev would continue to feel suspicious. Meanwhile, from time to time, I emitted orbs of energy that took on the ghostly appearance of people I didn't know as soon as they slipped through the crack in the glass. They came out in rapid bursts, one after another and at a greater frequency. It was as if they all had to do this before the bacterial robot found me.

Kibbutzes

As soon as Ze'ev cast eyes on Miriam, he lost his desire to see any Sophia Porno films, even the last tape they had seen together, the one that made Ze'ev laugh idiotically when it ended with her breaking into tears in the final shot. He no longer chuckled, masturbated, or wanted to freeze the picture on her right breast. In fact, he suddenly turned off the projector and said he wondered what had come over him. His face looked like a vacuum-sealed package containing someone else's face. But at least Ezer was now spared the obligation of masturbating to Sophia Porno films with Ze'ev.

The medical team often visited the room after I woke up from one of my long sleeps. They measured my energy levels and the rate at which my body was rotting. Then they checked Ze'ev and Ezer to see if they were carrying the bacterial robot. Ze'ev saw this as a humiliation in every sense of the word. But Ben the Elder said, 'Mistakes sometimes happen.'

Miriam was the least important member of the team. Just a young woman responsible for writing down their observations and carrying the scanner that, when placed near the earhole, scanned the whole body and measured the amount of energy the body would lose when it died. The first time they came into the room they were wearing plastic overalls specially designed to absorb as much energy as possible. But that didn't stop the plastic melting and catching fire. The overalls were so thick it was hard to make out their faces. Ben the Elder and his brother-in-law were in charge of the team. You could tell them apart from the rest of the team because their gestures were identical. Ze'ev, annoyed that he had to undergo a blood test for the bacterial robot, waved his Luger and said, 'You must be Ben Moshe and this your brother-in-law. How can you put up with someone imitating you all the time? Doesn't that make you paranoid? It must make you suspicious.' He laughed.

Ben Moshe was the one who won all the public attention. But Ze'ev never stopped provoking him. 'How are the kibbutzes?' he would ask. 'Will we have to defend our own kibbutz soon?' It was no secret that the kibbutzes had started to expand as soon as Falasta ceased to exist. It began with simple disagreements over land and borders, then it moved on to river water, fruit and other primary resources. It was no longer easy to control. Ze'ev seized every opportunity to provoke Ben, who ignored him as he walked around the glass cube taking notes and examining the small screen at the base of the cube that showed the temperature, humidity and types of gas being given off by my body, as well as the amount of radiation the cube walls had absorbed. As Miriam went over Ze'ev and Ezer's bodies with the bacterial-robot scanner, Ze'ev said, 'You know what? It's normal for all these conflicts to start up. This is what we've come to realise. Expansion. The Palestinians it turns out were actually a peace-keeping force between the Israeli factions.' This was too much for Ben to take, so he ordered Ze'ev to leave the room.

Miriam and two soldiers went with him. In the next room, Miriam took off her plastic overalls and Ze'ev saw her face for the first time. Her face was sweaty, but it captivated him. She walked up to him and whispered in his ear that although she found his opinions fascinating, he had better shut up. Then she folded her overalls under her arm and left. Ze'ev began to shout to the ceiling, 'Tell me, Ben, wouldn't it have been better for us to stay neighbours with the Palestinians, rather than live next to an area infested with bacteria? A kibbutz war is inevitable. I suggest we build rooms like Room 803 everywhere.'

One of the soldiers assigned to guard Ze'ev said nervously, 'Sir, no one can hear you. As you know, these rooms are insulated.'

'All the better! That way we can have a special, private audience next time I see him,' Ze'ev retorted. The soldiers treated him with respect because, like Eli, he was seen as a hero, not because he had saved the lives of dozens of Jewish children but because he had saved my life. Within my earshot, he was always saying, 'Imagine! They think I'm a hero for saving the life of the last Palestinian. I mean Falasti. What a joke! I have a feeling someone's making fun of me.'

Meanwhile, Ezer grew ever more disturbed by the bacterial-robot blood tests. He had been constantly sullen as it was, ever since Ze'ev had slept with Sophia Porno. By this point he was regularly coming up to the glass cube, staring at me and wielding his pistol, which contained an adrenaline shot. 'The idiots,' he would say robotically. 'They don't realise that the Lord planned all this for me. The last seven victims were my deliverance from the Lord. I said that to the judge. You should have seen his face. It was dripping with sweat, so much so that parts of his face were refracted upside down in the beads dripping from his nose. His face seemed to be falling apart cell by cell. Why? Because I told him that before every mission, I would go the Western Wall and pray to the Lord to help me succeed. You and I are similar. We know how to kill. I don't think anyone but another killer like me could understand my readiness to take a life. Tell your friends not to mess with me or I'll find a way to do them harm.' I didn't know who Ezer was referring to, but I felt it had something to with the three spectral brothers. On the medical team's last visit Ze'ev was forced to wear medical overalls. When they explained to him that if he wore the overalls any energy waves emitted by me would only give him second or third degree burns but not actually kill him, he said sarcastically, 'So instead of dying, we'd spend the rest of our lives disfigured? Great. Wouldn't death be better than that?' At this point Ben turned to him and said, 'We've developed a vaccine against the bacterial robots. We're going to assign you to manage the public launch of it shortly. It'll be shown in schools and you'll take it round all the kibbutzes promoting it. The Falasta weren't a peace-keeping force between us, but the Mud Ball Kid is a peace-keeping force on his own. No one would dare to open fire at him. Remember to explain to everyone how much energy there is stored in his body. He's the last specimen of the might of the enemy we fought for a hundred years. And they haven't disappeared completely. We are depending on you, Ze'ev, to end the chaos in the kibbutzes and calm people down. This is your chance to save thousands of children from civil war, to be a hero, to be even more important than Eli. As you know, the kibbutzes are surrounded by army forces and it's no longer safe for most people to leave them. I haven't seen my father for more than a month, even though his wife has left him.'

But I was scaring no one. The sight of me cowering in a glass cube, covered in sores and unable to do anything but shiver, wouldn't frighten a dung beetle. But what Ben said triggered the old passion for heroism that lay deep down inside Ze'ev. His brother-in-law came up to me and injected me with a germ programmed to be hyperactive and then suddenly die. At that moment, I emitted ghostly patterns of energy that looked like snapshots of my grandmother, school, the neighbours, my grandfather and the bull. I didn't see my sister. The images hung in the air for seconds, until the plastic overalls absorbed them and they splattered into shreds. 'We've just given him immunity to the bacterial robots,' Ben said. 'But the more energy he loses the more his cells will go on rotting. The glass in the cube will make sure they're absorbed. So far the amount of energy he has lost is no more than five hundredths of one percent of all the energy that was stored in him. He still poses a deadly threat.'

I realised I was gradually drying out. The energy that was stored in me didn't belong to me, but to the Palestinians killed by the bacterial bomb. And each one wanted to escape, taking their energy with them. It was also a question of time. Apparently each spectre needed some form of vessel for the emotions that had come to define them over their lives. Anger or frustration, for example. The three young men would not have exited my body if Sophia Porno hadn't been there. As I later discovered, they had an old score to settle.

Beer

Ze'ev didn't know that the injection I'd been given wasn't an antidote to the bacterial robot that was after me. It was a germ that was digitally programmed to hold my cells in a state of biological activity. The aim was to double my life without me needing food or drink. That would force the cells to consume the energy stored in me, instead of me emitting it all in the form of ghostly figures. But doubling my life expectancy meant that the memories I had acquired in my earlier life had to be erased, to be recorded over. This explains why when I projected an image, it was then lost to me forever.

On the CCTV footage, Ben watched as the three spectral brothers took shape outside the glass cube then left the room. It made him anxious when he first saw it. It shocked him. But soon he started to believe what he had seen was actually a heaven-sent salvation. Ze'ev didn't know that he was the one who had given Ben the whole idea when he dismissively described the Falastis as peace-keepers between the Israelis. 'We really needed them,' Ben said to himself, as he ordered Ze'ev to leave the room. If they could despatch some ghostly Falastis into rival kibbutzes, it would amount to deploying a peace-keeping force. And it would have less impact than living with a nuclear time bomb that threatened to obliterate everything at any moment. So he recruited Miriam to stay close to Ze'ev.

But Ben Moshe didn't realise he was doomed to fail. Not because, in the end, I would release all the energy stored in my body, but because a single batch of energy only had to remember a single incident that involved a strong emotional sense of injustice, and the contagion would immediately spread to the other batches of energy already out there, provoking a similar feeling in each new batch of energy it spread to, thus setting off a chain reaction. So I found myself bursting with feelings of tension I hadn't known before.

Ben Moshe would hide his failure from everyone, even from Miriam, the main player in his plan, and a fascinating one, with her white complexion, her thick, soft black hair and her grey eyes, as well as her slightly angled front tooth, which made her beauty more realistic in Ze'ev's eyes. She was the first woman to come into the room after Sophia Porno. Ze'ev, now full of the idea of becoming Israel's next hero, found himself stifled by his feelings towards her. He abandoned his childish behaviour and no longer spoke much to Ezer Banana, who teased him maliciously, as if he were also warning him: 'Are you now like your grandfather, who stopped speaking before his death? Be careful Miriam doesn't kill you.' But Ze'ev was confident that no woman would dare to kill him, now that everyone looked on him as a future hero. Even so, the first night he slept with her he kept his hand under the pillow clutching the Luger. As soon as he penetrated her, he came. But this time he didn't pull the trigger. He thought this marked an improvement in his performance, but Miriam had another point of view. 'Never mind,' she said, 'I'll make you come two more times.' And that's what happened. Right after that, he told her the story of his life, which she already knew from Ben, but she didn't tell him that of course. It's true that Miriam's job was to monitor my activity after I had the injection, but she fell in love with Ze'ev. She even made it clear she wanted to live with him, provided he asked to be relieved of his assignment as my minder. She begged him, and Ze'ev refused because, if it wasn't for me, he wouldn't become a hero. 'You'll get used to his presence and forget about him,' Ze'ev said.

'I don't think this is how Ezer feels!' she said.

'Ezer's been behaving strangely recently. He wasn't always like that.'

'I've never known him any other way. Apparently the only person who hasn't been struck by the curse of the Mud Ball Kid is you.'

But Miriam, consumed with guilt for deceiving Ze'ev, developed an addiction to beer. She would sit and read in her pyjamas in a dishevelled state. She looked all the time at Ezer, sitting on his rocking chair, holding the adrenaline pistol and staring at me curled up in the corner, motionless except for my shivering. He only left the room when Ze'ev wanted to sleep with Miriam or when they had an argument.

When Ze'ev found out that Miriam was pregnant he thought he was on his way to breaking the death curse that had struck his family. But whenever Miriam looked at me, she remembered she was an accomplice in Ben's deception of Ze'ev. She was consumed with guilt, and her body begged for beer to get that idea out of her head. And when she had to stop drinking because of her pregnancy, she became neurotic. She told Ze'ev the truth: that her body needed beer whenever she looked at me. Ze'ev begged her to resist the temptation, just as her unborn child urged her to abstain from alcohol. But in the end she settled the matter by having an abortion, throwing the blame on me. She was in her third month and Ze'ev was about to announce to her that he had decided to give me up, to be free for her and the child. It was the first time he'd realised that being killed sometimes hurts less than when someone close to you is killed. After the abortion, Ze'ev decided it wasn't safe to live with Miriam. The night she left, he sat on the floor beside my cube, leant his head against the glass where I usually curl up, and started to cry. There were two layers of glass between me and him. At that moment I wished I could raise my hand to caress the glass as if I were stroking his head. But all my body did was carry on shivering as usual. Then he said, 'You'll never be my friend. You're too decrepit to be my friend. I seem to be cursed with you.' Then he took out the Luger, shut his eyes tight, pointed the pistol at my eyes and pulled the trigger.

Strawberry Milk Ezer

Ezer wasn't there when that happened. He'd gone to visit Sophia Porno. Since I'd been injected with the germ, he'd been allowed to leave Room 803 for longer periods. But it was a personal matter for Ezer, more than anyone had expected. The rest of us never knew that Sophia Porno had, many years before, been Ezer's neighbours' daughter and he had fallen in love with her as a boy. When he found out she had become a professional porn star, he took a vow that he wouldn't watch any of her films. But the Internet and the shops where he bought films were full of pictures of her. On one occasion, when he and Ze'ev were talking about porn stars, Ze'ev told him frankly that she was the only actress he would like to sleep with. 'What's the difference? Since she has sex with so many men in films, I can pretend that Ze'ev is just a passing actor too, not a friend who has his birthday today,' Ezer said to himself. When Ezer called her as a special favour for a close friend, he didn't reveal that he was 'Strawberry Milk Ezer', the boy who used to chase her with a bottle of strawberry milk and beg her to take a sip of it so that she would suddenly grow a shiny new tooth to replace her lost tooth. In southern Palestine children called a lost tooth a gypsy tooth and the term had spread across the country. Sophia and her family had recently moved to Haifa from somewhere in northern Europe. She had a skin disease and needed plenty of sunshine. She slowly started to lose her hair and no young men would approach her at parties. He remembered how he used to tell her, 'I can't love you if you have a gypsy tooth,' in the belief that by saying this he was telling her it made no difference to him that her hair was falling out. Her response was, 'Why don't you find yourself an ant and rub its thighs?' Her fake moans when Ze'ev slept with her brought back all these memories for Ezer and his eyes teared up silently. His transformation into Ezer Banana, the killer, from the boy whose bones were in danger of bending and whom they called 'Strawberry Milk Ezer', took place the moment he pushed Sophia's twin brother down the stairs, breaking his neck and killing him. If her brother hadn't pissed into the milk carton and forced him to drink it that day, none of this would have happened. But Ezer got away with it. No one discovered that he was the killer.

Indeed the only effect it had on Ezer was the child inside him died too, as if he was the one who had fallen down the stairs and broken his neck. After that, Sophia and her family moved from Haifa to Cyprus. He lost all trace of her until she reappeared years later under the name Sophia Porno. The only thing that consoled Ezer after Ze'ev slept with the love of his life was that it meant Ze'ev no longer desired her. But Ze'ev wouldn't stop describing her right breast and saying, 'Imagine it scratched, not punctured, just scratched. And it bleeding profusely and spattering on you as you fuck her! No doubt that would please the great Ezer Banana, who's seen plenty of blood in his time.' It *did* please Ezer, he thought about her all the time, and when he found out she was no longer making porn films, he felt guilty. Eventually he was driven to call her, pretending to be a customer. He kept his cool and ended up having a deeper conversation with her than any he'd ever had.

'Don't think of me as a stranger. Think of me as a lover returning from past times,' Ezer said.

'Who are you?' she asked.

'I'm no one, just someone who'd like, if it were within his power, to give back to you everything you've lost.'

It was touching. Sophia was curious, not to sleep with him but to get to know him as a person. 'You can come any time after 9:00 PM, since you're returning from past times.' After her work was over she usually went home, drank a little whiskey and was sometimes so depressed that she even watched a compilation of her 50 best porn scenes. But when he reached her apartment in Haifa that night, the door had been broken open. Sophia Porno was sitting on the sofa in front of him, surrounded by three ghostly young men, the spectral brothers that had come out of me. They seemed to be angry and it was clear that they had business with her specifically. They kept asking her why she had lied and said it was their younger brother who had pushed her brother down the stairs. 'Sophia! Sophia!' Ezer called. But she didn't turn towards him. He might as well have been a ghost himself. She seemed to be taken with the young men around her. Overcome by them, in fact. Ezer took out his pistol and emptied the magazine into the three of them. But the bullets went right through their ghostly forms, doing them no harm. His hands were shaking and one of the bullets went through Sophia Porno's right breast. When he went up to her, she was gasping for air. She had been having a heart attack since the moment the young men first surrounded her, but now his bullet had created a pressure wave in her chest that kick-started her heart, so Ezer had inadvertently saved her life.

Bean Poison

I don't know if I should have been upset or pleased that Ze'ev had pulled the trigger on me. Whatever the case, the bullet didn't blow my face away. I had a terrible burning sensation in my eye and the side of my head started to fall away like clumps of ash. In its place a swelling emerged with lots of little rounded bulges like the little balloons I used to blow up for my little sister – remnants of the massive balloons Amir's grandsons used to send flying our way when they grew bored of playing with them. As soon as the balloons started to cross the wall, its electronic devices detected them and opened fire to stop them crossing, so their remnants would fall next to the wall. I would run out of the house, pick up the shreds of rubber and stretch them between my fingers like the skin of a drum. Then I put my mouth to the rubber and blew with all my strength until I made very small balloons that I tied at the neck. 'These are bobbles,' I would tell my sister, as I tickled her face with them. Anyway, that side of my head fell away and swellings like putrid bobbles appeared in the blink of an eye. The sight was quite a shock for Ze'ev. But that wasn't what made him turn and shout 'Doctor, doctor' like a madman, as he fumbled to open the first aid kit with trembling hands.

The bits of my face that fell away, drifted off and coalesced into ghostly body parts that floated around in the cube as if someone had blown on them. Like bits of arms, hands, fingers and legs. I recognised them immediately. They were my sister's. I remember when she died, I felt a pale blue flash in my right eye. That flash was the energy my sister deposited in me when she died. When she drew her last breath, she held something back, enough to form a new ghostly mass when the time came to come out of me. Only then did I realise that my sister wanted to give me a chance to save her. It was as if she wanted to fulfil my wish to really become a superhero, but the Luger bullet that pierced my right eye had torn it to pieces. The parts of her body were floating around in a way that made you think they came from someone sad, as when you see a dancer performing and it makes you want to cry, although the dance is silent. All this happened in a flash and was imprinted on the mind of Ze'ev who, unable to open the first aid kit, fainted.

As Ze'ev was taken away by doctors, I remained crouched in my usual corner. My body was shivering, although less violently than normal. I was taken to the research centre's medical bay, which also has rooms insulated against radiation. When I came around from another one of my long sleeps I was surrounded by a team of medics, all but one of them wearing plastic overalls – the exception being Ze'ev, who shouted, 'Ezer's here!' the moment he saw me open my left, and now only, eye. Ezer was in the next room with Sophia Porno. He had brought her to the same medical bay. All the way there, Ezer had apologised to her profusely and, as her right breast bled, he told her the whole truth, except about his role in the killing of her twin brother. His candour reassured her, and she felt in love for the first time in her life, so much so that even the bleeding seemed to slow down. 'She didn't even look at her breast. She just sat in the seat beside me listening, never losing consciousness for a moment,' Ezer whispered enthusiastically as they scraped layers of rotten skin off me, as well as what looked like smallpox blisters. Ze'ev and Ezer chatted away, holding their noses throughout.

'But that's not everything,' Ezer said. 'Did you know they've just discovered that Sophia is pregnant? I've been seeing her whenever I can since she came here, and I slept with her a few weeks ago. I pretended I was a client, but I made passionate love to her. Like an old lover. When I was inside her I felt I was pouring into her all the love I had saved up over a lifetime. She didn't make a sound. She just looked into my eyes as if to say, "Thank you." I decided to become a different person after that. I am handing in my pistol and moving out of Room 803.'

'We're working,' interrupted one of the medics, and Ezer apologised with a hand gesture. Meanwhile the medics were measuring the energy my body would release if I happened to die. They found it had noticeably declined, which led them all to shout, 'Hoorah!' spontaneously, except for Ben, who didn't like this development and considered it a bad omen.

That was all a few days before Ben Moshe killed himself. He knew he had failed. He insisted that the bacterial robot had struck me although the tests showed the opposite and no one would be able to stop the spectral bodies flowing out of me, which meant that the kibbutz residents would be doomed to have the ghosts of Palestinians living among them for the rest of their lives. This would turn the community into an environment that was permanently psychologically damaged. They found him dead after he injected himself with a poison he had extracted from beans. His brother-in-law, who had been prevented at the last moment from killing himself in the same way, and who had been assigned to lead the medical team, thought it would be best to keep discharging the energy inside me, 'on the grounds that a time bomb still threatens to obliterate everything at any moment', as he put it, taking the words of the late Ben Moshe completely out of context in his first heady rush of independence. But it was decided to declare Ze'ev a hero to raise the morale of the residents and to spread a story that his Luger was holy and the only thing capable of getting the energy out of my body.

So it was that Ze'ev was asked to fire one Luger bullet at me every month. He chose my bad eye as the target so that I wouldn't be disfigured any further. We stayed in the Aharon Kibbutz, the only difference being that we moved to an old stone house near the perimeter. Since Aharon sits on a hilltop, I enjoy a great view of the Galilee kibbutzes and from time to time see ghostly shapes moving around in the dark. Sometimes they seem to be looking back at me, and I find consolation in the fact that there is at least one spectral body out there that wants to be a superhero and extricate me from the glass cube.

Robomicrobe

When Ze'ev started shouting, 'Doctor, doctor,' and tried to open the first aid kit, I didn't know he wasn't doing it for me but for himself. Because the person the bullet did most harm to was him. As soon as it hit me, Ze'ev felt like all the muscles in his face had been torn and then reconnected in a different pattern. This made his face freeze with the expression by which he is now known: a panicked look that will always be a part of him now, whether he's telling a joke, or being kind to a child at school, or a dog in the supermarket. The massage experts couldn't do anything for him. And it didn't stop there. At the end of the day, whenever

Ze'ev fired a bullet at me, his expression became even more alarmed. Despite this, he didn't give up his mission. 'If that's the price for becoming a hero,' he said, 'I won't stand in the way.' He did his best to always look convincing as a hero and undo the initial impression his face had on people. He didn't like to be an object of ridicule, even when he was shooting at me. No one knew that, in reality, the bacterial robots weren't interested in me, given that I had in fact died on the day I ate mud with my grandfather. But my energy diminished noticeably. Ze'ev was free to go for a walk, now and again, or go shopping sometimes. He even joined a gym. Of course, he aroused curiosity whenever he trained. Everyone would sneak a peek at him. Some of them tried hard not to laugh, not while he was lifting weights but when he was running on the treadmill. With his panicked face he looked as if he were still running away from something that had frightened him when he was young and that his face had never been able to mature or grow, because the fear was so great. With every bullet he fired at me, he felt his face muscles being torn apart and then reconnecting again, to freeze on a face that reflected yet more horror. So he started to resemble his father, initially, then his grandfather later on. He hoped his face would end up looking like Eli's, but that didn't happen. The reason being that Eli never felt afraid in the German camps.

Ezer continued to visit us from time to time. He and Ze'ev would chat normally like old times, but as soon as Ezer left, Ze'ev would say, 'That bastard. He thinks my face looks like this because I'm afraid of him.' Despite all Ezer had done for him, Ze'ev still couldn't forget the psychological harm he had done to Sophia, who was now Ezer's wife. He imagines that on one of his visits, with his son Aaron, Ezer will jump up suddenly, shout, 'Son of a whore', and fire a bullet into Ze'ev's neck while still holding his child's hand. 'That child, I don't know why he brings him,' Ze'ev would say. Looking at Aaron made Ze'ev suspicious and sad, you see. He felt that Aaron was really his child, not Ezer's. 'He has my features. Then there's his smell. I think I had the same smell when I was young,' Ze'ev said to himself. But Ezer always kept himself busy with something else. As he rocked Aaron, Ezer said to him, 'They were three brothers, the children of our neighbours in Haifa. We called them the rabbits because all of them were born with cleft lips. I saw them in Mummy's house. Ghostly bodies. Your poor mother, sometimes she sees them in her dreams, and she wakes up in a panic. Except for that, everything in our life is beautiful.' In fact, the three rabbits had a fourth brother, the youngest of them and the only one that was born normal, but after Ezer Banana pushed Sophia's twin brother down the stairs, Sophia, for some reason, claimed it was the youngest brother who had done it. He was imprisoned, although he was no more than eleven years old. Some months later he was found dead, strangled by some juvenile inmates with their bare hands.

On the first Tuesday of every month throughout the year 2048, at 10:15 AM, Ze'ev puts a Luger bullet in my right eye, shouting, 'Death to our enemies.' On the road, afterwards, he says proudly, 'The shot hurt you, didn't it? You better get used to it.' But he doesn't understand that my emissions of energy have nothing to do with the Luger bullet. The stories that reach us from the kibbutzes make him convinced that they do though. One kibbutznik woke up terrified during the night and said, 'I dreamed there was a Falasti looking for something in the garden.' As soon as he went outside he saw the Palestinian he had dreamt of, really looking for something in his garden. The worst thing was that he was just as ghostly as he had appeared in the dream. Ze'ev, who had nothing to live for except his image as a hero, said, 'I'm going to keep shooting at you, even if all your energy is exhausted, because one thing will remain alive in you, the idea of the robomicrobe. Ben Moshe's brother-in-law recommends I don't stop shooting at you until you're so weak that I can steal the robomicrobe idea from you. That will be his greatest achievement, and it will make us immune to diseases – immortal.'

But until that happens, the kids in the schools ask me if I have anything to do with the death of Ezer Banana and Sophia and their child Aaron in the car crash – a question that brings tears to Ze'ev's eyes when we get home each night. Or they ask me if I really am the last Palestinian. Or 'Is it true that you have inside you a robomicrobe idea that can cure children?' As for the spectral bodies that the inhabitants of Greater Israel see, they act with complete confidence. They go for walks in the woods or in the markets or in the old towns. They go into shops or onto the beaches. They float over the houses or sit near an old school, looking at a tree or lying in the sun. Some of them can be seen putting their ears to the grass as if they're listening, as if they know the place well. But although the scene is normal and there's nothing disturbing about it, it strikes terror in the hearts of kibbutz residents. As far as Ben Moshe's brother-in-law is concerned, it's still better than seeing kibbutzes fighting each other with real weapons. The same goes for Ze'ev's frightened face, which turns firing a Luger bullet at me into an amusing scene for the children, who for a moment forget that the body into which the Luger bullet lands could, at any moment, wipe them and their school out. When Ze'ev feels that the children are about to start making fun of him, he brings up a fact that everyone is well aware of – that the ghostly bodies of the Falasti are now seen in every kibbutz and town, and that the ghostly Falasti completely ignore the kibbutz residents however hard they try to drive them out or harass them. In fact, the kibbutzniks might as well be the ones who are ghosts. Ze'ev raises this prospect in a question he poses to the children: 'Can any of you prove that *they* are the ghosts and not us?' But he doesn't hear any answer, so he repeats it: 'Can any of you prove that *they* are the ghosts and not us?' Looks of terror appear on everyone's faces, so now his face looks completely unexceptional. At that point he slowly and calmly puts me and the glass cube back on the motorcycle, like someone who has just regained control of the situation.

About the Authors

Tasnim Abutabikh (born 1996) grew up in Gaza and graduated from Al-Azhar University, before moving to the United States in 2018, where she now works as a dentist. In 2015, she was a winner in the Novell Gaza Short Story Award, and was published in *Novell Gaza 2*. Her grandfather was living in Kofakha at the time of the Nakba, although her great-grandfather was originally from Gaza City.

Emad El-Din Aysha (born 1974) is an academic, journalist, and translator and an author, currently stationed in Cairo. Having received a BA in economics and philosophy and an MA and PhD in international studies from the University of Sheffield, he currently teaches across a range of subjects, from international politics to Arab society, at various universities in Egypt. He's a regular commentator on Middle Eastern politics, an avid fan of history and science fiction, and a film reviewer and columnist for publications like The Levant, The Egyptian Gazette, Daily News Egypt and Mada Masr. He was born in the UK to a Palestinian father, from the Akka region.

Selma Dabbagh (born 1970) is a British Palestinian writer of fiction living in London. She grew up between the UK, Saudi Arabia and Kuwait and has also lived in Bahrain, Egypt, the West Bank and France. Her first novel, *Out of It* (Bloomsbury, 2012) was a Guardian Book of the Year. Several of Selma's short stories and plays have won, or been nominated for awards. Her writing has been published by *Granta, The Guardian*, International PEN, the *London Review of Books*, the British Council and Saqi Books.

Her radio plays have been produced by the BBC and WDR. Her father's family is from Jaffa.

Basma Ghalyini (born 1983) has previously translated short fiction from the Arabic for the KfW Stiftung series, *Beirut Short Stories*, published on addastories.org, and Comma projects, such as *Banthology* and *The Book of Cairo* (edited by Raph Cormack). She was born in Khan Younis, and spent her early childhood in the UK until the age of five, before returning to the Gaza Strip.

Saleem Haddad (born 1983) is a writer and aid worker, who has worked with Médecins Sans Frontières and other organisations in Yemen, Syria, Iraq, Libya, Lebanon and Turkey. His debut novel, *Guapa* was published in 2016, won the 2017 Polari Prize and was awarded a Stonewall Honour. His essays have appeared in *Slate, The Daily Beast, LitHub,* and the *LARB*, among others. He was born in Kuwait City to an Iraqi-German mother and a Palestinian-Lebanese father, and is currently based in Lisbon. His paternal grandparents were both from Nazareth, and fled to Beirut in 1948, where they later met and fell in love.

Anwar Hamed (born 1957) is a Palestinian novelist, poet, and literary critic. With a master's degree in literature theory, he lives in London and works for the BBC World Service. He speaks Arabic, English and Hungarian, in addition to French and a little Turkish, Persian and Hebrew. He has published eight novels in Arabic, and a number of other works in Hungarian, and has contributed to a number of non-fiction titles, most recently: *Being Palestinian: Personal Reflections on Palestinian Identity in the Diaspora*, edited by Yasir Suleiman. His novel *Jaffa Makes the Morning Coffee* was longlisted for the International Prize for Arabic Fiction (IPAF). His most recent novel is *Shijan* (published in Arabic in March 2019). He was born in Anabta in the West Bank near Tulkarm, where his family comes from.

Majd Kayal (born 1990) studied philosophy and political science in Jerusalem and is currently an editor at *Metras* and a writer at the *Arab Ambassador*. His first novel, *The Tragedy of Mr. Matar* (El Ahlia, 2016) won the Qattan Young Writer Prize, and his first collection of short stories *Death in Haifa* came out this year. He was born in Haifa to a displaced family from the village of Birwa.

Mazen Maarouf (born 1978) is a writer, poet, translator and journalist. Maarouf holds a bachelor degree in General Chemistry from the Lebanese University (Faculty of Sciences). He has published two collections of short stories J*okes for the Gunmen* (translated into English by Jonathan Wright, and winner of the inaugural Al-Multaqa Prize for the Arabic Short Story), and *Rats that Licked the Karate Champion's Ear*. He has also published three collections of poetry: *The Camera Doesn't Capture Birds*, *Our Grief Resembles Bread* and *An Angel Suspended On a Clothesline* (2012). He also works as a translator into Arabic. In 1948 all four of his grandparents (as well as his father who was six years old at the time) fled the village of Deir Al Qasi in the mountains of Galilee and travelled on foot to Lebanon. His parents lived in Tel El-Zaatar refugee camp until the late seventies when they had to flee again at the start of the Lebanese civil war.

Abdalmuti Maqboul (born 1987) studied graphic design at Al-Najah National University in Nablus and has a master's degree in management and international relations from the University of Ankara, in Turkey. He is a lecturer at the Ummah College in Jerusalem. An extract from his forthcoming novel

Al-Mukhtalson (The Embezzlers) has been serialised in *Specimen* magazine, and translated into Spanish and Italian. He was born and lives in Nablus.

Ahmed Masoud (born 1981) is a writer and director who grew up in Palestine and moved to the UK in 2002. His debut novel *Vanished: The Mysterious Disappearance of Mustafa Ouda* won the Muslim Writers Awards. His theatre credits include *The Shroud Maker, Camouflage, Walaa, Loyalty, Go to Gaza, Drink the Sea* and *Escape from Gaza.* He is the founder of Al Zaytouna Dance Theatre, for whom he has written and directed several productions for the London stage, and subsequent European tours. Following his PhD research, he has published numerous academic articles, including a chapter in *Britain and the Muslim World: A Historical Perspective* (Cambridge Scholars Publishing, 2011). His family is originally from Dayr Sunayd.

Talal Abu Shawish (born 1967) is Assistant Director of the Boys Preparatory School for Refugees in Gaza. He has published three short story collections – *The Rest are Not For Sale, The Assassination of a Painting* (2010) and *Goodbye, Dear Prophets* (2011) – as well as four novels: *We Deserve a Better Death* (2012), *Middle Eastern Nightmares* (2013), *Seasons of Love and Blood* (2014), and *Urban House* (2018). His work has won three awards (the Ministry of Youth and Sports' Short Story Competition in 1996 and 1997, and the Italian Sea That Connects Award, 1998). Shawish was President of the Association of New Prospects for Community Development, 2007-2011, and is a member of the Palestinian Writers Union. He was born in Nuseirat Refugee Camp. Until they had to flee in 1948, his father lived in the town of Beer el Sabea, and his mother in the village of Barqa.

Rawan Yaghi (born 1994) is a Gaza-based writer. She was a member at the Qattan Centre for the Child, where she used online resources to start her own blog. In 2011, her love of writing and languages led her to start a degree in English Literature at the Islamic University of Gaza. She was awarded the Junior Members' Scholarship by Jesus College, University of Oxford, to pursue an undergraduate degree in Italian and Linguistics. She contributed to the 2014 anthology *Gaza Writes Back*, and has just been awarded a Fulbright Scholarship to study journalism in New York. Her family originates from Al Masmiyya Al Kabira.

Samir El-Youssef (born 1965) has a bachelor's and master's degree in philosophy from the University of London, having lived in the city since 1990. He is the author of nine novels and collections of stories, including *Gaza Blues* with Etgar Keret. He has published in magazines and newspapers such as *Al-Hayat, Al-Quds Al-Arabi, Nizwa, Al-Ghardeen, New Testament* and *Jewish Chronicle*. He was awarded the Tucholsky Prize by the Swedish (Ben) Commission for the year 2005. He was Born in Rashidieh, a Palestinian refugee camp in southern Lebanon in 1965,his family having been displaced from the village of al-Bassa in Acre, northern Palestine.

About the Translators

Raph Cormack is a translator, editor and author with a PhD in modern Arabic literature. He is the co-editor *The Book of Khartoum* (2016), with Max Shmookler, and editor of *The Book of Cairo* (2019), both published by Comma Press. As well as other translations, he is currently working on a non-fiction book about the female entertainers of early twentieth-century Cairo, called *Martyrs of Passion* (to be published in 2020).

Mohamed Ghalaieny is an atmospheric scientist who has previously worked as a journalist for Free Speech Radio News in New York, and as a translator for the Gaza-based Union of Health and Work Committees. He has also worked as an environmental researcher for the Toxic Remnants of War Project and his work included regularly translating documents from Arabic to English. His previous translations for Comma include Mamoun Eltlib's 'The Passage' for *The Book of Khartoum* (edited by Raph Cormack and Max Shmookler).

Andrew Leber is a graduate student at Harvard University's Department of Government. He has previously translated Sudanese, Syrian, Palestinian, and Iraqi literature, including 'It's Not Important, You're From There' by Arthur Yak Gabro in *The Book of Khartoum*, 'The Worker' by Basra-based author Diaa Jubaili in *Iraq + 100*, and several works of poetry by Palestinian poet Dareen Tatour.

Thoraya El-Rayyes is a Palestinian-Canadian literary translator and political sociologist based in London, England. Her

English language translations of contemporary Arabic literature have won multiple awards, and have appeared in publications including *The Kenyon Review, Black Warrior Review* and *World Literature Today*. Her father is of Gazan heritage and was born in Jaffa, Palestine in 1945. Her maternal grandparents were born in the Palestinian cities of Jaffa and Lydda. Thoraya herself was a stateless Palestinian refugee until the age of 11, when she became a Canadian citizen.

Yasmine Seale has previously translated short fiction for Comma's *The Book of Cairo* (edited by Raph Cormack) and is currently working on a new translation of the *Thousand and One Nights* for W. W. Norton. She lives in Istanbul.

Jonathan Wright is a translator and former Reuters journalist. His previous translations from the Arabic include Khaled Al Khamissi's *Taxi*, Youssef Ziedan's *Azazeel* (Winner of the IPAF, 2009), Saud Alsanousi's *The Bamboo Stalk* (Winner of the IPAF, 2013), Hammour Ziada's *The Longing of the Dervish* (Winner of the Naguib Mahfouz Prize), Ahmed Saadawi's *Frankenstein in Baghdad* (shortlisted for the Man Booker International), Mazen Maarouf's *Jokes for the Gunmen* (shortlisted for the Man Booker International), and Hassan Blasim's *The Madman of Freedom Square* and *The Iraqi Christ* (winner of the 2014 Independent Foreign Fiction Prize).

Special Thanks

The editor would like to thank the following people for their help and inspiration: Ra Page, Mona El-Farra, Bahaa Ghalayini, Sondos Ghalayini, Mohamed Ghalaieny, Sarah Cleave, Becca Parkinson, Zoe Turner, Mohamed Yusuf, Kerry Bertram, Nikki Mailer, Adie Mormech, Theresa Ghalaieny, Khaled Soliman Al Nassiry, Nisreen Naffa, Angelina Radakovic, Jody Reeve, Bill Martin, Khalid Mansour, Liana Badr, Maya Abu Al-Hayat, Pam Bailey, Musheir El-Farra, Noor Hemani, Mosab Mostafa, Anas Abu Samhan, Refaat Alareer, Majd Abu Shawish, Najlaa Ataallah, Ramzy Baroud, Majd Abusalama, Ehab Bessaiso, Atef Abu Saif, Theodora Danek, Rafeef Ziadah, Omar Al-Qattan, Jon Fawcett, Daniel Lowe, Neelam Tailor and Anne Thwaite.

Thank you all
for your support.
We do this for you,
and could not do
it without you.

PARTNERS

ADDITIONAL DONORS, CONT'D

Mark Haber
Mary Cline
Maynard Thomson
Michael Reklis
Mike Soto
Mokhtar Ramadan
Nikki & Dennis Gibson
Patrick Kukucka
Patrick Kutcher
Rev. Elizabeth & Neil Moseley
Richard Meyer

Scott & Katy Nimmons
Sherry Perry
Sydneyann Binion
Stephen Harding
Stephen Williamson
Susan Carp
Susan Ernst
Theater Jones
Tim Perttula
Tony Thomson

SUBSCRIBERS

Caroline West
Margaret Terwey
Ben Fountain
Gina Rios
Elena Rush
Courtney Sheedy
Elif Ağanoğlu
Brian Bell
Dee Mitchell
Cullen Schaar
Harvey Hix

Jeff Lierly
Elizabeth Simpson
Michael Schneiderman
Nicole Yurcaba
Sam Soule
Jennifer Owen
Melanie Nicholls
Alan Glazer
Michael Doss
Matt Bucher
Katarzyna Bartoszynska

Michael Binkley
Erin Kubatzky
Martin Piñol
Michael Lighty
Joseph Rebella
Jarratt Willis
Heustis Whiteside
Samuel Herrera
Heidi McElrath
Jeffrey Parker

AVAILABLE NOW FROM DEEP VELLUM

SHANE ANDERSON · *After the Oracle* · USA

MICHÈLE AUDIN · *One Hundred Twenty-One Days* · translated by Christiana Hills · FRANCE

BAE SUAH · *Recitation* · translated by Deborah Smith · SOUTH KOREA

MARIO BELLATIN · *Mrs. Murakami's Garden* · translated by Heather Cleary · *Beauty Salon* · translated by David Shook · MEXICO

EDUARDO BERTI · *The Imagined Land* · translated by Charlotte Coombe · ARGENTINA

CARMEN BOULLOSA · *Texas: The Great Theft* · *Before* · *Heavens on Earth* · translated by Samantha Schnee · Peter Bush · Shelby Vincent · MEXICO

MAGDA CARNECI · *FEM* · translated by Sean Cotter · ROMANIA

LEILA S. CHUDORI · *Home* · translated by John H. McGlynn · INDONESIA

MATHILDE CLARK · *Lone Star* · translated by Martin Aitken · DENMARK

SARAH CLEAVE, ed. · *Banthology: Stories from Banned Nations* · IRAN, IRAQ, LIBYA, SOMALIA, SUDAN, SYRIA & YEMEN

LOGEN CURE · *Welcome to Midland: Poems* · USA

ANANDA DEVI · *Eve Out of Her Ruins* · translated by Jeffrey Zuckerman · MAURITIUS

PETER DIMOCK · *Daybook from Sheep Meadow* · USA

CLAUDIA ULLOA DONOSO · *Little Bird*, translated by Lily Meyer · PERU/NORWAY

RADNA FABIAS · *Habitus* · translated by David Colmer · CURAÇAO/NETHERLANDS

ROSS FARRAR · *Ross Sings Cheree & the Animated Dark: Poems* · USA

ALISA GANIEVA · *Bride and Groom* · *The Mountain and the Wall* · translated by Carol Apollonio · RUSSIA

FERNANDA GARCIA LAU · *Out of the Cage* · translated by Will Vanderhyden · ARGENTINA

ANNE GARRÉTA · *Sphinx* · *Not One Day* · *In/concrete* · translated by Emma Ramadan · FRANCE

JÓN GNARR · *The Indian* · *The Pirate* · *The Outlaw* · translated by Lytton Smith · ICELAND

GOETHE · *The Golden Goblet: Selected Poems* · *Faust, Part One* · translated by Zsuzsanna Ozsváth and Frederick Turner · GERMANY

SARA GOUDARZI · *The Almond in the Apricot* · USA

NOEMI JAFFE · *What are the Blind Men Dreaming?* · translated by Julia Sanches & Ellen Elias-Bursac · BRAZIL

CLAUDIA SALAZAR JIMÉNEZ · *Blood of the Dawn* · translated by Elizabeth Bryer · PERU

PERGENTINO JOSÉ · *Red Ants* · MEXICO

TAISIA KITAISKAIA · *The Nightgown & Other Poems* · USA

SONG LIN · *The Gleaner Song: Selected Poems* · translated by Dong Li · CHINA

JUNG YOUNG MOON · *Seven Samurai Swept Away in a River* · *Vaseline Buddha* · translated by Yewon Jung · SOUTH KOREA

KIM YIDEUM · *Blood Sisters* · translated by Ji yoon Lee · SOUTH KOREA

JOSEFINE KLOUGART · *Of Darkness* · translated by Martin Aitken · DENMARK

YANICK LAHENS · *Moonbath* · translated by Emily Gogolak · HAITI

FOUAD LAROUI · *The Curious Case of Dassoukine's Trousers* · translated by Emma Ramadan · MOROCCO

MARIA GABRIELA LLANSOL · *The Geography of Rebels Trilogy: The Book of Communities; The Remaining Life; In the House of July & August* · translated by Audrey Young · PORTUGAL

PABLO MARTÍN SÁNCHEZ · *The Anarchist Who Shared My Name* · translated by Jeff Diteman · SPAIN

DOROTA MASŁOWSKA · *Honey, I Killed the Cats* · translated by Benjamin Paloff · POLAND

BRICE MATTHIEUSSENT· *Revenge of the Translator* · translated by Emma Ramadan · FRANCE

LINA MERUANE · *Seeing Red* · translated by Megan McDowell · CHILE

VALÉRIE MRÉJEN · *Black Forest* · translated by Katie Shireen Assef · FRANCE

FISTON MWANZA MUJILA · *Tram 83* · *The River in the Belly: Selected Poems* · translated by Bret Maney DEMOCRATIC REPUBLIC OF CONGO

GORAN PETROVÍC · *At the Lucky Hand, aka The Sixty-Nine Drawers* · translated by Peter Agnone · SERBIA

LUDMILLA PETRUSHEVSKAYA · *The New Adventures of Helen: Magical Tales*, translated by Jane Bugaeva · RUSSIA

ILJA LEONARD PFEIJFFER · *La Superba* · translated by Michele Hutchison · NETHERLANDS

RICARDO PIGLIA · *Target in the Night* · translated by Sergio Waisman · ARGENTINA

SERGIO PITOL · *The Art of Flight* · *The Journey* · *The Magician of Vienna* · *Mephisto's Waltz: Selected Short Stories* · *The Love Parade* · translated by George Henson · MEXICO

JULIE POOLE · *Bright Specimen: Poems from the Texas Herbarium* · USA

EDUARDO RABASA · *A Zero-Sum Game* · translated by Christina MacSweeney · MEXICO

ZAHIA RAHMANI · *"Muslim": A Novel* · translated by Matthew Reeck · FRANCE/ ALGERIA

MANON STEFAN ROS · *The Blue Book of Nebo* · WALES

JUAN RULFO · *The Golden Cockerel & Other Writings* · translated by Douglas J. Weatherford · MEXICO

ETHAN RUTHERFORD · *Farthest South & Other Stories* · USA

TATIANA RYCKMAN · *Ancestry of Objects* · USA

JIM SCHUTZE · *The Accommodation* · USA

OLEG SENTSOV · *Life Went On Anyway* · translated by Uilleam Blacker · UKRAINE

MIKHAIL SHISHKIN · *Calligraphy Lesson: The Collected Stories* · translated by Marian Schwartz, Leo Shtutin, Mariya Bashkatova, Sylvia Maizell · RUSSIA

ÓFEIGUR SIGURÐSSON · *Öræfi: The Wasteland* · translated by Lytton Smith · ICELAND

DANIEL SIMON, ED. · *Dispatches from the Republic of Letters* · USA

MUSTAFA STITOU · *Two Half Faces* · translated by David Colmer · NETHERLANDS

SOPHIA TERAZAWA · *Winter Phoenix: Testimonies in Verse* · POLAND

MÄRTA TIKKANEN · *The Love Story of the Century* · translated by Stina Katchadourian · SWEDEN

BOB TRAMMELL · *Jack Ruby & the Origins of the Avant-Garde in Dallas & Other Stories* · USA

BENJAMIN VILLEGAS · *ELPASO: A Punk Story* · translated by Jay Noden · MEXICO

SERHIY ZHADAN · *Voroshilovgrad* · translated by Reilly Costigan-Humes & Isaac Wheeler · UKRAINE

FORTHCOMING FROM DEEP VELLUM

MARIO BELLATIN • *Etchapare* • translated by Shook • MEXICO

CAYLIN CARPA-THOMAS • *Iguana Iguana* • USA

MIRCEA CĂRTĂRESCU • *Solenoid* • translated by Sean Cotter · ROMANIA

TIM COURSEY • *Driving Lessons* • USA

ANANDA DEVI • *When the Night Agrees to Speak to Me* • translated by Kazim Ali • MAURITIUS

DHUMKETU • *The Shehnai Virtuoso* • translated by Jenny Bhatt • INDIA

LEYLˆA ERBIL • *A Strange Woman* • translated by Nermin Menemencioğlu & Amy Marie Spangler· TURKEY

ALLA GORBUNOVA • *It's the End of the World, My Love* • translated by Elina Alter • RUSSIA

NIVEN GOVINDEN • *Diary of a Film* • GREAT BRITAIN

GYULA JENEI · *Always Different* • translated by Diana Senechal · HUNGARY

DIA JUBAILI • *No Windmills in Basra* • translated by Chip Rosetti • IRAQ

ELENI KEFALA • *Time Stitches* • translated by Peter Constantine • CYPRUS

UZMA ASLAM KHAN • *The Miraculous True History of Nomi Ali* • PAKISTAN

ANDREY KURKOV • *Grey Bees* • translated by Boris Dralyuk • UKRAINE

JORGE ENRIQUE LAGE • *Freeway La Movie* • translated by Lourdes Molina • CUBA

TEDI LÓPEZ MILLS • *The Book of Explanations* • translated by Robin Myers • MEXICO

ANTONIO MORESCO • *Clandestinity* • translated by Richard Dixon • ITALY

FISTON MWANZA MUJILA • *The Villain's Dance,* translated by Roland Glasser • DEMOCRATIC REPUBLIC OF CONGO

N. PRABHAKARAN • *Diary of a Malayali Madman* • translated by Jayasree Kalathil • INDIA

THOMAS ROSS • *Miss Abracadabra* • USA

IGNACIO RUIZ-PÉREZ • *Isles of Firm Ground* • translated by Mike Soto • MEXICO

LUDMILLA PETRUSHEVSKAYA • *Kidnapped: A Crime Story,* translated by Marian Schwartz • RUSSIA

NOAH SIMBLIST, ed. • *Tania Bruguera: The Francis Effect* • CUBA

S. YARBERRY • *A Boy in the City* • USA

Printed in the USA
CPSIA information can be obtained
at www.ICGtesting.com
JSHW021704031024
71025JS00004B/33